MW01153441

Tim

Julian

Dave

d6

by

ROBERT BEVAN

TAKE A PEEK INSIDE MY SHORTS.

DO YOU LIKE WHAT YOU SEE?

Caverns & Creatures logo by EM Kaplan.
Used with permission by the creator.

C & C Gang Illustration courtesy of evilgiggles.com.
Used with permission by the creator.

20-Sided Die icon provided by Shutterstock.com and used and adapted in conjuction with its licensing agreement. For more information regarding Shutterstock licensing, visit www.shutterstock.com/license

All content edited by Joan Reginaldo.
Layout design by Christopher Dowell.

ISBN: 1492711128
ISBN-13: 978-1492711124

SPECIAL THANKS TO:

First, I'd like to thank Joan Reginaldo for her invaluable criticism. It's tough to find a good beta-reader. I went through a few before I met Joan. I can't stress enough how important it is to find someone who understands your vision and is able to help you achieve it. There's so much more involved than pointing out misplaced commas (though she did a lot of that, too). Go take a look at Joan's blog if you have a chance. She's got some good tips on writing. Leave a comment. She likes comments.

Next, I'd like to thank my beautiful wife, No Young Sook, for her constant support, and for getting up to get the kids ready for school every morning because I left early to go to the office to write some books.

Next in line to be thanked is my brother-in-law, No Hyun Jun. Every cover of mine you see is the end product of a communication struggle, his English being about on par with my Korean. But the guy can work some Photoshop magic. And he also helps out with the kids quite a bit. Thanks, Hyun Jun.

TABLE OF CONTENTS

Cave of the Kobolds

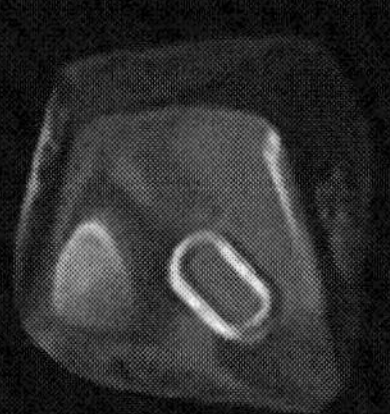

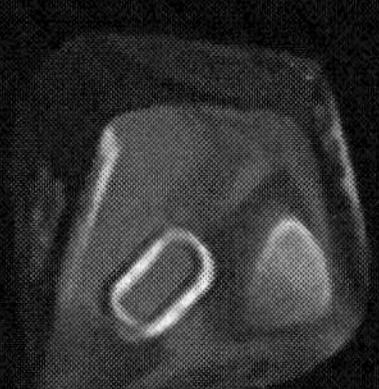

ROBERT BEVAN

CAVE OF THE KOBOLDS

(Original Publication Date: July 16, 2012)

Cooper reached a clawed hand under his loincloth and scratched his balls thoughtfully.

Julian, catching an unwanted glimpse of Cooper's balls, noticed that the hair on them was as sparse, long, and twisted as the hair on his face. No, that wasn't quite right. Cooper's ball hair was perfectly normal. The strange part was that Cooper looked to have a face full of pubes.

It wasn't his fault. He was a half-orc with a Charisma score of 4. But still, Julian didn't think he'd ever be able to look at Cooper's face again without making the connection.

When it occurred to him that he was staring at his friend's balls, Julian turned his head toward the entrance of the cave. "It's... um... dark in there."

Cooper plugged one nostril with his thumb, and shot a snot rocket out the other. "It's a cave. Caves are dark. Light up a rock and chuck it inside."

Julian picked up a stone from the ground. "Light," he said. It was too bright outside to see whether the spell had taken effect, so he tossed it into the cave. Light flowed into the cave as the stone clattered along the floor.

"Could you please explain to me what we're doing here?" asked Ravenus, flapping in from a nearby tree. He perched atop Julian's quarterstaff.

"Jesus Christ, could you shut that fucking thing up?" said Cooper. "I had a lot to drink last night. I don't even know what half of it was. My head is killing me and I really don't need that thing screeching in my ear this early in the morning."

"You'd be able to understand him if you'd just spend a skill point on learning the Elven language next time you level up. It's just English with a British accent."

"The day I speak with a British accent is the day I stick a baguette up my ass and slap a beret on my head."

"I think you mixed your xenophobias."

"Yes, I did," said Cooper, impatience rising in his voice. "And that's why I have a fucking hangover. So tell your fucking bird to shut the fuck up."

"He just wants to know what we're doing here," said Julian. "I wouldn't mind an answer to that myself."

"We need money," said Cooper. "I'm tired of pulling silver arrowheads out of my ass and melting them down for cash. We're going to get some gold the old fashioned way."

Julian squinted his eyes and peered in at the walls of the cave. "Mining?"

Cooper closed his eyes and clenched his fists. He breathed deeply a few times. An impressive snot bubble expanded and contracted from his right nostril. After one long, final exhalation, he spoke.

"I'm supposed to be the one with the low Intelligence score here. Look around. What do you see?"

"A cave."

"Or you might even call it a cavern, right?"

"Okay."

"We're stuck in a game called Caverns and Creatures. So it's a pretty good bet that there are some creatures living in this cavern. Creatures often have treasure."

"So we're going to go in there and steal their shit? What if they see us? We should have brought Tim. He's the sneaky one."

"Tim would have said no. It's too dangerous or some bullshit. And no, we're not going to steal their shit. We're going to claim their shit as our own after we kill whatever's in there."

"So we're talking about murder then?"

"We're just going to kill some monsters. If there are any people in there, we won't kill them."

"What about goblins?"

"Goblins are monsters."

"That guy Shorty was pretty cool."

"Yeah." Cooper picked between one of his lower tusks and the tooth next to it with a fingernail that looked like a rhinoceros horn. "Okay. No goblins, no humans. Anything else is fair game. Agreed?"

"How do you even know we can take what's in there? I mean, without Mordred running the show, we have no guarantee that we're going to be up against level appropriate creatures. There could be anything in there. Maybe a cockroach, maybe a horde of dragons. Maybe nothing."

"That's a good point. Okay, here's the plan. If we find something we think we can take, we'll beat the shit out of it and be on our way. If it looks like something tough, you can diplomafy it."

"What?"

"Use your high Charisma score. Talk your way out."

"That's a stupid plan."

Cooper unstrapped the enormous double-bladed axe from his back, and ran an edge against his cheek, leaving one patch of bald semi-cleanliness on his otherwise filthy face. "Let's go."

Cooper stepped across the threshold into the cave. Ravenus flapped down from Julian's staff to perch on his shoulder, and they followed Cooper inside.

When they reached the center of the light, Julian stooped down to pick up his stone. He stayed kneeling on the ground and scrunched up his face. His eyes started to tear. "You're right," he said between shallow breaths. "Something definitely lives in here. I just got a whiff of their waste."

"That was... um..." said Cooper. "That was me. SBD. Sorry."

Julian stood up. "Jesus, Cooper. How about a little warning next time?"

"Consider yourself lucky it was just a fart."

Julian waved his hands around in an attempt to stir up the stagnant, fart-filled air. Shadows leaped up and down violently on the wall before them.

"Stop waving that rock around," said Cooper. "You're making me dizzy. I don't think you want to add puke to your olfactory buffet."

Julian took a few steps to the left, holding the stone out in front of him, and then did the same in the opposite direction. A tunnel led out of this chamber in each direction perpendicular to the entrance. "What do you think? Left or right?"

Cooper shrugged.

"Ravenus."

"Yes, Julian," said the raven, hopping from Julian's shoulder to his outstretched forearm so they could talk face to face.

"Pick a direction. Left or right?"

"Um... right?"

"Ravenus says we should go right."

"So we go left," said Cooper, sticking up his middle finger at Ravenus. "Fuck you, bird."

Cooper started down the tunnel on the left. Julian threw the glowing stone at his head.

"Ow!"

"Oh, sorry!" said Julian. "I was just trying to throw it ahead so we could see where we were going."

Cooper rubbed the back of his head. "Oh, right. Good thinking." He bent down to pick up the stone. Julian winked at Ravenus.

Cooper chucked the stone at an angle, and light bounced back and forth along the tunnel as the stone ricocheted off the rocky walls. When it came to rest, Julian caught a brief glimpse of a small humanoid reptilian creature, no bigger than a human twelve-year-old, staring back at him through beady red eyes. He blinked and the creature was gone.

"Did you see that?" Julian whispered.

"I saw something," said Cooper.

Julian put his hand up to his shoulder for Ravenus to perch on, and then cradled the bird against his chest. "Cooper, I'm scared."

"Don't be a pussy," said Cooper, but his voice was distant, and his eyes remained focused on the darkness just beyond the stone's magical light. "Come on. Let's check it out." He stepped into the light and picked up the stone.

As soon as the light moved, the sound of running footsteps echoed off the cavern walls. They were running away from Cooper and Julian. The footsteps were soon accompanied by what might have been a yapping terrier, or what might have been a language. If it was the latter, it wasn't any language that Julian was familiar with.

Cooper grinned. The light illuminated his face from below, making his tusky grin all the more horrifying. "I think I know what these things are." He walked briskly down the tunnel, which gradually turned to the right.

Julian had to jog in order to keep up with Cooper's long strides. "What are they?"

"Kobolds."

"That doesn't mean anything to me. Why are you smiling?"

"Because kobolds are weak. We can take these fuckers down with no problem."

Julian looked down at Ravenus. "Do you know anything about kobolds?"

"I know they're kin to dragons."

"Jesus, Cooper," said Julian. "Did you hear that?"

"I heard 'Scrraaawwwww!'."

"Ravenus told me that kobolds are related to dragons. Is that true?"

"How the fuck should I know?"

Ahead of them the faint glow of firelight flickered on the walls of the cave. The fleeing creature's panicky yapping was met with more of the same. Whatever this thing was, it wasn't alone.

"Well what if it is true?" asked Julian, grabbing Cooper by the elbow to stop him. "Are you really so confident that we can take on a nest of dragon people?"

"Look," said Cooper. "Kobolds are the weakest, most generic monster in the game. They're what lazy Cavern Masters use for baddies in low-level dungeon crawls. Maybe the book says they're related to dragons. I don't know because I've never given a fuck. But they don't breathe fire and shit. You saw how big they are. They've only got a couple of hit points each. You can beat them to death with your shitty little walking stick. Hell, I bet even your stupid bird could take on a couple of them by himself. They are nothing to worry about."

This was of little comfort to Julian, but he kept his worries to himself. There would be time enough for I-told-you-so's while they were having their limbs gnawed off. He set Ravenus on his shoulder, readied his quarterstaff, and walked toward the flames.

A pair of torches mounted on the walls marked the entrance to a chamber, within which was the source of the excited yapping. When they were about twenty yards away, Cooper pressed a finger to his lips.

"Shh."

Julian nodded, and Cooper tossed the light stone into the chamber. The yapping came to a sudden halt.

"Dude!" Cooper whispered excitedly. "I can see in the dark."

"Seriously?"

"This fucking rules."

"Well I can't see shit," said Julian.

"Yeah, you kind of look like a jackass right now, reaching out your arms like that."

Julian jerked his arm away from something in the dark that tried to grab it. Then he realized it was just Cooper and relaxed. Cooper's attempts to tip-toe were laughable. He couldn't have been any louder if the floor had been made out of cats.

They hadn't gone more than five steps when light rushed into the tunnel toward them like water bursting through a hole in a dam.

"Goddammit!" Cooper shouted into the chamber, holding his hand over his right eyebrow. "What if that had gone in my eye, asshole?"

Julian looked down. His light stone had been returned to them.

After a brief bit of yapping from a single voice, a chorus of high-pitched laughter from maybe a dozen different voices echoed toward them. The yapping was definitely a language, and Julian had a strong feeling that someone in the chamber had just translated Cooper's shouting.

"Is he crying?" asked Ravenus.

"No, he's not cry—," Julian looked up to see Cooper wiping a tear away from his eye. "Cooper, are you crying?"

"It stung, alright," Cooper snarled.

Ravenus laughed.

"That's it," said Cooper. Apparently, He didn't need to understand Elven to know when he was being laughed at. "I don't need to take this shit from a fucking bird." He made a grab at Ravenus.

Ravenus flew out of Cooper's reach. Cooper raised his giant axe with both hands and swatted at Ravenus, trying to smack him out of the air with the flat of his blade. Ravenus flapped and dodged, but not by much.

"Cooper!" Julian shouted. "Knock it off. He didn't mean anyth—" He grunted and fell to his knees, a loud caw ringing in his ears.

Julian's vision was gone. All he could see was twinkling white lights in his periphery. He heard the clank of Cooper's axe falling to the ground, and he felt massive clawed hands grabbing him by the upper arms and lifting him.

"Julian! Are you okay? What's wrong?"

Julian's vision was slow in coming back to him, but he could feel the warmth of Cooper's breath on his face, and the smell... it was like meat that had gone so bad that flies wouldn't go near it. He bent his head back to breathe in some nice stagnant cave air.

"Where's Ravenus?"

"I'm sorry. I didn't mean to hit him so hard. I was just trying to —"

Julian didn't need sight to make a pretty good guess at where his foot was in relationship to Cooper's balls. His right foot connected with the first kick. He heard a grunt and the all too familiar squirt of Cooper's bowels letting go, and then he was on the ground again.

His vision was blurry, but coming back to him. "Ravenus!"

"I'm here, Julian," said Ravenus, flapping down into Julian's lap.

Julian stroked the feathers on the bird's head and neck. "Are you okay?"

"Yeah," said Cooper. "Don't sweat it."

"I wasn't talking to you," said Julian curtly. "Ravenus, are you okay?"

"Yes," said Ravenus. "He just knocked the wind out of me. That's all."

"For fuck's sake, man," said Cooper, rolling around on the ground with his hands on his balls. "My fucking nuts."

Julian blinked a few times until his vision became clear. "Cooper. Is there something you'd like to say to Ravenus?"

"I'm sorry I hit you with my axe, Ravenus," said Cooper. "It won't happen again."

"Thank you," said Julian. "Ravenus. Cooper said he's sorry for hitting you. Is there something you'd like to say to Cooper?"

"Go fuck yourself, shithead."

"Ravenus said he's sorry for laughing at you. Are we all cool now?"

Cooper lowered his head. "Yeah, we're cool. I'm really sorry, dude."

"Forget it," said Julian. "I've suddenly got an urge to beat the shit out of something. What say we go in there and kick some ass?"

"All right," said Cooper. "Let's roll." He took a step toward the firelight and Julian grabbed his arm.

"Shouldn't we have some sort of a plan before going in there?"

"Okay, fine. So what is it?"

"You don't have to heap all of the responsibility on me, you know."

"I'm a fucking moron. Strategy and planning are not what my character was made for. Any plan that I come up with is bound to be shitty."

"Okay okay," said Julian, tossing the light stone up and down in his hand. He caught it and looked at it. "Ravenus. Can you fit this stone in your beak?"

"I think so," said Ravenus. "I once ate the eyeball out of a dead sheep. It was a little bigger than that stone."

"I really wish I didn't know that about you." Julian held up the stone to Ravenus's beak. Ravenus accepted it and they were once again in total darkness save for the distant flicker of torchlight.

Julian suddenly felt a wave of nausea sweep over him, which passed as the cavern lit up again. The stone lay on the ground in front of Ravenus.

"What was that?" said Julian, crouching down with his hand over his belly. "What's wrong?"

Ravenus flapped his wings and shook his head. "It tastes like Cooper."

"That's worse than dead sheep eyes?"

"Why don't you go lick him and tell me which you prefer?"

Julian looked at Cooper, who was staring blankly back at him, and shuddered. He grabbed his wineskin. No. He needed something stronger.

"Cooper. Do you have any of that dwarf booze that Dave was drinking?"

"Stonepiss?" said Cooper. "Yeah. I swiped a flask from his bag while he was praying yesterday morning. It's some strong fucking shit."

"Good," said Julian. "Give it here."

Cooper handed over a steel hip flask. Julian unstoppered the flask and sniffed.

"Jesus wept! You're not kidding." He poured the stonepiss

over the light stone in the hope that it would neutralize whatever funk and superbacteria Cooper had infected it with through the mere act of touching it. Then he poured some of his own wine over the stone to take the edge off of the stonepiss.

"Try this." Julian held the stone up to Ravenus. After a quick peck, the cave went dark, and this time it stayed dark. Julian's stomach gave a small rumble of objection, but it wasn't unmanageable.

"Fly ahead," Julian said to Ravenus. "When you enter the chamber, fly up to the ceiling and try to find a perch or something. Wait for me to give the order, and then drop the stone. Okay?"

With a small disturbance in the air and the sound of flapping wings, Ravenus was gone.

Julian took Cooper's arm. "Okay," he whispered. "Let's go."

As they approached the twin torchlights, a third fire came into view in the center of the chamber. It was a small campfire, burning just brightly enough to illuminate the three creatures standing on the other side of it.

The creature on the left made some excited yipping noises and pointed its staff at Julian and Cooper as they passed between the torches. Julian let go of Cooper's arm. He could see well enough now.

"Are those cobalts?" Julian whispered, not looking away from the three figures.

"Kobolds," Cooper whispered back.

"Whatever. Is that what those things are?"

"Yeah, I'm pretty sure."

"They're kind of cute." Said Julian. "Try not to look threatening. Let's try to talk to them."

Cooper hugged his axe.

"Hi there, little guy," said Julian to the creature in the center. He took it to be their leader, due to its Billy goat beard and the fact that it stood up straight, looking confident despite its lack of any visible weaponry.

The creature on the right gave three sharp yips and thrust its spearhead toward Julian. He didn't need to be a linguist to understand the message.

Julian held his quarterstaff to one side, and raised his other hand to show it concealed no other weapon. He and Cooper stepped forward slowly. "We don't want to hurt you."

"We don't?" said Cooper.

"Look at them, Cooper." The creatures backed away from the fire as Julian and Cooper approached. The one with the spear continued to prod it forward and yip threateningly. "They're scared. We can't kill them. They look like little Jar-Jars."

"You're not making a very compelling case against killing them."

When Julian and Cooper reached the fire, the creature in the center spoke. He sounded like Stephen Hawking, if Stephen Hawking was a Chihuahua.

Julian and Cooper looked at one another. The awkward silence that followed was soon interrupted by another high-pitched voice beyond the light of the fire, but this one spoke in the common tongue.

"He says that you will be permitted to leave with your lives, but not with your weapons, your belongings, or your dignity."

The elder kobold smiled. Julian had seen enough movies about prison rape to know this smile for what it was. He noticed that both of his hands were now wrapped tightly around his quarterstaff.

Julian whispered, trying to keep his lips as still as possible. "Are you sure these things are as weak as you think they are?"

"Yeah," said Cooper. "But I'm not sure about how many of them there are in here. If you had some sort of plan in mind, now might be a good time to set it into motion."

Julian looked up and shouted, "Ravenus, now!"

A loud caw echoed from the top of the chamber, and the three kobolds directly in front of Julian and Cooper glanced up nervously.

"Ow!" said Cooper as an ordinary stone bounced off of his head.

The kobolds went into fits of laughter. The old one in the middle sounded like a car engine that didn't want to turn over.

Cooper rubbed the top of his head and looked up. "He did that on purpose."

"I'm sure he didn't," said Julian.

"Why isn't your rock glowing anymore?"

"Spell duration must have expired."

"Well can you light up another —"

"Cooper!" Julian whispered urgently.

"Huh?"

"Be careful. I think the one at your eleven o'clock is a spellcaster."

"Which one is that?"

"Eleven o'clock. Like on a watch."

"I can't tell time."

"Jesus, dude. The Mississippi public school system must have sucked even worse when you went through it than when I did."

"I'm illiterate, asshole. I can't read letters or numbers. It's part of being a barbarian."

"Oh, right. Sorry. It's the one on the left."

"Your left or mine?"

"We're both facing the same direction!"

Cooper laughed. "Oh yeah... I meant my left or its —"

"He's the one casting the fucking spell right now!"

"Huh?" said Cooper. He turned to the kobold on the left. It was making a whiny moaning chant that sounded like it was recalling getting a severe kick to the nuts. Its hands began to shine blue light.

Cooper punched it in the face. It was a quick, left-handed jab, but it sent the creature to the floor.

The old one wheezed out a couple of barks, and Julian heard movement behind him. He picked up the stone and repeated his incantation. "Light."

The two kobolds in front of them shielded their eyes from the sudden brightness, but Julian turned around to find four more standing behind them, all armed with spears.

He dropped the stone and held his quarterstaff like a baseball bat. "Take it easy guys. Which one of you speaks English?"

"Common," said Cooper.

"What?"

"One of them speaks Common. There is no English."

"Whatever. Which one of you can understand what I'm saying?"

"I can understand you, elf." The voice didn't come from any of the Kobolds that Julian could see. The elder kobold made some yaps and barks, and the voice translated. "This is your last chance. Drop your weapons and your bags, leave this cave, and do not return."

Cooper lifted the front of his loincloth and waved his cock around at the elder. He spoke slowly and loudly. "You can suck my balls." He pointed a finger at his balls to make sure the message got across.

Diplomacy was probably off the table at this point.

Cooper's cock-wagging was interrupted by a series of commands.

"Yip!"

"Bark!"

"Yap!"

Thwack.

"Son of a bitch!" said Cooper as a smooth round stone bounced off his temple.

They weren't screwing around anymore. That stone had been propelled by something more powerful than one of these guys' scrawny reptilian arms. Blood streamed down the side of Cooper's face.

"Looks like we're going to have to fight our way out of here after all," said Julian. "You'd better do your barbarian rage thing."

"Okay," said Cooper. He wiped some blood away from his eye.

"I'm really angry."

As soon as he'd said the words, his muscles bulged and grew veiny. If he'd been wearing a shirt, it probably would have ripped. The whites of his eyes turned red with fury and blood.

The effect was not lost on the kobold leader, who ditched his young subordinate and ran into the darkness. He was replaced by three more spear guards, none of whom looked to be very happy about their chances of making it through the impending battle alive.

None of the kobolds wanted to make the first move, but someone was bound to, and soon. Julian still didn't want to actually kill anyone, but his options were running out. An idea came to him.

"Sleep!" he said.

Six of the kobolds surrounding them collapsed instantly to the ground. The remaining two yawned, but shook it off. Cooper kicked one in the face. It did a backward somersault through the air and landed face down. It did not get up again.

The last one took a desperate stab at Julian's waist, but he swerved his hips in time to dodge it. He swung his quarterstaff around and felt the crunch of it smashing into the side of the kobold's head. It crumpled into a heap on the cavern floor.

"Shit," said Julian. "You don't think I..."

"He'll be all right," said Cooper. "Come on. Let's go find the —"

Another stone hit Cooper in the shoulder. It left a nasty welt.

"You sons of bitches!" he shouted. He charged off in the direction the stone had come from.

"Cooper, wait!" Julian shouted after him, but Cooper had already left the sphere of light provided by the stone. Julian felt suddenly alone and very vulnerable. He considered putting the stone in his pocket, but didn't like the thought of being alone in the darkness any more than he liked being the only visible target in the light.

From the direction Cooper had stomped off in, Julian hear the sounds of a brief scuffle, Cooper swearing a lot, and something

like a cat with its tail caught in a food processor.

A kobold flew toward Julian, but landed just short of him and not on its feet. Its short flight had apparently not been of its own volition. It flipped onto its back and scrambled away from Julian. In its hand it clutched a small length of rope with a leather pocket tied in the center. The pocket was just about large enough to accommodate one of the stones that Cooper had been being pelted with.

Julian kicked the creature in the gut. It curled into a ball, vomited on Julian's shoes and passed out.

"Nicely done," said Cooper, walking back into the light.

"There's still at least two more," said Julian. The leader and whoever was translating for him. Maybe we should just cut our losses and—" He dropped to one knee and looked up at toward the ceiling.

"What's wrong?" asked Cooper.

"Ravenus!"

"What about him?"

"He's not with me."

"Relax," said Cooper. "He's probably off somewhere fucking a bat or something."

"No," said Julian. "I mean his mind. We share feelings. I can't feel anything from him right now. I guess I haven't for a while. Why wasn't he down here fighting with us?"

"Have no fear, elf," said the voice that spoke the common tongue. "Your bird is unharmed for now."

Julian turned toward the direction the voice was coming from. "Where is he? What have you done with him?"

"To be honest, I didn't think holding your pet bird was a strong enough card to play, but I see you really care about it. Perhaps we can come to an arrangement."

Julian dropped his quarterstaff and raised his hands. "What do you want?"

"That's a good start. Now the orc."

Julian looked pleadingly at Cooper. Cooper nodded, bent

down, and set his axe on the ground. He picked up a couple of stones, including the light stone, which he tossed in the invisible voice's direction.

A new section of the chamber lit up. The walls were purposefully carved. The elder kobold stood behind a stone altar, holding a dagger over Ravenus, who slept peacefully on top of it.

To the left of the altar stood an obese kobold with colorful tattoos all over its face. It offered Julian and Cooper a smug grin.

"We finally meet. My name is—"

"Fuck your name," said Cooper. "Give my friend back his bird or I'll rip your heart out through your asshole."

"You are not in a position to negotiate," said the fat kobold. "One thrust of that dagger will end that bird's life."

"I don't give a shit about the bird," said Cooper. "And my friend here will get over it."

"Come on," Julian pleaded with Cooper. "Let's just give them what they want and leave. You don't understand the bond between a wizard and his familiar."

The fat kobold grinned.

"I'm sorry, Julian," said Cooper. "This might sting a little." He threw the remaining stone in his hand at Ravenus.

Julian winced at a phantom pain in his side. "Dammit, Cooper!" He punched Cooper repeatedly in the arm. "You stupid selfish piece of sh—"

He was cut off by a loud caw, which was followed by a scream that sounded like a buzz saw cutting through a sheet of steel.

Julian stopped punching Cooper and turned toward the altar. Ravenus was flapping wildly on the elder kobold's face, beak deep in its left eye socket. Having secured his prize, he flew away as the elder kobold collapsed behind the altar.

Cooper held up a hand, and Ravenus landed on it.

"We square, bird?"

Ravenus greedily slurped down the eyeball. Julian nearly threw up watching the bleeding optic nerve flap around before disappearing down Ravenus's throat.

Julian, Cooper, and Ravenus turned their attention to the fat kobold. Its grin was gone, and a stream of urine trickled down its right leg.

They walked a few yards away from one another as they approached the last kobold, so that he had nowhere to run to.

Cooper towered over it. "My friend didn't want to kill you guys before. He may have changed his mind since then, but I honestly don't give a fuck. I will tear you limb from fucking limb. I will tear off your nuts and feed them to you. Tell me where you keep your treasure."

The kobold turned its nose up at Cooper. It was trembling, but it managed to keep its voice steady. "I'll tell you nothing," it spat. "I'm not afraid of you."

"Seriously?" said Julian. "Because frankly, I'm a little frightened of him right now."

"Why you fat little shitbag," said Cooper, raising a fist.

"Hold on, Cooper," said Julian. "Let me try."

"If it's not afraid of me, what makes you think it's going to be afraid of you?" asked Cooper. "I mean, no offense, but you're not exactly a scary-looking dude."

"I took a couple ranks in Intimidation."

"What the fuck for?"

"It was a Charisma-based skill."

"Knock yourself out."

Julian turned to the kobold. "Now listen, you." He pointed a finger at it sternly. "You'd better look like talking, or else I'm going to—"

"All right! All right!" the kobold pleaded, dropping to its knees. "I'll talk."

Cooper sighed. "I don't fucking believe this."

"Our valuables are stored in a small chamber to the right of the cave entrance."

Ravenus looked at Cooper.

"I'll wipe that smirk right off your face, bird."

"It's just sitting there unguarded?" asked Julian.

"The guards were the four that surrounded you from behind."

"Oh," said Julian. "Cool. Thanks." He gave the kobold a swift smack in the head with his quarterstaff, bent down to feel for a pulse, and stood up again. "You guys ready?"

*

"Sixty-seven copper coins, and three silver," moaned Cooper.

"Hey," said Julian, digging through a rotted wooden chest full of garbage. "There's a little vial in here. I think it's a potion."

"What kind?"

"I don't know."

"Does it have a label?"

Julian rubbed some dirt off the side of the vial with his thumb. "It says 'Cure light wounds'."

"Sweet," said Cooper. "Give it here. Those rocks really fucked me up."

Julian handed the vial to Cooper, who gulped the contents down, shoving his tongue as far as he could into it to lap up any residue left on the sides.

"I don't feel any better," said Cooper.

"That's because I lied," said Julian. "The label actually said 'Truth serum'."

"You know, there's a certain irony in that."

"I want to know why you hate Ravenus so much, and now you have to be honest with me."

"Fuck you, dude. How's that for honesty?"

"Come on. Spill it. You've hated him ever since he became my familiar. What's the deal?"

Cooper sat on the ground and lowered his giant head. "I'm jealous, all right? We've been delivering pizzas together for like two years now. We always hang out, watch movies, get fucked-up together. And then on the second day we arrive in fantasy land, you start spending all your time with a fucking bird. I'm insecure. My feelings hurt easily."

"Dude," said Julian as comfortingly as he could. "Ravenus can't replace you. He's my familiar. It's hard to explain. He's his own person, but he's also an extension of me."

"Is that sort of like the God and Jesus relationship?"

"Yeah. Well probably. I don't know. I'm Jewish."

"Oh right," said Cooper. He stood up. "We should probably get out of here before all of those kobolds wake up."

Julian followed him out of the entrance of the cave. Ravenus launched himself into the fresh midmorning air.

"Hey Cooper," said Julian. "I haven't been completely honest with you."

"No shit."

"It wasn't actually a truth serum. The label said 'Fire resistance'."

"You really are a piece of shit."

Julian smiled. "Yeah, I guess I am."

Cooper shook his head and laughed. "Come on. Let's get back to town before we're missed. My head hurts. I need a drink."

The End

ZOMBIE ATTACK!!!

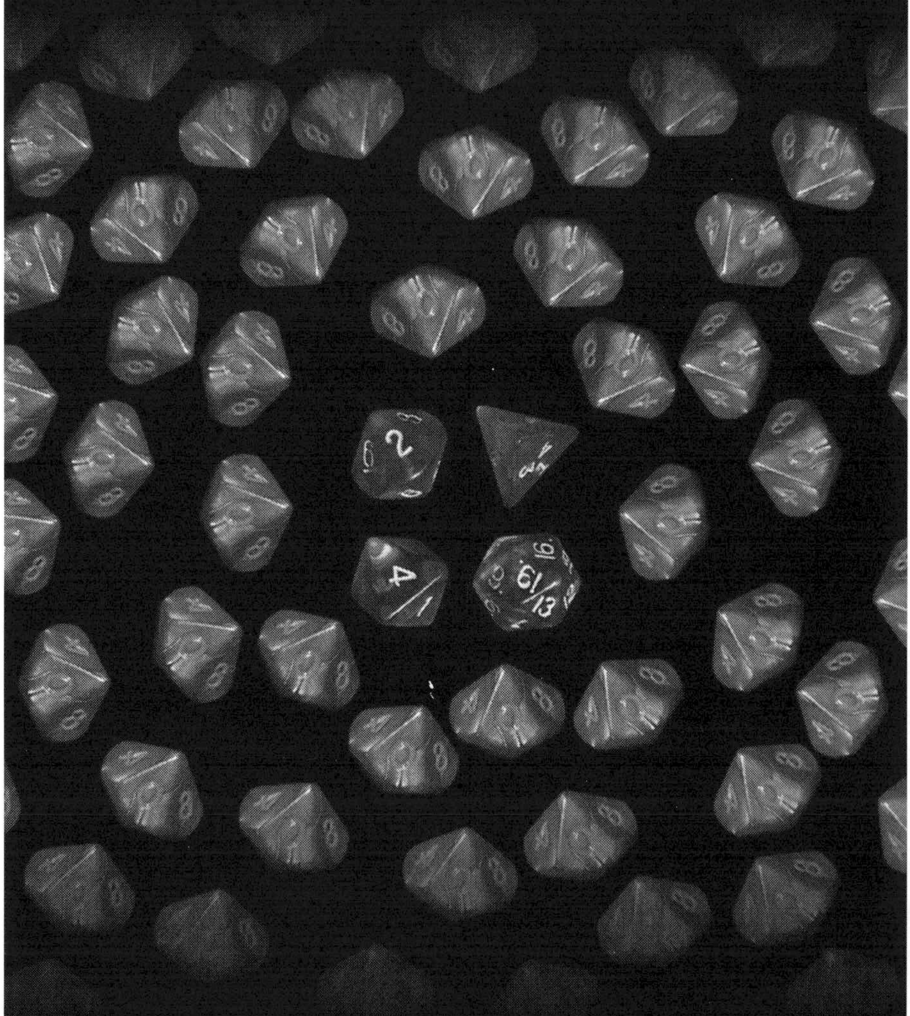

ROBERT BEVAN

ZOMBIE ATTACK!!!

(Original Publication Date: October 4, 2012)

"Well," said Tim. "That ought to just about do it." He ran a finger lightly along the rope, feeling the tension. It was stretched as tight as a bowstring. His eyes followed it up to where it was tied to the tree limb above. The knot was partially hidden with pine needles, but the whole branch was bent just short of its snapping point, which didn't look natural at all. This trap would be obvious to anyone with a mind to look out for such things, but that didn't matter. The creatures they were hunting today had no minds at all. "Now everybody, take a step back. Whatever you do, make sure you don't step on this circle of leaves. Anything heavier than a rabbit that steps on this is in for a nasty surprise."

"Impressive," said Dave, taking a step as far back as his short dwarven legs would allow. "I didn't know you could do that."

"I can't," said Tim. "Just like you can't magically cure wounds or grow a proper beard in the real world. But we're not there. We're here, stuck in this stupid fucking game where I look like pedophile bait and know how to set a trap."

"Sorry, man. I was just saying —"

"Cooper!" Tim shouted.

"Huh?" said Cooper. He had a finger so far up one nostril that he might have been scratching his tiny half-orc brain, and he was stepping dangerously close to the snare.

"What did I just say?"

Cooper pulled out his sticky, snot-covered finger and wiped it down his chest. "I wasn't listening. You were bitching about how hard your life is or something?"

"Fuck you, Cooper. Just stay away from the trap, will you?"

"Oh, right." He stepped back.

"Go on, Ravenus," said Julian, lifting his arm for his big black raven to perch on. "Scout the area. Come back if you see anyone or anything approaching."

"Very good, sir," said Ravenus, and took to the air.

Julian walked over to Tim. "Something on your mind, dude?"

"I just don't like this," said Tim. "I wish I hadn't let you guys talk me into it. I mean, it was Cooper's idea, and he's a complete idiot. No offense, Coop."

"None taken," said Cooper.

Julian leaned on his quarterstaff and tugged at one of his long pointy ears. "We've got a slim chance to get back home if that little gambit of yours even works. But we need to level up some before we even attempt it. You said that killing monsters is the most effective way to do that."

"I know," said Tim. He pulled his cloak tight around himself, holding a shiver at bay. "But does it have to be zombies?"

"We've fought zombies before," said Cooper.

"Yes," said Tim. "I've also had my face shoved into your armpit before, which gives me firsthand knowledge of why I never want that to happen again."

"We were unprepared for them last time," said Dave. "This time we have a lot more going for us."

Tim folded his arms and glared up at Dave. "I'm listening."

"Um, well," Dave stammered under the spotlight. "We're at full strength, for one. Also, we are choosing where we fight this time. We have a nice defensible position. It'll be impossible for them to surround us like they did last time."

"We're on the edge of a cliff," said Tim. "Who knows how far up we've climbed. We're looking down on the tops of clouds, for Christ's sake. A pessimist might say we're backing ourselves in a corner."

"Just stay quiet," said Julian. "If we don't make too much

noise, we shouldn't have to fight more than a couple of zombies at one time. And if we get lucky, we might get a lone zombie to spring that trap of yours."

Cooper grinned. "He'll just hang there defenseless while we beat the shit out of him like a meat piñata."

"Or we could get unlucky, and have swarms of the living dead wash over us and rip our faces off."

"You're really a fucking downer today, dude," said Cooper. "Lighten up. Zombies aren't social creatures. They're mindless shitheads. There's no way they'd be swarming together unless —"

"Somebody's coming!" said Ravenus, flapping excitedly to the ground.

"Okay," said Tim. "Action time. Everybody behind the tree trunk."

Julian vaulted over the trunk on his quarterstaff, landing almost silently on the ground behind it. Cooper simply stepped over it and ducked down. Dave, weighed down by his armor, struggled to climb over it. He looked like a turtle trying to climb a ladder. Cooper grabbed him by the breastplate and yanked him over the log. Tim was small enough to crawl under it. They had already packed leaves, dirt and sticks into the gap between the log and the ground to keep themselves hidden. Included in the gap-stuffing were four lengths of bamboo so that each of them could see what was going on on the other side.

The four of them lay on their stomachs, each with one eye searching for something through their bamboo tubes.

"What the hell is that?" said Tim.

"I don't see anything," said Dave.

"I don't either," said Tim. "I hear something. Julian, do you hear it?"

"Yeah," said Julian. His giant elf ears were even keener than Tim's halfling ears. "It sounds like someone singing."

"And laughing," said Tim.

"Are you sure we're in the right haunted forest?" asked Cooper.

Tim sat up straight. "What the hell is going on?"

"I hear it too!" said Dave. "Shit! Tim, get down. I think I see something."

Tim lay flat on his belly and squinted into the bamboo tube again, focused in the direction of the hooting and laughing and singing. Whatever it was appeared to be on fire.

No, now there were two flames. They waved about wildly as they drew closer. It wasn't long before Tim could clearly see a man running toward him waving two lit torches over his head.

"What the fuck is that jackass doing?" asked Cooper. The man stopped, turned around, and waved his torches at something in the direction of where he was coming from. He was naked but for a deerskin loincloth and a leather satchel slung over his shoulder.

The approaching man's voice was clear now. "Hoo hoo! Haa haa!" he shouted. "Come and get me, you dead bastards! Woogie woogie! Boogie boogie!"

"He's out of his god damned mind," said Tim. And then Tim saw what he hoped he wouldn't but knew he would. The first of the zombies stumbled into view. "You were saying something before, Cooper? I think the last word you said was 'unless'? Did you want to continue with that thought?"

"I'm not taking the blame for this," said Cooper. "How could I have known some crazy ass fuck would purposely try to lead every single zombie in this whole fucking forest straight to us?"

When the first line of zombies got within ten feet of the crazy asshole with the torches, he moved back, still taunting them, still screaming nonsense. "Hoo haa! Hoo haa! Hoobily boobily boo!"

"We have to get out of here," said Tim.

"There's nowhere to go," said Julian. "The whole area is crawling with zombies. Look, there are dozens of them."

Tim shook his head. "I knew this shit would happen. It doesn't matter. We're just going to have to fight our way through and make a run for it."

"Julian's right," said Dave. "We'll never make it."

"Goddammit, Cooper!"

"Chill the fuck out, dude," said Cooper. "And keep your voice down. Let's just lie low and see if this guy has some sort of plan."

"Are you fucking with me?" said Tim, straining to keep his voice to a whisper. "Does that fucking lunatic look like he is acting according to any sort of plan?"

The fucking lunatic ran forward another twenty feet, turned around, and shouted some more taunts at the zombies. "We're almost there, you hell-spawned fiends! Prepare yourselves, for true death awaits you all!" He waved the torches above his head, waiting for the zombies to catch up to him again. He looked over his shoulder, and Tim followed his gaze. There was no mistake. He was looking at the cliff's edge.

Tim was no psychologist, but he didn't think the man looked crazy. His blond hair was windblown and sweaty from all the running he'd been doing, but it could hardly be considered wild or filthy. His grey-green eyes looked to be filled with determination rather than madness.

"I think I know what he's planning to do," said Tim.

"So you don't think he's crazy?" asked Julian.

"I think he's batshit insane," said Tim. "He's going to jump off the edge and hope that they follow him like lemmings."

Julian's eyes went wide. "We've got to stop him!" He started to push himself up to his feet.

Cooper pushed Julian's face into the dirt. "Fuck that guy," he said. "If he wants to jump off a cliff, it's not our place to stop him. His retarded plan might be the only thing that lets us get out of here alive."

"Wiggy jiggy poo ha haa!" sang the man as he ran forward another twenty feet. "Down to the depths of hell with you all!"

He turned around again, and Tim caught the glint of gold on his left hand. A ring. Great, the idiot is married. A story began to form in Tim's mind. Dude probably had a wife, a couple of kids, a golden retriever... all eaten by zombies. Must have broken the poor fucker's will to live. That was a sad story to think about, but it was the only explanation Tim could think of that made any sense.

The smell of rotting flesh swept over them as the zombie horde drew ever closer. These zombies were in some pretty rough shape. The ones he'd seen last time looked like your garden variety movie zombie. Just a grey dead dude walking around. The ones approaching now looked like they'd been through a number of deaths. Some of them dragged their intestines behind them. Most had huge gouges of skin missing from various parts of their bodies. And almost none of them wore more than a shredded scrap or two of clothing. Males shambled forth with their junk swinging between their legs. Females that hadn't had their tits bitten off had them out on display as they reached out their arms in search of one more life to extinguish. Cooper was most likely boring a hole into the ground with his erection.

The man with the torches slowed his pace now that he was nearly at the cliff's edge. He walked backwards, waving the torches like he was signaling a plane to land. Tim and his friends pressed themselves as flat as they could against the ground as he walked past their position. They didn't dare to breathe.

"Behold!" the man shouted, raising the torches so that he looked like a flaming letter Y. "For today marks the end of your tortured existence. The beginning of your eternal slumber. Today you will find rest. Today you will find pea—"

The trap sprung as he stepped on the trigger panel. The rope tightened around his lower leg and swung him up into the air. The tree limb bounced him up and down a few times before he settled, hanging upside down, his head a mere two feet from the ground.

"No!" he screamed. "This can't be! What fool's game is this?" He struggled and writhed as he bounced up and down on the rope. But his efforts brought him no closer to freeing himself from the snare. Tim could only lie still and helpless while the zombies closed in around him.

He clung desperately to the torches he had impressively managed to keep a hold of. His screams were no longer fragments of silly rhyming gibberish. These were screams of terror and disbelief. Tim couldn't believe that this was a man who was ready to die.

But Tim wasn't in a position to do anything to help. The approaching zombies that Tim could see numbered at least thirty or forty. Considering the limited field of view from his current position, the actual number could easily be three or four times that many.

The dangling man swung his torches wildly at the first two zombies to approach him. A completely nude one-armed corpse batted the torch out of his right hand with ease. He caught a female zombie's hair on fire, causing her to stumble away from him blindly, and apparently in a lot of pain. Tim watched her stagger over the edge of the cliff. By the time he looked back, three more zombies had taken her place, the second torch was gone, and the man's screams had either subsided or been drowned out by the sounds of fist pounding flesh and the tearing of skin and leather.

Julian turned to lie on his back. "What the fuck are we going to do?"

"You've got all those scrolls in your bag, right?" asked Dave. "Do you have anything that might help us here?"

"They're all first level spells!" said Julian. "There's like a billion zombies over there. What use are any of these going to be?"

"He's right," said Cooper. "Our only hope is to stand up and fight."

"Fuck you," said Tim. "That's not a hope. That's suicide. Julian, look through your god damned scrolls and find something useful. Now is the time to use your imagination."

Tim kept a careful eye on the carnage while Julian rummaged through his bag. He pulled out a bunch of rolled up parchments.

"No... no... no," said Julian as he looked over each scroll and tossed them aside. "There's nothing here. Oh man we are so fucking fucked." He looked over another scroll, gave it some thought, and tossed it into the growing reject pile. "No... no... no... wait."

"What is it?" asked Dave excitedly.

"Ventriloquism," said Julian.

Cooper hung his head. "What? You think you're going to impress them with a vaudeville act?"

"Shut up, Cooper," said Tim. "What do you have in mind, Julian?"

"If I can make them think there's someone over in the opposite direction, they might start moving away from us."

Tim shrugged. "I've heard worse plans. Today, in fact. Give it a try."

The zombies began to quiet down. Tim looked through his bamboo tube to find only a severed piece of bloodied rope dangling from a broken tree branch. This was all that remained of his former snare. The zombies were dispersing, having presumably beaten all the life they could out of that poor crazy bastard. He looked at Julian and mouthed the word "Now".

Julian nodded, and then silently read over the parchment one more time. He rolled it into a conical tube, closed his eyes, and spoke. Tim could see Julian's lips moving, but the sound was coming from the other side of the zombie horde.

"Oh my heavens!" said Julian's disembodied voice. "I seem to have pulled my big meaty hamstring! However will I deliver this basket of raw human flesh to the orphanage?"

Everyone looked at Julian. His face was covered in sweat and his hands were trembling. He gave a weak shrug and kept talking.

"My sweet fat sister!" the voice continued. "Please shoulder this burden on your thick, elephantine legs. Be swift!"

"They're buying it!" Tim whispered. The zombies, which had until that point been walking around aimlessly, were once again united in the direction they traveled, and it was toward Julian's phantom voice. "Keep talking!"

Julian's eyes darted back and forth as he scrambled for something to say.

He started talking again, only this time in a poorly imitated, high-pitched, female voice. "I cannot leave you, my brave brother. We have come too far only to fail now! The feelings I have for you can no longer be ignored. Come, make sweaty meaty love to me here in this wood, my beloved darling!"

"What the fuck, dude?" said Cooper.

"Shut the fuck up, Cooper!" said Tim. "Keep talking, Julian. They're going."

The walking corpses had all cleared out of the snare trap area. One corpse remained, mangled and bloody. Tied to one of its legs was a length of red sticky rope. Tim turned his head away and threw up.

"Speak you the truth, my dear portly sister?" Julian's voice continued in the male voice again. "For many years I have longed to bury my face in the soft folds of your neck. What joy it does bring me —" As Julian continued to speak, his voice originated once again from within his own body. "to hear you say —"

Cooper clapped a giant clawed hand over Julian's mouth. "Your spell just tapped out," he whispered. "Shut up."

Dave looked through his bamboo tube. "A couple of them turned around. They're headed this way."

"Shit," said Tim, looking through his own tube. "It's okay. We should be able to handle a few. Julian, do you have any more of those ventriloquism spells?"

His mouth still held shut by Cooper's massive hand, Julian answered with a shake of the head.

"Damn," said Tim. "I guess we'll just have to fight the ones who didn't leave. Cooper, swing hard but try not to make a lot of noise if you can help it. Dave, the same goes for you. But break off and do some healing if anyone gets hit. Julian, use whatever spells you've got in your arsenal, but try to keep the incantations as quiet as possible. Got it?"

Julian nodded. Cooper farted.

Dave never took his eyes off the tube. "Guys," he said. "We're in some deep shit."

"Fucking hell," said Cooper. "What is it now?"

"You know those zombies that were moving away?"

"Yeah?" said Tim.

"Well they're not moving away anymore. A lot of them are starting to wander back this way."

"Shit!" said Tim. "Shit shit shit! We were so close. Julian, are you sure you don't have any more ventriloquism scrolls?"

"Yes, I'm sure."

"Why the hell not?"

"Because it really seemed like it sucked."

"Well find something else," said Tim. "And hurry. We've only got about a minute before we have to make our stand or run like hell."

"I don't have anything else," said Julian, looking desperately through his scrolls again. "I've got a couple of magic missiles. I've got a charm person. I've got..."

"What?" said Tim.

"I've got an idea."

"Well come on," said Cooper. "Is it a fucking surprise? Spit it out."

Julian looked up. Tim, Dave, and Cooper turned onto their backs to see what he was looking at. Ravenus looked down at them. He raised a black wing. The four of them waved back at him.

"Ravenus!" Julian whispered excitedly. "Go! Fly away! Talk!"

The bird nodded and launched itself into the air. When it was far enough away, it picked up the disturbing conversation Julian had started. "My sweet sister. Oh how I long to rub my cloaca on your cloaca!" Ravenus's voice grew fainter as he continued to fly away.

All of the zombies followed the bird as he continued spouting more and more of Julian's incestuous dialogue.

Tim breathed what he felt was a long deserved sigh of relief. "Well done, Julian. Way to think on your feet."

"What was all that shit about you wanting to fuck your fat sister?" asked Cooper.

Julian looked at Tim.

"Don't look at me," said Tim. "He's right. That was pretty fucked up."

"Screw you guys," said Julian. "I was just trying to say what I thought might appeal to a zombie."

"They're fucking zombies, dude," said Cooper. "They can't understand what you're saying."

"Well I didn't know that."

"So," said Cooper. "Just to be clear. Do you want to fuck your fat sister?"

"My sister isn't even fat."

"But do you want to fuck her?"

"No!"

"Can I?"

"Fuck off, Cooper."

"You guys shut up," said Tim. "We don't know how long Ravenus is going to be able to hold off those zombies." He crawled under the log and stood up to survey the carnage. What a fucking mess. The torch guy was barely recognizable as human. If Tim had just stumbled upon this scene randomly, he might have just as easily taken this pile of bloody guts to be the remains of a deer that had been mauled by a pack of angry bears.

Cooper, Dave, and Julian joined him.

"Man," said Cooper. "They really tore this poor bastard up."

"I don't guess there's anything you can do for him?" Tim asked Dave.

Dave looked back with an expression of shocked disbelief. "I think he's well beyond negative ten hit points. Look at him. His spleen is way over here." He gestured at a pulpy lump of flesh on the ground next to Cooper's foot.

"How do you know what a spleen looks like?" asked Julian.

"I took a couple of ranks in the heal skill. It came with some basic knowledge of anatomy."

"Cool."

"Julian," said Tim. "He's wearing a ring. Can you use a detect magic spell on it?"

"Sure," said Julian. "No problem." He closed his eyes and put his fingertips on his temples. "Annatto Bixine." When he opened his eyes, they shone like balls of white fire.

"Damn," said Dave. "That looks pretty badass for a zero level spell."

"Holy crap, you guys," said Julian.

"What's wrong?" asked Tim. "Is the ring magical?"

"Yes," said Julian glancing down at the ring briefly. "Everything is magical."

"Are you fucking high?" asked Cooper.

"We're in an extremely evil place, guys."

"How can it be evil?" asked Dave. "It's just a forest."

"I'm telling you. This forest is crawling with dark magic."

"Is the ring dark as well?" asked Tim.

"No. Maybe. I don't know. It's different from the rest of the magic around here, but I can't get a proper reading on it."

"Good enough for me," said Tim. There wasn't any part of the man not absolutely slathered in blood, so Tim was forced to put his squeamishness aside as he slid the blood-soaked ring from the red slippery finger. "Cooper, get over here."

Cooper stepped forward and Tim wiped the blood off of the ring and his hand on Cooper's loincloth.

"Did you want something?" asked Cooper.

"No," said Tim. "Never mind." He looked closely at the gold ring. It had a feather pattern engraved around its edge. "No, wait. I think I know what this is." He slipped the ring on. It constricted until it was comfortably snug around his finger. "It's magic all right."

"So what does it do?" asked Dave.

"I've got a pretty good idea, but we're going to have to try a little experiment. Cooper, I need you to throw me as high in the air as you can."

"Okay," said Cooper. He grabbed Tim by the arms and swung him back.

"Wait!" cried Tim.

"What?"

"I'd like to be thrown away from the cliff's edge, if you don't mind."

"Oh, right. Good idea." He turned around and swung Tim back. "Ready? One, um.... Fuck it." He threw Tim a good thirty feet into the air.

Having reached the zenith of his flight, Tim began to descend. The descent, much to Tim's surprise, was at normal speed. He'd been wrong. He was in for some serious pain. He — Oh, there it was. After falling for a distance of only five feet, the ring betrayed the secret of its power. Tim's fall suddenly slowed as if he'd deployed an invisible parachute. He drifted to the ground and landed harder than he expected, but unharmed.

"That torch guy wasn't committing suicide," said Tim. "He was just clearing out a bunch of zombies. The idea was brilliantly simple. Can you imagine the experience points he would have gotten?"

"Pity you killed him," said Cooper.

"Fuck you, Cooper," said Tim. "That was an accident."

"You have to admit," said Dave. "You're accidental death count is beginning to get alarming."

"Fuck you too, Dave. I only count two."

"Some people go their whole lives without accidentally murdering anyone."

"I don't have to defend myself to you ass clowns. It wasn't my idea to come out here in the first place. I'm going back to the Whore's Head Inn. You idiots can stay out here and get eaten by zombies all you like." He turned around and stomped his tiny legs as he walked away.

"Come on man," said Cooper, following behind him. "We were just fucking with you."

"I'm not in the mood, Cooper. Just leave me —"

"Jesus Christ!" shouted Julian. Tim and Cooper whirled around.

The corpse of the torch guy was grasping Julian by the ankle. The body convulsed as broken bones snapped back into place.

"Get it off me! Get it off me!" Julian cried. Dave grabbed him around the waist and tried to pull him away from the zombie, but its grip was too tight.

Dave's stout form had the advantages of good traction on the ground and a low center of gravity. The zombie was still in the middle of being reformed, so Dave was able to drag it and Julian back a few steps, keeping the zombie from getting properly balanced on its feet. It stumbled to its knees, and its small intestine spilled out of the gaping hole in its belly.

"Come on," said Cooper.

"No," said Tim. Cooper turned around to give Tim a severe glare, but lightened up when he saw Tim smiling. "I've got an idea. Follow me."

Tim ran around to get behind the zombie, and Cooper followed. They gave it a wide berth, but that precaution proved unnecessary. The creature's focus was completely fixed on Julian's leg.

"Where the hell are you guys going?" Julian shouted. "Get over here and help me!"

Tim ignored him and ran up to the tree that he'd used for his snare trap. He pointed to the branch that was only still hanging onto the trunk by a few green splinters. "Cooper. I need that branch. Can you rip it off the tree for me?"

"Not a problem," said Cooper, and proceeded to tear the branch right off. It must have weighed as much as six Tim's, but Cooper tossed it on the ground as if it was nothing more than a rolled up newspaper.

Dave continued his struggle to pull Julian away from the zombie, but all he was succeeding at was to keep the three of them moving.

Tim ran up behind the zombie until he was only about ten feet away from it, grabbed the end of its small intestine, and pulled it back to the tree branch. That got its attention. It let go of Julian's leg at once and got to its feet. It stumbled along the path of its own guts, but Tim was not worried in the least. He tied the end of

the severed rope to the end of the zombie's intestine.

"Okay, Cooper," said Tim. "Do your thing."

Cooper farted and stood looking confused.

"Jesus, Cooper. Grab the branch and chuck it off the side of the cliff."

"Ooh," said Cooper. "Good idea." He picked up the branch and hurled it like a javelin over the side of the cliff.

The zombie tried to grab its intestine with both hands, but it was too slippery for him to get a good grip. More and more intestine spilled out of the creature. Tim had no idea the small intestine was that long. And then he ran out of gut and fell to his knees with a jerk. He tried to gain traction but lacked the coordination. He fell to his face and slid along the stony dirt until he disappeared over the edge. Tim whispered a quiet apology for the man whose death he felt at least partially responsible for.

Dave sat on the ground. "Do you think that next time you could find a more disgusting way to kill something?"

Tim frowned, scanning the edge of the forest. There was nothing to see but trees. "Something's wrong," said Tim. "He shouldn't have been a zombie."

"Why not?" asked Julian. "He was killed by zombies. It's only natural that he becomes one."

"That's not how zombies work in Caverns and Creatures. It's not a communicable disease. Zombies are corpses animated by evil magic. Without an evil cleric here to cast an animate dead spell, there shouldn't be any new zombies."

"I told you before," said Julian. "This place is crawling with evil magic. The whole forest is cursed."

Tim looked at Cooper. "Can that happen?"

Cooper shrugged. "The cavern master can make up any kind of shit he wants. If Mordred put a cursed forest in his campaign, it's a little late to argue with him."

"Don't fucking start with me again, Cooper."

"Is that Ravenus?" asked Dave.

Tim looked to the sky. There certainly was a large black bird flying in toward them.

"Julian!" said Ravenus as he landed. "Are you okay?"

"I'm fine," said Julian. "Just a little shaken up."

"Ravenus," said Tim, switching over to his British accent, as the bird was only able to communicate in the Elven tongue. "What the hell are you doing here? You're supposed to be leading the zombies away from here."

"I couldn't keep the story going," said Ravenus. "I just don't know that much about human sexuality. I felt like they weren't buying it, so I just started telling them about my youth while they clawed against the tree I was perched in. And then I heard Julian scream, so I —"

"Shit," said Tim.

"What?" asked Julian.

"What are you guys talking about?" asked Cooper. "You know I can't understand you when you talk like that."

Tim switched back to his normal dialect. "Ravenus heard Julian scream. If he heard it, then it's a good bet the zombies heard it too. We've got to move now."

"Too late," said Dave, getting to his feet. He was looking past Tim into the trees.

Tim turned to see what he was looking at and found a corpse shambling out of the trees toward them. Two more emerged to her left, and then another three on her right. "Fuck." He ran as fast as his tiny legs would carry him and made a baseball slide under the log.

"What are you doing?" asked Cooper. "They've already spotted us. We can't hide from them."

Tim stood up and cocked his crossbow. "Who said anything about hiding?"

"Shit," said Cooper. "He's right." He, Dave and Julian ran to fetch their weapons from behind the fallen tree.

The zombies continued to shuffle forward.

Cooper leapt over the log and sprinted toward the nearest zombie. He shouted as he ran. "I'm really angry!"

"Cooper!" Tim shouted. "Don't get surrounded!" He knew it was useless to reason with him. He'd turned on his rage and was now in a killing frenzy.

Dave and Julian made their way over the log while Tim scrambled under it. He emerged just in time to see Cooper follow through with his axe in an underhand golf swing that tore a zombie in two from crotch to armpit. The blade then smashed through the exposed collarbone of a second zombie, lodging deep in its chest, but that wasn't quite enough to drop it. It reached out for Cooper's throat with its still-functional right arm.

Tim took aim with his crossbow and pulled the trigger. The bolt pierced through the zombie's brittle cheekbone and it slid off of Cooper's axe.

Dave ran forward, brandishing his mace, to fend off three more zombies that were threatening to surround Cooper. Watching an armored dwarf in a hurry was like watching a normal person wake up from a nap.

Julian didn't waste any time getting tricky. He fired off a magic missile. Tim had to admit, Julian's form was improving. The glowing arrow didn't sputter about like a fourth-hand used car in desperate need of a tune up. It sailed through the air like a shiny cruise missile and blasted a bit of flesh off the chest of the zombie that Dave was running toward, exposing its ribs. It didn't even flinch.

Cooper roared as he swung his axe horizontally. The blade sliced through the necks of two zombies. Neither of their heads was separated entirely from the body, but they both dropped to the ground.

Dave's target caught Cooper from behind before Dave could reach it. It jumped onto his back, hugging him over one shoulder and under the opposite armpit. It sank what remaining teeth it had deep into Cooper's neck. Cooper was already screaming with rage, so it was difficult to tell if his current screaming was a reaction to pain.

If there was any silver lining, it was that Dave's zombie, now latched onto Cooper's back, made for an exceptionally easy target for Dave. He dropped his shield, grabbed the handle of his mace with both hands, and swung as hard as he could. The mace crunched into the creature's back, collapsing the chest cavity entirely. Its arms and legs went limp, but it remained dangling off Cooper's neck from the force of its bite. Cooper shrugged it off and it fell to the ground.

Tim might have been encouraged by how the fight against that first wave had gone. He might have held out hope that they could make it through this if they stood their ground and got a bit lucky. He might have thought it possible that he'd live to see another sunrise. But the massive numbers of zombies currently emerging from the trees snuffed out any hope he had. Even Cooper, maddened with his barbarian battle rage, was taking small steps backward, even while screaming and brandishing his axe. Tim fired his crossbow listlessly into the crowd, not even looking to see if he hit a zombie. He loaded another bolt as he walked over to where Cooper and Dave were convening. He'd never see his sister or his parents again. He'd never again see moonlight sparkle down on the Gulf of Mexico. But if he was going to die today, at least he could meet his end standing alongside his friends.

Julian fired off another magic missile at a random zombie who didn't even seem to mind that its shoulder just exploded. "Hey Tim! Where are you going?" He hopped over the log and followed after Tim.

The four of them converged on the cliff's edge as their imminent death stumbled excruciatingly slowly toward them.

Cooper turned around to face the others. The battle rage was gone from his eyes. Fuck. Even Cooper, who had seemingly spent his entire life building a resistance to the psychological effects of failure, had given up. He got down on one knee and spread his arms. "Come on guys," he said. "How about a hug?"

"Um, okay I guess," said Julian, hesitantly lifting his arms.

Dave pretended not to hear and kept focused on the approaching zombie horde, apparently feeling more comfortable with that than with Cooper trying to hug him.

"Are you fucking serious?" said Tim.

Cooper frowned. The sides of his giant lips sagged over his lower tusks. "Don't be a dick, Tim. Give us a hug."

"Fuck that," said Tim. "I'm going to go out with at least a little bit of dignity."

Cooper sighed. "Dignity is so overrated. Well I'm sorry, Tim. I don't have time for your whiny bullshit right now." As quick as a wink, he scooped up Tim and Julian in one of his giant leathery gorilla arms, and Dave in the other.

"Jesus fuck, Cooper," cried Tim, gagging at the smell of Cooper's sweaty armpit. "I told you I don't want—" He was moving. "Cooper! What are you doing? Sweet Jesus no!"

Dave and Julian also shouted a barrage of objections and expletives, but Cooper was hearing none of it. He clasped his hands together, locking his friends against his body, and ran toward the edge of the cliff.

"Get ready, Tim!" Cooper shouted.

"Ready to die?"

"Fuck that!" said Cooper, and took a running leap off the cliff's edge.

They dropped through the air like a sweaty, foul-smelling stone. Over the roar of the air rushing past them, Tim heard Cooper shit himself. Perfect.

"What the fuck are you waiting for, Tim?" Cooper shouted. "Turn on that fucking ring!"

"It's automatic!" Tim shouted back. "It can't support this much weight!"

"Give it here!" shouted Julian. "I've got an idea!"

"Yeah," said Tim. "Nice idea. Save yourself and let the rest of us fall to our deaths. Here's an idea. Fuck you!"

"Trust me!" said Julian. "It's our only chance!"

Tim looked down. The ground was rushing up toward them at an alarming rate. He looked up. The first couple of zombies had already jumped off the cliff after them. What did he have to lose?

He opened his hand.

Julian scrambled to grab the ring off of Tim's finger, nearly dropping it in the process. What a selfish dick. But Tim was surprised to see that Julian didn't put the ring on his own finger. He wrestled one of Cooper's fingers free from where his hands were locked together, and attempted to shove the ring on.

"You've got to be kidding me!" shouted Tim. "You fucking homo!"

The ring expanded to the size of what Tim might wear for a bracelet. Julian slid the ring onto Cooper's finger, and a fraction of a second later, the four of them were gliding gently toward the ground.

"What?" said Tim. "How...?"

"Feather fall is a first level spell," said Julian. "I read about it in my spellboo—"

"Aaaaahhhh!" everyone shouted as they suddenly started to free fall again. An instant later, the ring's magic kicked back in again.

"Holy shit," said Dave. "What the hell just happened?"

"The ring must have been crafted by a first level wiz—"

If Julian finished his sentence, Tim didn't hear it, being too distracted by his stomach leaping up to his throat. They were in another split-second free fall. And then they weren't.

"Brace yourselves," said Julian. "I think this is going to happen once every six seconds."

Tim shook off a wave of nausea. "Why the hell would it —"

Free fall. Glide.

"The spell only lasts for one round per caster level," Julian explained. "But it's permanent on a ring, so it —"

Free fall. Glide.

"So it kicks back in," Julian continued, "after another five foot drop."

Tim closed his eyes. "That's so fucking retarded. This is going to take forev—"

Free fall. Glide.

Tim abandoned his previous thought. "So why does it work for Cooper, but not for me?"

"The spell —"

Free fall. Glide.

"The spell allows for the wearer to glide down gently while carrying his maximum weight allowance. You can't carry the three of us, but—"

Free fall. Glide.

"But Cooper is strong as shit."

Tim conceded that there was a certain kind of stupid logic in that. He looked up at Cooper's face. It was unnaturally pale. "Coop. What's wrong?"

"I think I'm going to —"

Tim was braced for the next free fall, but not for the shower of half-orc vomit that came just after it. He and Julian spit out chunks of whatever Cooper had eaten for breakfast. Judging by the taste, Cooper's breakfast had been a mixture of corn and dog shit. He was about to shout at Cooper again when he saw a dead body fall past, reaching out to grab him. He looked up. "Shit! Cooper!"

A zombie landed squarely on Cooper's back and sent the lot of them into a tumble. By the time Tim got his bearings, they'd been through another brief free fall, and Dave was missing.

"Dave!" cried Tim.

"Fuck!" cried Dave.

Tim followed Cooper's left arm. Cooper held the zombie in a wrist lock, and Dave was holding onto the zombie's leg. "Hang on, Dave!"

Zombies were raining down all around them. The ground was a whole lot closer now, and Tim could see the bodies smashing into the rocky ground below, kicking up tiny explosions of dust and debris.

The zombie dug its long fingernails into Cooper's wrist, and Cooper dug his claws into the zombie's wrist. The next free fall gave the zombie a jerk, and Cooper clawed straight through the decayed flesh. Tim heard the sound of cracking bone. The next free fall was going to leave the zombie short one hand and send Dave falling to his death with the rest of it.

Tim shouted as loud as he could. "Take off the ring, Cooper!"

"What?"

"Just fucking do it! We've only got one shot at this!"

Cooper pulled up his arm to where Tim could reach his hand. As Tim grabbed the ring, the zombies hand snapped completely off, and everyone was in a full free fall once again. Cooper lost his grip, and Tim found himself falling through the air alone with the ring.

The ground was racing up toward them. Tim could now hear the zombies crashing into the ground. Cooper was still holding onto Julian, and Dave climbed up the zombie's back as they fell. Cooper caught them both in his bloody left arm and hugged tightly. Tim guided the path of his fall toward Cooper, trying his best to minimize his wind resistance.

He reached Cooper, wrapped his arms and legs around his thigh, and passed the ring up to Julian, who slipped it back on Cooper's finger.

They were only about a hundred feet in the air when they began to glide again. Cooper screamed as the zombie bit into his face, but he held on. There was nothing anyone could do but wait.

Free fall. Glide. Free fall. Glide.

The zombie continued biting and Cooper continued screaming. He was rapidly running out of face. He wasn't going to make it.

"Dave!" shouted Tim. "Do something!"

"My hands are pinned!"

"Heal him, you asshole!"

"Oh, right!" said Dave. "I heal thee!"

Cooper's expression was a mix of agony and ecstasy as the skin on his face grew back even while the zombie continued to eat it.

Free fall. Glide.

"I heal thee!" Dave shouted again. It was an uphill struggle. The zombie appeared to be doing more damage than Dave was healing, but Cooper was hanging on.

Free fall. Thud.

Cooper landed on his back with Tim between his legs, knocking the air out of Tim's lungs. Dave, Julian, and the zombie spilled out of Cooper's arms and rolled to either side of him.

Tim let go of Cooper's leg and sucked in as much air as his flattened lungs would allow. With that he got a generous whiff of the inside of Cooper's shit-caked loincloth. It was more than he could bear. He curled into a ball and threw up.

Cooper staggered to his feet. Half his face hung down in bloody tendrils. He stumbled backwards, trying hard to keep his balance. The zombie didn't look to be in much better shape, but it also managed to get on its feet. They limped toward one another, both seemingly unaware of the bodies exploding on the ground around them.

Cooper removed the dead hand still digging into his wrist and threw it on the ground. He spat out a gob of blood and phlegm and beckoned the zombie toward him.

It stumbled forward and took a swing at Cooper with its stump of a right arm. Cooper didn't have to move far to dodge it. He waited for the zombie to strike with its good arm, ducked out of the way, and grabbed it. He spun the zombie around by one arm like an irresponsible parent. After three rotations the arm broke off at the shoulder and the rest of the body flew through the air toward the cliff wall.

The dead bastard still had a bit of life left in him. With no hands, it was unable to stand up, but it pushed itself toward Cooper with its legs and opened its mouth wide to dig its teeth in one last time. It never got close. Cooper thrashed the thing with its own arm, swinging down as hard as he could again and again until it stopped moving. And then he thrashed it some more until the arm broke away from the wrist. And then he got down on his knees and punched it until its head was a pulpy mess of blood, brain, and bone fragments. And then he passed out on top of the handless headless mess.

"Come on, guys," said Tim. "Let's get him out of here. It'd be a shame to go through all that and then get hit by an errant corpse."

Tim, Dave, and Julian dragged Cooper out of harm's way. Dave used up the rest of his daily allotment of healing spells, bringing most of the skin back to Cooper's face and knuckles. He still looked like he'd survived a prison beating, but he was going to pull through.

Ravenus glided down in a wide spiral on his magnificent black wings. "Glad to see everyone's doing well."

Julian spit out some blood and gave a weak laugh. He and Dave helped Cooper to his feet and started the long walk back to the boozy comforts of the Whore's Head Inn.

Tim walked alongside Julian. "Hey, listen. I'm sorry I called you a fucking homo up there."

"It's all right."

"I was just upset. I don't actually have anything against homosexuals."

"I'm not one."

"Okay, but if you were, I just want you to know that I'm totally cool with that."

"But I'm not."

"Hey, it's none of my business, right? I'm just saying, it wouldn't bother me if—"

"I want to set the record straight," said Julian. "I'm not into fucking dudes, my sister, or fat girls."

"That's kind of shallow of you," said Tim.

"I'm kind of partial to big girls," said Dave.

"I wouldn't mind having a crack at your sister," said Cooper.

"Fuck you guys," said Julian.

The End

Orcs, Bears, and Assholes
ROBERT BEVAN

ORCS, BEARS, AND ASSHOLES

(Original Publication Date: December 15, 2012)

"Okay guys," said Julian. "Stop. Just stop." Tim, Cooper, and Dave turned around to look at him. "We're done."

"What are you talking about?" said Cooper. "We haven't done shit all day."

"That's exactly what I'm talking about. You said this was supposed to be a half day's journey. We've been walking for hours, and I haven't seen a single landmark referenced on that map of yours. If we turn around now, we can get back to Cardinia before nightfall."

"The half day's journey could be meant for people on horseback," said Tim. "There's no scale on the map. Even on foot, Dave's a dwarf and I'm a halfling. We've both only got a base movement speed of 20."

Julian snatched the map from Cooper. "Come on, man! A smoldering volcano? A pyramid? A rock formation in the shape of a lion's head? It's time to face the fact that we've been duped."

"You haven't played Caverns and Creatures before," said Dave. "In the game world, these things aren't as uncommon as you might suspect."

Tim wiped the sweat from his brow. "Maybe we missed something."

"Look around!" said Julian. "What's there to miss? The land barely has any topography. How could we have missed a fucking volcano?" He looked up into the branches of a nearby tree. "Ravenus. You've been flying around. How many volcanoes have you seen today?"

"None that I recall, sir," answered the giant black bird from where he perched.

Julian glared up at Cooper.

"Well?" said Cooper. "Don't leave me hanging. What did he say?"

"He said you're a moron."

"Not about me," said Cooper. "About the volcanoes."

"I've had enough," said Julian. "You guys go chase this wild goose as far as you like. Ravenus and I are going back to the Whore's Head Inn. Come on, Ravenus!" He turned around and started walking northward.

"Wait," said Dave. Julian turned around. "Here comes a wagon from the south. Let's ask them if anything on the map looks familiar. If they say no, we'll head back."

Julian pursed his lips and thought about it for a moment. "Fine. I'll do the talking."

"Of course," said Dave.

"Cooper, put your axe away. You're offensive enough to look at without it."

"Good call," said Cooper. He fastened the axe to the strap on his back.

"And try not to shit yourself or anything while we're talking."

Cooper's leathery jowls sagged as he frowned. "You know I can't always help that."

Julian sighed. He walked up and patted Cooper on his huge arm. "I'm sorry, Cooper. I just don't want to spook these guys, you know?"

"All right," said Cooper.

"I hate meeting new people," said Julian. "I never know what to say."

"Just go with the old stand-by," said Tim.

"The old stand-by is stupid."

"Do whatever you want. You've got the highest charisma score. You get to be the face of the party."

"Fine," said Julian. He led the group to the approaching wagon with arms raised in a gesture of peace.

The man driving the cart slowed his horses to a stop, but kept his hands conspicuously on the reins. He was fat and sweaty. His white hair was tufty on the sides, absent up top, and long in the back. It was the worst mullet Julian had ever seen. His whiskers were just long enough so that you couldn't tell if it was the beginning of an intentional beard, or the result of a couple of weeks' worth of laziness. He took a handkerchief out of the satchel slung over his shoulder and wiped the sweat off of the part of his head which was best reflecting the sun.

"Hi ho, friend or foe," said Julian.

The wagon driver squinted down at Julian and then surveyed the rest of the group. He spit something brown on the ground. "You fellers make a queer group of traveling companions. I don't recall never seein' a dwarf travel all friendly-like 'long side no orc before."

"I'm only half-orc," said Cooper.

The man's squinty eyes went round. "Bucky, Micah!" As quick as a flash, Julian found himself staring up at the points of two crossbow bolts aimed right at his face. Beyond them were the faces of two younger men. Their features betrayed a close blood relationship to the driver. No doubt his sons. "We don't want no trouble, hear?"

Julian stretched his arms out even wider, attempting to demonstrate that he couldn't be any less threatening. He twisted his head around to Cooper and mouthed the words "Shut the fuck up!" He turned to face the wagon driver again. "We don't want trouble either, sir. Honestly, we mean you no harm. We would only like to inquire about where you come from."

"What business is it of yours where we come from?" The old man spat on the ground again.

"Your personal affairs do not concern us," said Julian. "We simply require knowledge of the terrain in the direction from whence you came."

"Bucky," said the driver. "If'n he don't shut up all that fancy talk, you go on an' shoot him, hear?"

"You got it, Paw."

"Be clear now, boy," said the driver. "Just what is it you want?"

"I'd like you to take a look at this map for us." Julian shook the rolled up parchment in his hand.

"Micah, hop down an' get that map."

One of the younger men hopped down from the back of the wagon. The remaining son steadied his crossbow on Julian, as if daring him to try anything.

The one called Micah took the map out of Julian's hand and passed it up to his father.

The white whiskered man dug in his satchel until he found a small lens. He held the parchment at arm's length and scanned it with his lens. "The hell kinda map is this?"

"A treasure map?"

The driver glanced up at Bucky, who was peeking at the map over his shoulder. They shared a snicker.

"And what do you reckon this is a map of?" asked the driver.

"The lands south of Cardinia?" said Julian.

The old man flashed a wide grin. Two of the five teeth Julian could see were gold, and one was rotted away to a brown nub. "I think you boys done been had."

Julian lowered his hands and put them on his hips. He looked back at Cooper. "So there are no pyramids down that way?"

"We're from the south, boy," said the driver. "We're just headed up to Cardinia on a matter of business. I can assure you there ain't no pyramids down that way."

"How 'bout volcanoes, Paw?" said Bucky.

The old man tipped back his head as if in thought. "I don't seem to recall any volcanoes either. What do you think, Micah?"

"I think these fellers got about as much good sense between the lot of 'em as what the gods gave a bag of dog shit."

"That was uncalled for," said Cooper.

Micah's face went instantly serious, to the point of anger. He raised his crossbow right up to Cooper's snout of a nose. "You shut yer mouth, orc," he said. "I'll split that little brain of yers in two."

"You ever have an orc foot up your ass before, Billy Bob?"

"Micah!" snapped the driver. "Back in the wagon."

Micah backed off slowly, taking neither his eyes nor his crossbow off of Cooper. "You got a big mouth, orc. One day it's gonner get you into trouble."

"Try every day," said Dave.

"Shut it, Stumpy," said Micah, climbing back into the back of the wagon, his crossbow arm now shifting from Cooper to Dave. "You dwarves ain't any better than them orcs. I can't wait until you finally all kill each other."

"You have charming sons, sir," said Tim, his hands still raised.

"They got more spirit than sense at times," said the driver. He rolled up the parchment. "Listen, boys. I don't know where you got that map, but I hope you didn't pay too much for it. It ain't worth demanding yer money back for if'n you got to admit to havin' been stupid 'nuff to follow it."

"I'm sorry," said Tim. "Were you talking just now? Or just massaging your tooth?"

Julian threw up his hands and walked away from the wagon. "So much for diplomacy."

"It's startin' to get dark out," said the driver. "I had half a mind to offer you fellers a ride back to town, but now I think I'd rather see how those sharp tongues of yours defend you against the creatures that come out at night." He tossed the map to the ground and snapped the reins on his horses. "Yah!" The wagon started moving down the road toward Cardinia.

"Bite my little halfling ass!" Tim called out after them. "You toothless fucking hillbilly bastards!"

Tim was answered with a couple of lazily fired crossbow bolts. One sailed clear over the lot of them, but the other pierced Cooper in the ass.

"Ow," said Cooper, removing his finger — as well as an orange layer of filth — from his ear.

"You know," Julian said to Tim. "I can't really use my diplomacy skill if you guys are going to break into the conversation and insult people."

"I just can't stand rednecks. "

"I don't think I've ever seen you lose your shit like that."

"They're right about one thing," said Dave. "It is going to be dark pretty soon." The sky was pink as the sun touched the western horizon.

Julian picked up the map from off the ground. "Is everyone now satisfied that this map is useless?"

Tim sighed. "Yeah."

Dave nodded.

Cooper winced slightly as he plucked the bolt from his ass. "Maybe we were holding it upside down." He bent over and lifted the back of his loincloth to expose his grey leathery ass. Dark red blood — almost black — trickled out of the hole where the bolt had been. "Dave, you mind?"

"Jesus, Cooper!" said Dave. "It's magic. I don't actually have to touch the wound." He waddled over to Cooper's front and touched him on the shoulder. "I heal thee."

Cooper's wound healed over and was soon indistinguishable from the rest of his ass. Cooper farted in relief.

Tim took the lead on the long road back to Cardinia, but was soon outpaced by Cooper and Julian.

"The more I look at this map," said Julian, holding the map uncurled in front of him as he walked. "The stupider it looks to me. I mean, look at this. Even if we did find the volcano, there's just a curvy dotted line leading out into the middle of nowhere until it hits an X."

"How can you even read that?" asked Tim. "I can barely see where I'm going anymore."

"I've got like super elf eyes or whatever," said Julian. "I can see in almost total darkness."

"That must be nice," said Tim. "I can't see shit. Dave, let me hold your arm."

"Okay," said Dave.

Cooper turned around and snorted. "Fags."

Julian glared up at him briefly, but let it go. He had bigger issues with Cooper. "Where the hell did you get this map anyway?"

"In the open market," said Cooper. "There was a guy selling scrolls and shit, so I asked him if he had any treasure maps. I gave him a gold piece and he drew it right then and there."

"You spent a whole gold piece on that?" said Dave.

"It seemed like a good investment," said Cooper.

"How hard did the scroll guy laugh while he was drawing this?" asked Julian.

"He and his apprentice laughed quite a lot, actually," said Cooper. "But I thought it was because I farted."

"You are a piece of work, my friend," said Tim. "Remind me never to trust you with—"

A loud caw cut Tim off. Ravenus flew down out of the sky. Julian stopped to let him perch atop his quarterstaff.

"Trouble ahead," said the bird.

"What kind of trouble?" asked Julian.

"Those men in the wagon who stopped to talk to you earlier."

"Yeah? What about them?"

"A bunch of orcs came out of the woods and ambushed them."

"Good for them," said Tim. "Why should we give a damn?"

Julian furrowed his eyebrows at Tim. "I'll overlook, for the moment, that you are celebrating the murder of three human beings, but—"

"Oh come off it," said Tim. "They're not even real. Get it through your pale slender head." He waved his arms around. "None of this exists."

"You don't know that," said Julian.

"He's right," said Dave. "Who can say what exists and what doesn't?"

Tim shifted his rant to Dave. "What are you, a fucking philosopher now?"

"I'm just saying that we're in a seemingly impossible situation right now," Dave shouted right back at him. "And I'm not going to rush into any snap decisions about what exists and what doesn't. We're all either suffering from some complicated mass delusion, or else—"

"Will you guys shut the fuck up?" roared Cooper. A flock of black birds erupted out of a nearby tree and flew away, but otherwise, they all stood in momentary silence. "I'm sorry," Cooper continued. "My head was starting to hurt from all of your bullshit." From the way he was rubbing his forehead, he might have been serious. "We've got more important shit to talk about."

"Like what?" snapped Tim.

"Like there's an angry mob of violent orcs between us and Cardinia."

"Oh, right."

"Yeah," said Dave.

"Yeah," said Julian. "That's pretty important."

"So what do we do?" asked Dave.

"We could just camp out here for the night," said Julian."Go back to town in the morning."

"No good," said Tim. "There's every chance we'll encounter something far worse than orcs if we stay out here tonight. We're not high enough level to be camping in the wilderness at night yet."

"We slept in the woods on our first night here," said Julian.

"And we got mauled by a fucking leopard," said Tim. "Anyway, that was back when Mordred was around to keep encounters level-appropriate. Mordred's not here anymore. There's no telling what we could run into at night."

"Could we go around them?" asked Dave.

"We could try. But if we give them too wide a berth, we risk getting lost in the woods, which is worse than camping out here."

"They're just orcs," said Julian. "Aren't they supposed to be first level mooks? Why don't we just smash through them?"

"I'm a half-orc," said Cooper. "The half of me that makes the big badass you see before you is the orc half. The other half is just as much of a pussy as you guys. The guys you want to 'just smash through' are all orc."

"But we've got intelligence," said Julian.

"Is that racist?" Cooper asked Tim.

"That's not what I'm talking about," said Julian. "I'm talking about military intelligence. We know their position, their plan of attack. That sort of thing."

Everyone spent a moment in silent contemplation.

"Shit," said Tim. "Is that the best we've got?"

Dave, Cooper, and Julian answered with halfhearted shrugs, nods, and grunts.

"Okay then," Tim continued. "We'll get as close to their position as we can. And then we'll wait."

"Wait for what?" asked Dave.

"Wait for them to spot a target."

"Oooh, I like it," said Julian. "Ambush the ambushers."

"That's right," said Tim. "Hopefully whoever they attack is going to have at least some power to defend themselves, and we'll hit those fuckers from behind."

"Aren't you guys forgetting one thing?" asked Dave. Everyone turned to look at him, but no one spoke. "How is waiting around in the wilderness over there any different than waiting around in the wilderness over here? Except, of course, that if we're randomly attacked by bears or whatever over there, we'll be sandwiched between angry bears and angry orcs."

"Even better!" said Tim. "If we get attacked by bears or whatever, we'll just make a run for it."

"How is that not an incredibly stupid plan?" asked Dave.

"We'll run right through where the orcs are hiding. The orcs will have to deal with whatever is chasing us, preferably before they deal with us. We might be able to escape them without a fight."

Cooper nodded slowly. "I like it."

"I'm still not convinced," said Dave.

"Then stay here, fuckhead," said Cooper.

"I'm in," said Julian.

All eyes turned to Dave.

Dave sighed. "Fine. I guess dying with you guys is a little better than dying alone."

They walked along the road for another half hour before Ravenus warned them that the ambush site was coming up soon. They took cover behind a large oak tree.

"I see one!" whispered Julian excitedly. "I think he's alone. He looks to be taking a dump."

"If we could take one out now," said Dave. "It would be one less we'll have to deal with if it comes to a fight."

Everyone looked at Tim.

"What?" said Tim. "Have you forgotten? I'm the only one here who can't see in the fucking dark!"

"You're the only one who has any chance of sneaking up on him. You'll be able to see him if you get close enough," said Dave.

Julian pointed in the direction of the lone orc. "He's next to that tree over there. Can you at least see the tree's silhouette against the sky?"

"Yeah," said Tim, licking his lips. "Which tree?"

"The coniferous one."

"Good," said Cooper. "Maybe it will eat him."

"What?" said Tim.

"Shut up, Cooper," said Julian. "Stay focused, Tim. We'll be here to back you up if things go wrong. I'll make a couple of Light stones to distract them. Are you up for this?"

"I think so," said Tim. "It feels weird. I've never outright murdered anyone before."

"Sure you have," said Dave. "Don't forget Mord—"

Cooper punched Dave in the head.

Tim didn't even bother to glare at either of them. "Okay," he said. "I've got this." After patting himself down the sides to make sure his weapons were in order, he bolted off into the tall dark grass. He was surprisingly quick and nimble for someone who couldn't see. And so quiet. If Julian didn't have super elf ears and wasn't actually focused directly on Tim, he probably wouldn't have heard him moving at all.

He slowed down as he got to within about forty feet of the squatting orc. Julian guessed that Tim knew he was getting close, but was still unable to see his target. Every step was deliberate, almost exaggerated, like someone in a silent film who wants the audience to know they were being sneaky. He slowly unsheathed his dagger and crept ever closer. When he was almost on top of the orc — maybe fifteen feet away at best — he stopped dead in his tracks. Four heartbeats later, he darted forward, leapt onto the orc's back, pulled back its head by the topknot of hair, and drew his dagger swiftly and silently across the creature's neck.

Julian heard the faintest hint of a grunt which quickly gurgled away into nothing. The next sound was the orc's bowels letting go, which told Julian that Tim's mission had... Julian thought of Cooper. No, an orc's bowels letting go didn't actually tell him much of anything.

The orc fell forward, and Tim tumbled off of its back and popped up ready and alert, dagger in hand. He had a quick look around, nodded, and started running back.

"He did it," Julian whispered to Dave and Cooper.

"Nice," said Cooper.

"I hope he's okay," said Dave.

Tim didn't bother with sneakiness as he sprinted back, but he was still remarkably quiet for someone running as fast as... well, as fast as a normal-sized person casually jogs.

When he reached the others, he bent over with his hands on his knees to catch his breath. "One down," he said between breaths.

"How..." Julian forced out the rest of the question. Insensitive or not, he had to know. "How did it feel?"

Tim looked up at him with big bright eyes. "It was exhilarating," he said. "That's actually got me a little concerned."

"I wouldn't worry about it," said Cooper.

"Yeah," said Julian. "At least not until we get out of this — Shit! Get down!"

The other three lay down flat as roadkill while Julian focused his ear in the direction of the dead orc.

The sound was like nothing Julian had ever heard before. It was like a pig choking to death. "What is that?"

Cooper answered. "He said the blood is still warm. The kill is fresh."

"You can understand that?" said Tim.

"He's speaking orcish," said Cooper. "It sounds perfectly natural to me."

"Of course it does," said Dave. "Keep listening."

"Okay, um... I missed the beginning. Something about groups of four. Keep within visual range of one another. Do not engage."

"We're fucked," said Dave.

"No we're not," said Tim. "Just keep quiet and stay calm. We'll think of something before they get here."

"What does it sound like?" Julian asked Cooper.

"What does what sound like?"

"Orcish," said Julian. "You can't understand us when we speak Elven, but to those of us who can understand it, it sounds like British English. So I wanted to know. What does the Orcish language sound like to you?"

Cooper scratched under his arm as he thought about it. "The shrimp guy," he said finally.

"Seriously?" said Tim.

"Who's the shrimp guy?" asked Julian.

"He's an old Vietnamese guy who sells shrimp out of the back of his van on highway 90," said Dave. "He's got a bit of an accent, but his English is pretty good."

"You guys shut up," said Julian. "A group of them is coming this way.

Tim lay flat on his back with his crossbow on his chest. He groped around in his bag until he finally pulled out a bolt. He carefully pulled back the string until the weapon clicked. "If it comes to a fight, you guys jump up before me. I'll want to get in at least one sneak attack."

The others nodded. Julian held his breath as the four orcs continued to move toward them. The sweat under his robes was warm and sticky, but the sweat on his forehead felt refreshingly cool.

"How far off are they?" Dave whispered.

"I don't know," said Tim. "To me it sounds like they're right on top of us. Can you hear them?"

Dave and Cooper shook their heads.

"Good," said Julian, relieved. "Then they're probably still a good ways away." Tim's ears were nearly as sensitive as Julian's. It was easy to misjudge distance in times of extreme duress.

"Fuck it," said Dave. He was sweating like a rapist, and beginning to shiver. "I can't take it anymore. I say we take these four down and rush toward one of the groups on the side. If we can keep fighting them while they're in groups of four, we'll have a better shot at running away once they start to gather together." He looked at Tim.

Tim looked at Julian, and then at Cooper.

"I'm with Dave," said Cooper.

"Damn," said Tim. "I never thought I'd hear that. Julian?"

Julian shrugged. "Whatever."

"Count of three," said Tim. He held up one finger, then a second.

Before Tim could raise a third finger, a horrible noise echoed through the night air, full of snarls and phlegmy growls. Tim put his hand down. The orcs started moving in the opposite direction.

"What was that?" asked Tim.

"The orc leader, I guess," said Julian.

Everyone looked at Cooper.

"Well," said Tim. "What did he say?"

"I couldn't make it out," said Cooper. "It was too faint."

"Shit," said Julian. "It sounded like someone throwing up and

sneezing at the same time."

"All right," said Cooper. "That means 'Get back to your post. There's a target approaching from the north.'"

"Really?" said Tim.

Cooper nodded.

"That's what the shrimp guy sounds like to you?" asked Dave.

"Sort of," said Cooper. "Except that I can understand the orcs."

"What do you think?" said Julian.

"I think Cooper's a racist."

"Fuck you, Dave," said Cooper.

"Would you guys shut up?" said Julian. "I mean what do you think we should do now?"

"The plan was to ambush the orcs during their ambush," said Tim.

"Yeah, I remember," said Dave. "That plan seemed a lot less scary a couple of hours ago."

"If we do nothing," said Julian, "we're just sentencing some poor schlubs to an untimely death. Are you comfortable with that?"

Dave wiped the sweat from his brow with his leopard-spotted furry forearm. "I'm not completely uncomfortable with it."

"If we don't act now," said Tim, "we'll just be back at square one, but with a few more innocent deaths on our conscience. I say we—"

"Holy shit!" shouted Cooper without regard for the noise he was making. He jumped to his feet.

"Cooper!" said Julian. "Get down!" He chanced a peek up at the orcs who had indeed turned around. "They're going to see—" Julian was suddenly engulfed in a shockwave of reverberating air. A roar like a moose being fucked by a whale in a cave rumbled low, but loudly, from behind him. His insides shook. Julian knew he had to turn around, but the fleeing orcs strongly suggested that he wasn't going to like what he saw when he did so.

He turned around. "What the fuck is that?" The beast stood on its hind legs, brown and furry and huge. At this distance, he couldn't make out exactly how big it was, but it was easily more than twice as tall as a man.

"It's a bear," said Dave.

"Screw you, man," said Julian. "I've been to the zoo. That's no fucking bear."

"It's a dire bear."

"Dire bear?" Even in the presence of enormous furry death, Julian couldn't help but laugh. "Are you fucking with me?"

"Does that not look dire to you?"

"We'll talk about it later," said Tim. "Let's go!"

Cooper scooped up Tim in one arm and Julian in the other.

"Hey guys!" shouted Dave, huffing as he stomped after him on his short, thick legs.

"Put me down, Cooper!" said Julian.

Cooper stopped and looked back at the bear. It dropped down to stand on all four of its legs and the earth shook beneath them. It started moving toward them.

"You're not fast enough," said Cooper. "Hell, I'm probably not fast enough."

"You keep running," said Julian. "I'll summon up a horse for me and Dave."

"I don't know," said Cooper. "What if—"

"It's a good plan!" shouted Tim from under Cooper's arm. "Just fucking do it already. Go!"

Cooper started running.

Julian waved his hand in a small circle before his face. "Horse!" he said.

Dave caught up just as a white stallion materialized out of the air. "Hey. Thanks for—" He flew backwards through the air like he'd been shot from a cannon.

"Dave!" Julian ran over to him. He looked up to check on the bear. It was moving slowly in their direction, sniffing the air.

"Fucking horses," Dave moaned as he propped himself up on his elbows. There was a second hoof-shaped indentation in the breastplate. If it had been a little straighter, he might have been able to pass it off as a deliberate design.

"You know you're not supposed to approach them from behind," said Julian. He reached down to help Dave to his feet.

"I didn't approach it at all!"

"Just make sure you don't wear that armor around a stable. People will think you're retarded."

Dave looked back toward the bear. "Shit," he said. "I think Teddy has a taste for horse."

The ground shook. The bear was running at them. Hind legs reaching past forelegs as it bounded forward. "Come on, man. Get on the horse!"

"I can't!" shouted Dave. "I'm too short!"

Julian wove his fingers together to offer Dave a boost. Dave struggled, but couldn't manage to get his other leg over the horse's back. Julian let go.

"Shit!"

"What are we going to do?" asked Dave.

"I've got an idea," said Julian.

The bear had halved the distance between them. Julian pulled a coil of rope out of his bag. He tied one end around his waist and climbed into the saddle.

"Does your idea involve me at all?" asked Dave anxiously.

"Hold this," said Julian, tossing Dave the other end of the rope. "And try to keep your chin up."

Dave caught the rope. "Huh?"

"Yah!" shouted Julian. The horse bolted forward. Julian looked back at Dave, who was just standing there staring at the end of the rope like it was his dick in his hand. "Hold on, Dave!"

Dave appeared to have caught on just in time. Right before the rope pulled taut, Dave wrapped it around his leopard-spotted forearm and grabbed it with the other hand as well. He sailed forward over the same ten-foot patch of earth that he had, only a moment before, sailed backward behind.

Up ahead, Cooper and Tim were almost to the trees. The orcs running ahead of them had already disappeared into the forest.

Once they made it there, they would have some time to breathe. There was no way that big-ass bear would be able to move so fast through the trees.

While Julian was gaining on Cooper, the bear was gaining on him a lot faster. Dave's armor would probably have glided on the grass a lot more smoothly if it didn't have two hoofprints in it. It didn't matter. They would all make it into the trees with seconds to spare.

Julian was looking back at the approaching bear when his heart sank down to his feet. The horse took flight briefly. His heart started beating again when hooves met earth, but he only had time to spot the rock the horse had leapt over a split-second before Dave met it with his face. Julian felt the rope jerk him around the waist as he flew off the back of the horse.

Shit.

Julian hit the ground hard. Not so hard as Dave's face had hit that rock, but hard enough that he scarcely had time to figure out which way was up before the bear monster reached Dave.

From a distance, the beast had looked big, but only now that it was right up next to him did Julian fully appreciate the size of this creature. It was like being engulfed in a furry brown tsunami.

It sniffed at Dave with nostrils that Julian could have stuck his whole head in without messing up his hair. Julian didn't know if Dave was playing dead or actually dead, but whichever it was, it seemed to be working out well enough for him. Julian let his head drop to the ground, closed his eyes, and hoped for the best.

Playing dead was a lot more difficult than Julian expected it would be. With eight thousand pounds of fur and claws and teeth sniffing around him, lying still went against his basest instincts. The only reason he existed at all was because thousands of generations of natural selection had filtered out most of the people whose instincts, when presented with a giant bear, said anything but "You get the fuck out of here!" Add to that the effort he had to expend not to cry or piss himself, and playing dead was a remarkably astounding feat.

The ground shook as the bear smashed a car-sized paw into the earth toward him. Its breathing sounded like Darth Vader with a sinus infection. It felt like wind blowing the heat of a bonfire at his skin. And the smell. It was like a sewer filled knee-deep with dead bodies and fish. If Julian survived, he would add 'not vomiting' to his list of accomplishments during this encounter.

And then the rancid hot breath was gone. Julian chanced a breath and a peek. The big bastard was up on its hind legs, its giant bear dick looking down at him. The roar this animal let out was so long and loud that Julian wasn't sure if he was deaf or not until it ended. That was all Julian's bladder could take. It let go. So did the bear's. In the space of about five seconds, Julian had been sprayed with enough bear piss to swim in if it had been contained.

"Yah!" shouted Tim. Julian wiped the bear piss out of his eyes in time to see Tim hauling ass toward the trees on the back of his horse. The bear gave chase, and Julian could just barely make out a tiny crossbow bolt poking out of its back. It might as well have been a sewing needle for all the damage it did, but it got the bear's attention.

Julian got up and ran over to Dave. His face was covered in blood. His nose was smashed in, but he was breathing. Julian slapped him on the cheek a couple of times. Wet, sticky, bloody slaps. Dave moaned and Julian sighed in relief.

"Come on, man. Get up!"

"My face," Dave groaned.

"Dude," said Julian. "You're a cleric. Heal yourself."

Dave winced as he brought a fingertip to his cheek. "I... heal... thee." It was all he could do to get out the words, but it was enough. He moaned in a mixture of agony and ecstasy, like he was having an orgasm while his nose sprouted back out like an inflating balloon. "Damn that feels good!"

Julian helped Dave to his feet. "Let's go. Tim and Cooper are sandwiched between a horde of orcs and a giant bear."

Dave nodded. They both started running. Julian easily outpaced Dave, but he had no time to waste. The bear was tearing through trees like they were made out of balsa wood. It roared and stood on its hind legs every now and again as it was hit with an arrow or bolt, presumably fired by Tim and any number of scared orcs.

"Julian!" Dave cried out from behind him. Whatever it was could wait. As soon as Julian made it to the tree line, he would fire a —

Julian felt like he had just been smacked in the gut with a piece of swinging rebar. It knocked him off of his feet and he landed on his back. He looked down at his abdomen and remembered that he still had an umbilical cord between himself and Dave. He turned around to find that Dave, too, had fallen. Oops.

"Sorry!" Julian shouted as he hastily untied the rope from around his waist.

Dave got up and started moving again, pulling the rope into loops as he ran. Julian, now no longer attached to Dave, broke off to the right, giving the bear a wide berth. It wasn't paying any attention to him, but this wasn't the sort of creature you gambled with.

When he made it to the trees, he had a better view of the action. Tim and Cooper were right there alongside the orcs. They must have put their differences aside to deal with the common threat. Tim took pot shots at the bear with his crossbow, for whatever that was worth, but Cooper dared not close in with his axe. They all backed off at the same pace as the bear tore down trees. A couple of them made to back out of the fight entirely, but an authoritative voice shouted what Julian guessed must be the Orcish equivalent of "You'd better get your asses back in there," and they took up their positions once again in the front line trying futilely to stab at the bear.

"Ravenus!" Julian shouted.

"Up here," said the bird.

Julian looked up and found Ravenus perched on the branch of a tree just behind him. "Fly ahead and find out who's coming up the road," said Julian. "Try to talk to them. If any of them speak Elven, tell them about the orcs, and tell them about our current situation. If they've got any strength to them, see if you can't get them to come and help us out."

"Right away," said Ravenus. He flapped up through the treetops and into the night.

Julian had a couple of Magic Missiles at his disposal, but those weren't likely to decide whether that huge bear lived or died. They might, however, decide the fate of a few orcs in the meantime. He moved deeper into the forest, trying to stay out of sight and assess the orc threat. There wouldn't be much point in taking out the spear-wielding orcs on the front line next to Tim and Cooper. But an archer... yes, he might be able to take down an archer or two before the bear situation was resolved without the rest of the orcs even noticing. And he could pick up a bow as well.

He took a moment to look for an orc archer who wouldn't be missed immediately if he suddenly dropped dead. The one nearest him looked like a good enough target. Only about fifty feet away — well within the range of a Magic Missile — and the next one beyond him was another thirty feet away still. Pick them off one by one, Sergeant York style.

He focused on his first target. The orc was pulling back his bowstring, taking aim at the massive bear. Julian whispered the words "Magic Missile" and a small glowing yellow bolt of energy materialized in the air beside him and hovered. He waited until the orc loosed its arrow.

The arrow flew, joining a few dozen more sticking out of the dire bear, which was now beginning to look like a dire porcupine. Attention back to the orc.

"Have some!" said Julian, and the glowing arrow homed in on its target. It hit the orc in the side, just below his ribs, and exploded in a shower of sparks.

The orc's reaction was not exactly what Julian was expecting. It shouted a single orcish syllable. Julian didn't have to understand orcish to make a pretty good guess as to what it might have translated to. It looked down at the softball-sized third degree burn on its side, and then it looked up at Julian. The one thing it did not do, however — the one thing Julian had been counting on — was fall down and die. Shit.

The orc looked pissed. Not the normal kind of 'someone-just-shot-me' kind of pissed. This was a special kind of pissed that Julian had only seen in one other person before. The whites of its eyes turned blood red. Its bare arms and pectoral muscles hulked out and grew veiny. Julian knew what this was. Barbarian rage. Double shit.

The enraged orc ran at Julian nearly as fast as one of the arrows it had shot. As it ran, it pulled a large rusty sword from a sheath on its back.

"M-m-m-magic M-m-m," Julian tried to conjure up another magic arrow, but he stood there like a deer in headlights, knowing he was about to get chopped the fuck in half. He stuttered and stammered until a black blur whizzed from the right, straight into the orc's side.

The orc screamed in rage and pain so loudly that it drowned out the noise from the fighting. Ravenus's head was completely buried in the orc's Magic Missile wound. The bird's feet found purchase on charred orc flesh, and he pulled his head out. He actually had bloody meat hanging out of his beak. When the orc's scream finally subsided, the noise of battle did not filter back in. Either the bear was dead, or even it had been momentarily distracted by the orc scream. The orc grabbed Ravenus, no doubt a bit miffed at seeing part of its pancreas sticking out of his beak. As big a bird as he was, the orc's hand wrapped around him easily. Just as the orc was bringing Ravenus to his mouth for a little payback, Julian's wits came back to him.

"Magic Missile!" The glowing arrow flew straight into the orc's mouth. Light and sparks shone through his mouth, nostrils, ears, and the sockets where its eyes had just been. Red liquid eyeballs ran down either side of its face. A gush of blood and brain poured out of its mouth as it dropped to its knees. The body fell forward, mercifully hiding the molten orc face.

Ravenus struggled out of the dead hand and slurped down his bit of orc innards. "That was a close one, sir."

"What are you doing here?" asked Julian when he determined that he had successfully willed the contents of his stomach to stay where they were.

"There was no point in warning the approaching travelers," said Ravenus. "They're already engaged in combat with the orcs. So I thought I'd come back and check on you."

"Thanks."

Julian started at something crashing through the brush behind him. He whirled around just in time to see a large figure charging right at him.

"Magic Missile!" he shouted, and the arrow slammed right into the beast's chest, knocking it off its feet.

"Fucking hell, dude!"

"Shit, Cooper. I'm sorry. Are you okay?"

Cooper struggled back to his feet. "No I'm not fucking okay. I've got a goddam hole in my chest."

"Dave should be able to take care of it," said Julian.

"We don't know where Dave is."

"He's not with you and... hey, where's Tim?"

"He's doing his rogue hiding bullshit. Waiting for me to find you." Cooper started back in the direction he'd come from, and Julian followed close behind.

"Dave was supposed to meet up with you guys. Do you think he... whatever happened to the bear?"

"It just fucking ran off. And then the orcs ran off in the other direction. I don't know what the fuck is going on."

"The orcs went to do their ambush thing."

They ran through the trees for a couple of minutes until Cooper stopped to catch his breath. "That Magic Missile hurts like a sonofabitch."

"I said I was sorry."

"What happened to you?" said an otherwise innocuous patch

of shrubbery. And then it suddenly had eyes, and took on the form of a small person.

"Damn, Tim," said Julian. "Your rogue skills are improving. I might have walked by you a thousand times without spotting you in there."

"Cooper?" said Tim. "Your chest?"

"Julian shot me."

Tim looked at Julian.

"It was an accident."

"Where's Dave?"

"I thought he was with you guys," said Julian.

"Shit." Tim chewed his lower lip. "Well it looks like we're relatively free of danger right now. No point in keeping quiet. Dave!"

Julian and Cooper joined in. "Dave! Dave!"

"Help me!" Dave's voice came from somewhere in the grass beyond the trees.

"Dave! Dave!" Cooper continued shouting.

"Shut up," said Julian. "He answered already."

"I didn't hear anything."

Julian pointed to one of his freakishly long ears. "Come on."

Cooper carried Tim in order to make better time. The three of them made their way out of the trees, to the site of the bear fight. They peeked out. There was no sign of the dire bear, but neither was there any sign of Dave. Outside of some orc bodies and stray arrows, the land was grassy and featureless.

"Dave?" Tim whispered.

"Down here." Dave's voice was only a few meters ahead.

They walked forward. Dave was smashed into the earth, stuck in a Dave-shaped hole. His right hand was covered in blood and appeared to be clutching a broken stick.

"Are you okay?" asked Julian.

"Do I look okay?"

"What happened?"

"The bear stepped on me," said Dave. "I fucking hate animals."

"What happened to your hand?"

With some effort, Dave pried his forearm out of the ground so that it stuck straight up. The leopard fur was matted with mud. His gaze moved to his raised hand. He opened his blood-covered sausage fingers and dropped the back half of an arrow.

"That's not my blood," he said.

"Who's blood is it?" asked Tim.

"It's bear blood. Just before that big bastard stepped on me, I was able to grab a stray arrow and brace it upward."

"That must be why it took off," said Tim. "It's got an arrow stuck in its foot."

"Poor thing," said Julian.

"When you're done lamenting the minor foot wound of the giant monster bear beast," said Dave, "would you mind pulling me out of this hole?"

Cooper did the honors with a tug that would have straight up pulled the arm right off anything built less sturdily than a dwarf. Dave left a perfect imprint of his backside in earth and flattened grass. If a bear were to step on him while he lay face down, he might be able to fill both holes with wax and make a life-sized statue of himself.

Dave had no visible wounds, but no one could begrudge him using up another Heal spell after having been stepped on by an eight thousand pound bear.

"You mind?" said Cooper, pointing at the charred and oozing circle of burnt flesh on his chest.

"Sure," said Dave. They touched fingers, E.T. style, presumably so that Dave could minimize surface contact with Cooper's filthy half-orc body. "I heal thee," he said. Cooper shuddered and farted as his eyes rolled up in his head. The burnt flesh smoothed out and left a circle of clean grey skin in the filth.

Now that the group was back together and had their immediate problems sorted out, Julian's attention refocused on the distant sound of fighting up the road. Not so much axes and swords clanging together, but quite a bit of shouting and bowstring twanging.

Tim turned his head in the direction that the sounds of fighting was coming from. "We might still get there in time to help."

"I just used my last healing spell on Cooper," said Dave.

"And I used up my last Magic Missile," said Julian. He looked down at his feet. "Also on Cooper."

"Dude," said Cooper. "I don't want to sound like a dick, but I honestly don't give two fucks about whoever that is up there. I just want to get back to the Whore's Head and drink myself to sleep."

"Are you a fucking moron?" said Tim.

Cooper scratched his head. "I'm not sure where the line is drawn. I've got an intelligence score of seven, so I'm probably on the fence."

"The whole reason we got into this fight is because those orc bastards are blocking our way back to the Whore's Head."

"Shit," said Cooper. "I'd forgotten about that. Well let's get moving." He started walking toward the road.

"Hold on," said Tim. "Julian is out of spells. If we're going to fight, he needs something more than a stick. Julian, can you use a bow?"

"I think so," said Julian. "The book said all elves can use bows."

"Good. Go see if there are any functional bows lying around near the orc bodies."

There was no shortage of available bows, so Julian took a moment to pick out one that was less covered in blood and gore than the others. He was less picky about arrows as he scooped up as many as he could carry.

"For the record," said Dave, "I'd like to renew my objection to charging blindly into battle."

"Less queefing and more moving," said Cooper. His axe was out and ready to chop.

"Ravenus!" said Julian. "Come on!" He ran over to Cooper with his new bow and an arrow ready to nock. Ravenus appeared out of the dark sky shortly afterward and perched on his shoulder.

Tim cocked his crossbow and ran his hand over the belt quiv-

er on his side. He nodded. All eyes turned once again to Dave.

Dave rolled his eyes and trudged forward, resting his mace lazily on his shoulder.

They kept to the road until they were nearly on top of the fight. They couldn't see anything because there was a sharp bend in the road and it was heavily forested on both sides, making it an ideal location for an ambush, but they could hear it all right. Bowstrings twanged. Crossbows clicked. Orcs shouted orders at one another that Julian couldn't understand, occasionally peppered by a grunt or gurgle that he understood all too well.

"Okay," said Tim, keeping his voice lower than what was probably necessary. "Dave, you and Cooper cut through the trees and surprise as many as you can from behind. Julian and I will try to pick some off from the other side of the road."

"Your courage is inspiring," said Dave.

"We've got to play to our strengths," said Tim. "Look at me! I'm only three fucking feet tall. I'm not made for hand to hand combat."

"You only get your Sneak Attack bonus if you're within thirty feet of your target, though."

Tim stopped to think, then looked up at Julian. "He's right. I should go with them. Will you be okay over here by yourself?"

Julian shrugged. "I've got Ravenus to keep me company."

"Okay," said Tim. "Let's go. He darted silently into the trees with Cooper and Dave crashing awkwardly behind him.

Julian ran along the road on tiptoes until he was able to see what was going on. The first thing he saw was four horses lying dead on the road, forests of arrows poking out of them. Inching forward, he discovered that they were hitched to a fantastically large carriage. The wood was sturdy. There were at least as many arrows on the ground next to it as there were poking out of it, and those which were poking out were only barely hanging on by their steel tips. It was like a rolling fortress.

Three small windows on the side of the carriage allowed the occupants to return fire, but the security they enjoyed came with the price of a lousy angle to shoot from. The front had a larger window, but it was currently shuttered.

Julian watched the arrows fly out of the besieged carriage one at a time, at a glacial pace. More importantly, though, he listened. He was waiting for the sound of an orc's dying grunt that didn't coincide with an arrow being fired from the carriage. He only had to wait a moment before he heard what he was waiting for, but it came in the form of an agonized howl instead of a death grunt. Apparently, the guys had only wounded their first target. Julian could relate.

He made his move anyway. He ran to the side of the wagon that wasn't being attacked, drawing the fire of a couple of orcs. Those arrows sailed harmlessly behind him. His heart beat hard and fast as he pressed his back up against the protection of the carriage.

After a second had passed, Julian heard arrows begin thunking into the wood again. He pulled back his bowstring. Three. Two. One.

He jumped out, locked eyes with the first orc he found, and loosed an arrow. It was a respectable shot, catching the target in the chest, up near its left shoulder. Not a mortal wound, but — A bolt sprouted out of the orc's neck, even as Julian assessed his own shot. Dark blood sprayed out like beer from a can that had been shaken up and thrown against the wall. The orc fell. Score one for Tim.

Julian scanned the trees and underbrush, seeking out another target, but couldn't make any out. Arrows continued to fly at the carriage, but their sources were obscured by foliage. He held his bowstring back, waiting for the breeze to blow back a concealing branch, or for one of them to take a peek in his direction.

By the time the pain in his thigh registered, he was looking down at three inches of wood poking out of it.

"Yeow!" he cried, letting go of the bowstring.

His cry was echoed a second later by a much deeper voice, and followed with "Mother fucker!" Oops.

Julian hopped on his good leg back to the cover of the carriage, slamming his back against it. He looked at his leg. The arrow had gone all the way through. He had to pull it out.

The shutters opened above Julian's head. "Be away with you, filthy beggar!"

Julian looked up. A gaunt human face was looking down at him. He had long, curly brown hair spilling out from under a blue velvet cap. He had a waxy pointed beard, and a moustache that curved up at the ends, like he was wearing an upturned fleur-de-lis on his face.

The shaft of the arrow burned in Julian's thigh. "We're trying to help you, asshole." He shut his eyes, gripped both ends of the arrow, snapped off the fletching, and pulled the shaft through. "Fuck, that hurt," he said, breathing heavily.

The dandy coughed a dismissive laugh and sniffed. "The day Leopold Lioncrest requires assistance from a vagabond elf is the day I eat my—"

"Wha!" came the shrill screech of the other occupant of the carriage as an arrow thudded into the interior window frame, an inch away from Leo's head.

"Is that your daughter in there?" asked Julian, trying to appeal to the protective instincts of a parent. "For her sake, let me—"

"That's my son," said Leopold, taking his startled eyes off the arrow that had nearly ended him. "You're distracting us. Now be gone with you, or the next arrow you catch won't be from an orc bow. Hmm?" He held up a fine polished crossbow and raised his eyebrows to demonstrate that Julian was supposed to be impressed.

"Father!" cried the other voice from inside. "I hit one! I hit one!"

"Well done, lad!"

"That's really your son?" asked Julian. "Because he kind of sounds like a—"

Father's pride winked out of Leopold's face as he turned back toward Julian. "Now I'm warning you, elf. You had best move along by the time I count to three." He hefted his fancy crossbow out the window and pointed it awkwardly at Julian. "One!"

"Why are you being such a dick about this? I was only trying to—"

"Two!"

Julian put his arms protectively over his head. "Jesus Christ, man! Just hang on a second. Let's talk about this!"

"Thwargh..."

Something heavy landed on Julian's arms.

"Ow," he said. He opened his eyes. Leopold's crossbow was in his lap.

"Father!" cried the feminine voice from within the carriage.

Julian looked up. Leopold's lifeless eyes were staring down at him. His silk-gloved hands dangled a foot above Julian's face. An arrow protruded from his mouth.

"Look, man," said Julian. "I understand you're upset, and I'm sorry about your dad. But I was just trying to help, and he was being a total — hey, what are you doing?"

The young man gesticulated with his hands while reciting an incantation that Julian was all too familiar with.

"Oh shit." Julian attempted to shield his face with his arms, but knew in his heart that it wasn't going to make a difference. The Magic Missile caught him in the gut like a flaming steel-toed boot.

Julian's mind flashed back to the orc's open wound, and had a pretty good idea of what his abdomen must look like, though the Magic Missile did no harm to his clothes. He fell back against a tree, trying to favor his left ass cheek so as to mitigate the pain in his right thigh.

"Julian!" shrieked Ravenus, flying toward the face in the window. The man inside yelped, and managed to close the shutters just in time for Ravenus to smash into them with his face. Julian grimaced as he shared the bird's pain. It seared through his head like a hammer-induced migraine. Ravenus fell to the ground. With a considerable effort, he picked himself up and stumbled

toward Julian like a hobo at four in the morning.

Julian lay on the ground and wished that whatever was going to finish him off would just hurry up already. His robes were sticky with blood seeping out of his abdomen and flowing out of his thigh.

He brought Ravenus to his chest and resigned to sleep through the short and painful remainder of his life. He closed his eyes. It felt strange. Unnatural, somehow. Then he remembered. Elves don't sleep. Damn.

After a moment, it occurred to Julian that most of the commotion had stopped. No more arrows were thudding into the other side of the carriage. The predominant sound in the night air was that of crickets chirping, only interrupted occasionally by the clash of metallic weapons banging together or orcish grunts.

Sometime between four seconds and four hours later, Julian snapped out of a trance. Tim, Dave, and Cooper were looking down at him. Tim didn't look any worse for the wear, but Dave and Cooper were covered from head to toe with splattered blood.

"You okay?" said Cooper.

Julian turned his head and spit. It was pink. "Do I look like I'm okay?"

"You look like shit."

"You don't look much better. What happened out there?"

"We tangled with a few orcs," said Tim.

"You didn't tangle with shit," said Cooper.

"I did my part," Tim snapped back at him. "Anyway, as soon as things started to look bad for them, most of the rest of them ran away."

"Looks like you were right," said Cooper. "Orcs are just mooks after all."

"What's up with the guys in the carriage?" asked Dave.

"I don't know," said Julian. "It seems like everyone in this world is a complete asshole to people they don't know."

"That's understandable," said Dave. "It's a more dangerous world than the one we're used to. That sort of mistrust might save your life."

Cooper banged on the side of the carriage with his fist. "Hey! Are you guys okay in there?"

"Go away!" came a muffled voice from inside. It sounded like he was trying not to cry.

"Don't even bother," said Julian. "The guy is a total cockbag. He fucking Magic Missiled me."

Cooper shouted at the shuttered window. "Did you Magic Missile my friend? Not cool, man."

"Your friend killed my father!" No attempt was made to hide emotions this time. His voice was full of fire and venom.

"Shit, dude," Cooper whispered. "Did you kill his father?"

"I most certainly did not!" Julian shouted.

The man inside the carriage broke into a fit of heavy sobbing.

"Poor guy," said Dave. "What can we do?"

Tim shrugged. "We go back to town."

"We can't just leave him here in his grief and a horseless carriage. What if the orcs come back?"

"I was thinking the same thing," said Tim. "They could come back at any time, so we'd better get moving while we've got this window."

"You're essentially condemning an innocent man to death."

"Innocent?" Julian shouted, suddenly finding the energy to accept Cooper's hand and pull himself to his feet. "I've got a fucking hole in my gut thanks to him!"

"Well you shouldn't have attacked his father," said Dave. "You were supposed to be fighting orcs."

"I didn't do shit to his father, you fat fucking—"

A loud caw stopped Julian mid-sentence. Ravenus didn't even bother with language. He just let out a primal bird scream.

Julian was taken aback. "Ravenus?"

"Apologies, sir. But it appears we are no longer alone."

Julian, Dave, and Tim looked southward down the road. The dire bear, still peppered with dozens of arrows in the front, and limping on one of its hind legs, moved cautiously toward them.

"We can lose him in the forest," Dave whispered.

"What about your friend in the carriage?" asked Tim.

"Fuck him," said Dave. "Let's go."

Cooper threw Julian over his shoulder, slamming most of his weight right down on his Magic Missile wound. It was excruciating. But as severe as the pain was, it couldn't hope to match the offense to his nostrils as his head hung so near Cooper's ass.

As short as his legs were, Dave was the first into the trees, and Tim wasn't far behind him. Julian bounced up and down on his bleeding gut as Cooper took up the rear. The bear roared like a stuttering jet engine, shaking the leaves on the trees. But it couldn't hope to move through this dense a forest.

They ran for what seemed like an eternity, what with Julian being in as much agony as he was in. When they felt like they were safely out of harm's way, they stopped to rest. Cooper brought Julian around to his front, carrying him like a newborn baby. This was a massive relief to the pain in his gut, but Cooper's armpit smelled only marginally less offensive than his asshole. The stop was a short one, but when they continued north, they walked.

"I hope that guy in the carriage is okay," said Dave.

"He's fucked," said Cooper. "That's not a carriage to a creature that big. It's a fucking lunch box."

"Still," said Tim, unnaturally cheerfully. "This trip wasn't a total waste of time. I swiped the dead orc leader's money pouch." He held up a small, rough leather bag. "Three gold pieces!"

"Sweet," said Cooper. "I'll take it to that scroll guy in the morning and try to get a better treasure map."

The End

Shipfaced

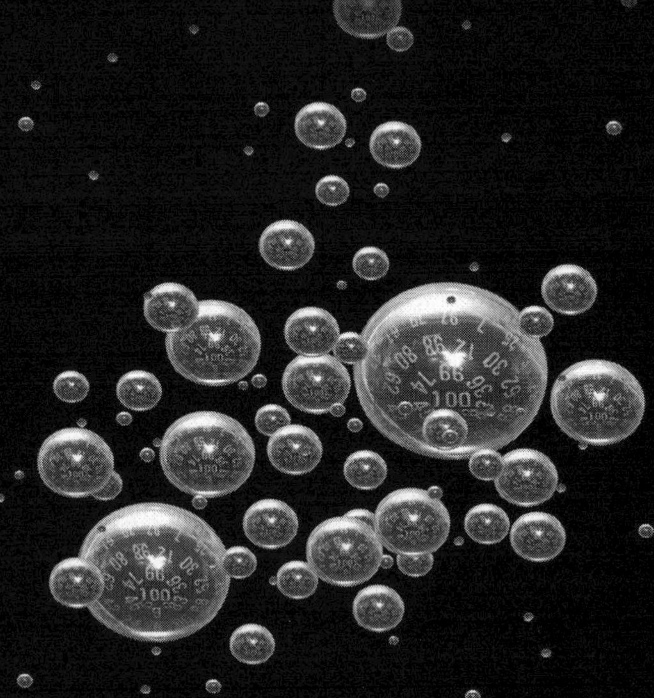

ROBERT BEVAN

SHIPFACED

(Original Publication Date: May 11, 2013)

"You'd be more helpful," said Dave, "if you just stood out of the way." He stopped to adjust his grip on his end of the large wooden crate he was holding.

Tim let go and stepped aside. It made little difference in the weight. "Sorry," he said. "I just want to look like I'm working. You know, it probably wasn't a good idea for you to wear your armor out here at the harbor."

Dave took a step backward and tried, unsuccessfully, to blow away a drop of sweat that was hanging off the end of his nose. A rotten plank, one among hundreds nailed haphazardly together to form this rickety pier, creaked beneath his boot. Two inches of waterlogged splinters of wood held together by termite shit was all that stood between him and a watery grave. "This armor is the only clothes I've got."

"Come on, guys," said Julian, who was carrying the other end of the crate. "Less talking, more walking. My back hurts." The difference between his height and Dave's was such that Julian had to stoop while he walked.

Dave continued moving backward, trying not to think about drowning in the sea.

Julian's familiar flapped down and landed atop the crate they were carrying. "This place is fantastic," he said. "I feel like I've been wasting my whole life out in the forest, scrounging around for dead squirrels and whatnot. The gulls have the right of it. Fish don't waste any time starting to decompose. They're lovely!" The sailors and dockworkers who'd obviously never seen such a big raven before, had been spoiling him, throwing chopped bits of fish and squid for him to catch in the air.

"I'm glad you're enjoying yourself, Ravenus," said Julian. If anyone else had said it, Dave would have assumed it was sarcasm. But Julian said it with a warm smile, despite his aching back. He cared more for Ravenus than a man — or an elf — should care for a bird.

"Hey, fuckers!" said Cooper, strolling by with one of the huge crates resting on his shoulder. "Slow down, why don't you? She's not due to sail for another few days yet." Cooper fit right in with the sailors and dockworkers. More than half of them were also half-orcs, though few of them even came close to being as offensive to look at as Cooper. The rest were mostly human, with a scattering of half-elves. As far as he could make out, he was the only dwarf around.

Dave considered telling Cooper to fuck off, but he didn't have the breath to shout. He had more than adequate breath, however, for grumbling. "I can't believe we're living in a fantasy world, and we're doing manual labor. This is worse than stocking shelves at Grocer Greg's."

"It's better than fighting monsters, isn't it?" said Tim. "At least here we aren't constantly risking our lives."

"I'm not so sure," said Dave as another board creaked under his weight.

"This wind is annoying the shit out of me," said Julian.

"I actually find it refreshing," said Tim. "I've always enjoyed the salty sea air."

"That's because you've got short hair. You wouldn't enjoy it as much if your hair was blowing all over your face."

"You should have tied it back."

"You should blow me."

"How close are we to the ship?" asked Dave.

"About another thirty feet," said Tim.

"Okay," said Dave. "I can do that."

"Hey Dave!" shouted Cooper, coming back for another crate. Dave closed his eyes and tried to ignore him. "What's short and fat and full of seamen?" He barely paused before answering his own stupid question. "Your mom!"

A few of the dockworkers laughed.

"How is that funny?" asked Dave, knowing full well he should just continue to ignore Cooper. "It doesn't even make any sense."

"It's a pun," explained Cooper. "A play on words. You know... semen, sea men."

"I know what a fucking pun is, you asshole," said Dave. "But for the joke to work, there has to be a double meaning. It's supposed to go 'What's long and hard and full of seamen?' so you think they're talking about a dick, but really it's a submarine. See? That's funny because it can be taken two ways. Your joke was just stupid."

"Mine can be taken two ways as well," said Cooper. "Your mom is full of sea men, and she's also full of semen. Both are true."

"Fuck you," Dave huffed.

"What's a submarine?" asked one of the dockworkers.

"I don't know," said another. "The dwarf isn't very funny."

Dave shook his head and ignored them. It was one thing to mouth off at Cooper, but he didn't want to start any shit with guys he didn't know. He couldn't wait to put this goddamn crate down.

They were only halfway up the loading platform when Dave saw Cooper approaching again with another crate. "This sucks."

"Quit your bitching already," said Tim. "You're almost there."

"This way, fellas," said the first halfling Dave had seen, outside of Tim, all day. He stood on a railed platform built around the main mast, holding a clipboard and pointing to the cargo hold. "Just down those stairs."

"Dammit," said Dave. "Stairs?"

"Turn around," said Julian. "Let me go down the stairs first."

"Okay."

"Oh my god that's better," said Julian as he straightened his back.

"Hey Dave," said Cooper, who was right behind him.

"Not now, Cooper," said Dave.

"What's the difference between your mom and a big bag of shit?"

"Would you just shut the fuck up for once?"

"Yeah, I couldn't think of any differences either."

Laughter followed Dave into the cargo hold. Even that little halfling bastard was laughing. Fuck them.

"Okay," said Julian once they'd reached the bottom of the stairs. "Set it down."

Dave let go of his end. The crate landed with a thunk and a few clinks from inside it.

"Sounds like glass," said Tim. "Hope you guys didn't break anything."

Dave didn't give a damn if anything was broken or not. He wiped the sweat from his nose and his forehead. He scratched his cheeks through his beard. He scratched the top of his head. He scratched places that didn't even itch, just because he finally could. "I'm taking a break," he said, sitting down and leaning against the crate.

"Good idea," said Julian. He sat down as well.

"Pussies," said Cooper. He set down his own crate on top of another one. There were a dozen in all, eleven of which had been hauled up by Cooper. "I wonder what's in here." He ran his giant fingers along the lid.

"Cooper, don't," said Tim.

"It's stuck," said Cooper, pushing up with his thumbs.

"That's because it's nailed shut," Tim explained.

"Huh?" said Cooper as he inadvertently ripped the top off of the crate. "Oops."

"Dammit, Cooper!" said Tim. "Put that back on right now!"

Cooper's half-orc eyes went wide. "Booze!" he whispered. He pulled out a purple glass bottle. It had a foot-long slender neck which opened to a round base, somewhere between the size of a cantaloupe and a basketball. It was sealed at the top with an ornate-looking stopper. It looked like top shelf stuff.

"Don't even think about it," said Tim. "Put it back right now and put the lid back on—"

The cargo hold suddenly went dark as the hatch slammed shut. Dave's Darkvision kicked on. Everything was black and white.

Julian stood up carefully, reaching out until he felt a wall. He blindly made his way up the stairs and pushed on the hatch. "It's locked," he whispered.

"Great," said Dave.

Cooper pulled the stopper out of the bottle. It came out with a loud plunk.

"Dammit Cooper," said Tim, turning his head sort of toward Cooper, but several degrees off. "That better not be what I think it is."

"They're not going to miss one bottle," said Cooper. "Anyway, I'd say they owe us a bottle for locking us in the cargo hold. What if I was afraid of the dark or something? It's just insensitive." He took a pull from the bottle. "Hey, that's some good shit."

"It sounds like they're fighting outside," said Julian.

Dave didn't need elf ears to hear that. The sounds were muffled, but he could make out screams, swords clanging together, angry shouting. There was definitely a brawl going on outside.

"Sweet," said Cooper. "Let's go help." He took another swig from the bottle.

"Help who?" asked Tim.

"Like I give a fuck. I just want to fight something."

"What are we going to fight with?" asked Tim. "Our dicks? We left all our weapons at the Whore's Head."

"None of that matters," said Dave. "Because we are on the wrong side of a locked hatch, in the cargo hold of a — what was that?" The floor had been noticeably less still than solid earth since he boarded the ship. That was all a part of being on the water, and Dave hadn't paid it any mind. But now it was moving in a discernible direction.

"Wha!" said Tim as he fell over. Nimble as he was, he couldn't see, and the ships's sudden movement caught him by surprise. Still, he rolled with the fall and was upright again in one fluid motion. "What was that?"

"Ship's moving," said Cooper. He held the bottle upside down over his head and pursed his lips around the mouth of it, squeezing in his wormy tongue to lap up the last few drops.

"Thanks for the news, shithead," Tim said to a stack of crates about five feet away from Cooper. Cooper waved to get his attention, but it was no use. "Why is the ship moving? Didn't you say it wasn't due to leave for a few days?"

"That's what the harbormaster told me," said Cooper. He grinned at Tim flailing his arms around to find a wall, and quietly placed the empty bottle back in the crate, replacing it with a fresh one.

Plunk.

"Knock it off, Cooper!" Tim barely kept his voice below a shout. "We've got to find out what's going on."

"Maybe they changed their minds?" offered Cooper.

"Maybe they're trying to get ahead of an approaching storm," said Julian, hopefully.

"Give it a rest, guys," said Dave. "You all know full well what's happened." From the looks on their faces, they didn't. Dave spelled it out for them. "We've been hijacked by pirates."

"Sweet!" said Cooper.

"No," said Tim. "It's not sweet. They're going to murder us and use us for chum if they catch us. Also, we have no idea where they're going. We've got two choices. We either stay hidden down here and hope nobody finds us, and then sneak off the ship when it docks somewhere else. Or we try to make a break for it now, jump over the side, and swim like motherfuckers back to the city."

"I'd sink like a stone in this armor," said Dave.

"I vote for option two," said Cooper.

"Fuck you, Cooper," said Dave.

Cooper let out a long belch.

"You'd have to ditch the armor," said Tim. "What do you think, Julian?"

Julian walked down the stairs. "I think we're screwed. That hatch is pretty solid. Cooper might be able to bust through it, but not without alerting all hands on deck that we're here. We'll be surrounded before we can jump off the side of the ship."

"But we could be at sea for weeks!" said Tim. "Months, even! We can't live on booze that whole time."

"Don't say that until you've tried it," said Cooper. "This shit is— hiccup— fantastic."

"Jesus, Cooper!" said Tim. "Are you wasted already?"

"I'm telling you, man," said Cooper. "This stuff goes down like Dave's mom."

Dave chose to be the bigger person, in spirit if not in stature. "Fuck it," he said. "It's not like we're going to get in any more trouble than we're in right now." He got slowly to his feet. His stubby dwarf legs were not meant for the sea. He grabbed a bottle from the open crate. "We'll have a drink and figure out our next move."

Plunk.

"Do you really think it's a good idea to get shitfaced when we could get attacked by pirates at any minute?" asked Tim.

"Sounds like a fine idea to me," said Julian. "It'll take the edge off of being murdered." He stretched out his arms in front of him as he carefully walked past Tim. And then he stopped. "Wait a second. This is stupid." He took a knee and felt around on the floor until he found a loose, rusty nail. "Light."

Dave's vision blurred as color flooded in. He shook his head until it cleared. "Good idea. Thanks."

"Dammit, Cooper!" said Tim. "Did you piss on the floor already?"

Dave peered around the crate. Sure enough, Cooper was standing in the middle of a circle of wood noticeably darker than the rest of the floor.

"Where the fuck am I supposed to piss?"

"I don't know," said Tim. "Maybe piss on the stairs or something. Give those fuckers something to slip on when they come to kill us."

Cooper nodded and pointed a finger at Tim. "Now that's smart thinking."

Julian grabbed a bottle and unstoppered it. Plunk. He took a small sip, and the tips of his long ears turned red. "Wow," he said. "Cooper's not wrong. This is amazing."

Tim sighed. "Fine. Give me a bottle.

Somewhere between thirty minutes and five hours later, by Dave's best estimate, the four of them were completely hammered. The stairwell was covered in piss. At one point they held a contest to see who could reach the highest step, but it wasn't really a contest at all. Cooper's stream was nearly forceful enough to blow the hatch off its hinges. Tim gave it his best effort, but only barely managed to reach the fourth step.

The slipperiness of the stairs was tested when Cooper decided he had to throw up. As soon as he got that familiar look in his half-orc eyes, Tim urged him to do it at the top of the stairs. He didn't make it three steps before a misstep sent him face first into a stair. The ensuing crunch sent a chill up Dave's short spine, but he'd be lying if he said he didn't enjoy it a little. Hell, Cooper breaking his face on a stair incited hysterical laughter in all of them, but the warm feeling it gave Dave inside was something that he thought he'd still treasure in his heart even after he sobered up.

Cooper's broken face nearly made the big idiot forget he'd gone over there to vomit. When the memory came back, it came back in force. It looked as though his head had just exploded. Dave couldn't believe how purple it was. Cooper was obviously drinking on an empty stomach. It almost looked good enough to drink again.

Dave immediately wished that thought hadn't occurred to him, but the damage was done and he couldn't unthink it. His stomach began to rise into his throat, and he had only just enough time to make it to the staircase before he dropped to his knees and joined Cooper in spilling his guts all over it.

Tim and Julian were nearly pissing themselves, they were laughing so hard. Even Cooper, who was bleeding profusely from his broken snout, wheezed out a laugh at Dave's expense.

Dave crawled away from the stairs feeling like a hollowed out pumpkin. The ship rose suddenly on a big wave, sending empty bottles rolling around on the floor and spilling the one he hadn't yet finished. Dave wished he had something more to throw up. He reached out to rescue what little was left in his bottle, but his supporting hand slipped out from under him. His face hit the floor hard.

*

When Dave woke up, he determined that doing so had been a serious error in judgment. The air was moist and salty and fresh, with no trace of piss or vomit. The light which flooded into his pounding head through his stinging eyes was not the light of an enchanted nail. It was natural sunlight. They were on the deck of the ship, and he was as sober as a fencepost. Fuck.

He forced his eyes open and saw a makeshift table in front of him. It was really nothing more than two crates with some planks hastily thrown on top. On the planks sat eight empty glass bottles. The bases were wide and round, and then necks were long and slender. The sight of them turned Dave's stomach.

His eyes opened wider, and he noticed about two dozen sets of eyes staring back at him. The eyes were all human and half-orcish, and they all looked curious. None of them, interestingly enough, looked at all angry or threatening. Well... one of them did. One of the sailors, whose arm was in a sling and whose clothes were stained purple, gave Dave a quiet snarl and a threatening glare. He must have been the first one to discover them. But aside from him, everyone else merely looked curious.

Before Dave had time to be relieved by that, he realized the reason why they weren't threatening. They didn't need to be. Dave and his friends were completely helpless. His left arm, his leopard arm, was in a manacle. About a foot and a half of heavy iron chain secured his manacle to the one on Cooper's right wrist. Looking further along, he saw that Cooper was chained to Julian, who was then chained to Tim. They were all still asleep. Dave made a quick survey of his surroundings. They were all on the edge of the deck, with only a chest-high wooden wall keeping them from falling into the sea. They were fucked.

"Ahem," said a little voice at the back of the crowd, which immediately parted in the middle as if a truck were about to drive through.

What they revealed was not a truck. It was a halfling. And not just any Halfling. It was that little guy who was taking inventory down at the docks. Only, he was no longer dressed like a dockworker. He was decked out in brightly colored silk, gold jewelry studded with gemstones, and a hat with a brim at least as wide as he was tall. On his belt he wore an ornate scimitar. It must have been for show, because this wasn't the sort of weapon you'd want to get any blood on.

"You fellows have a good time last night?" said the halfling.

Dave's jaw moved up and down, but no words came out of his mouth. He tugged on the chain connecting his arm to Cooper's a couple of times, but to no avail. He sat up straight, grabbed Cooper's forearm, and used it to slap him in his own disfigured half-orc face.

"Ow!" shouted Cooper. "Fuck, that hurts! What happ—where are we?"

"You are aboard the Seventh Serpent, my friend," said the halfling. He patted the main mast affectionately. "And a fine ship she be."

Cooper flicked Julian in the head a couple of times. After that failed to wake him up, he sucked on his finger and put the tip of the claw in Julian's ear.

Julian batted Cooper's hand away. "Hey, knock it off, man. I'm — holy fucking shit!" He sat bolt upright and started shaking Tim.

"Huh?" said Tim. "What's going on?"

"We've been captured," said Dave.

Tim yawned. "Of course we have."

"Who the fuck are you?" Cooper asked the halfling. Dave slapped his wrist.

"Do you see the hat atop me head, mate? Don't nobody here wear a bigger one. Now you tell me, my boy. Who do you think I be?"

"Um..." said Cooper. "You kind of look like the Hamburglar."

Tim and Julian giggled. Even Dave let out a little snort. He couldn't help it. It was true.

The halfling squinted his eyes and shot curious glances at a few of his crewmen, but only got blank stares and shrugs in return.

"I'm the captain, you daft bastard!" He nodded up at the sailor next to him.

The sailor stomped forward and kicked Dave in the ass. "You stand up when the captain addresses you!"

The four of them rose unsteadily to their feet. Dave, ever aware of his own armor and the open sea just behind him, gripped the wall firmly with his right hand. He caught a glimpse of Julian shielding his eyes as he peered up at the crow's nest. When Julian furrowed his brow and shook his head ever so slightly, Dave followed his gaze. Ravenus was perched up there with his wings outstretched, maybe trying to look intimidating. He lowered his wings in response to Julian's order. He must have been hiding out up there. How appropriate.

The sea behind him was quiet, still, and vast. The only disturbance on the water was the ship cutting through it. Dave had a pretty good view, and the only land in sight was a speck of an island off on the eastern horizon. He didn't think he could swim that far. Not that it mattered. With his armor on, he'd have to make the trip on foot.

"That's more like it," said the captain. He spread his arms out, gesturing at the empty glass bottles lined up on the table. "Now, who can tell me what we have before us?"

One of the crewmen, a half-orc on the pudgy side, raised his hand. The captain shot him a wicked glare, and he immediately lowered it.

"Look," said Tim. "We get it. We drank your booze. We're sorry. Let's roll this along, huh?"

Dave felt his bladder let go as a warm stream of piss flowed down his leg. What the fuck was Tim doing?

"I'm sorry, lad," said the captain. "Am I boring you?"

"Yeah," said Tim. "You kinda are."

Dave looked up at Cooper, but even he had a stupefied look on his face.

"Hey," Julian whispered at Tim. "Chill out, man."

"Don't tell me to chill out!" Tim snapped. "I'm tired, my neck hurts, I've got a massive fucking headache, and I'm not in the mood for games. If this little prick wants to kill us over some fucking booze, I'm just about ready. I'm sick of being three feet tall. I'm sick of sleeping on the floor of a fucking tavern. I'm sick of getting my feet chewed off by giant fucking rodents. I've had enough. Let the slaughter commence."

The captain unsheathed his scimitar, walked around the table, and held the blade up to Tim's throat. Tim lifted his head, exposing as much of his tiny neck as he could. The captain's grimace slowly melted into a grin, and he lowered his weapon. He walked back around to the other side of the table and continued talking.

"If I didn't know any better, I'd say your friend has been captured by pirates before."

"Doubtful," said Cooper.

"That's a smart thing he did," said the captain. "If you ever find yourself in this situation again," he said, smiling at Cooper. "Doubtful. Always try to antagonize the captain. You might get lucky and be rewarded with a swift death by hanging or stabbing. Sadly, that won't be the case for you today."

"You're not going to—" Julian started, but then doubled over to throw up. The chain connecting his wrist to Cooper's made him sway that way and throw up on Cooper's foot. It must have digested some since last night, as it was a significantly paler shade of purple. He wiped his mouth on his sleeve. "... kill us?"

The captain looked at Julian with disgust. "Not just yet." He glared at Tim. "That fucking booze you spoke of. Do you have any idea what that is? How rare? How valuable?"

"I'll grant you it was tasty," said Cooper.

"That's Whistlethorn Brandy you idiot's were gulping down like goblin grog! That fucking booze sells for over six thousand gold pieces per bottle!"

"Sorry," said Cooper.

"Not half as sorry as you're about to be, my friend." The captain's smile returned. "It's a lonely life out here at sea. I've decided to let my men have their way with you for the next couple of weeks. If any of you are still alive when we reach the Slaver Islands, I'll see if I can't recoup any of my losses."

With that, the captain took his leave and stepped below deck. The sailor who had kicked Dave, clearly the first mate, took over the proceedings.

"Softy," said the first mate. "You won the first pick of round one. Which will you have?"

Dave took another look at the sailors' faces. He wasn't sure if he had mistaken lusty hunger for simple curiosity before, or if it had since turned into that since then, but there was no mistaking it now. The whole crew eyed them like big slabs of rape-meat.

Julian wiped some of his vomit-sticky hair out of his face.

"I'll take the elf," said Softy, a bare-chested and heavily tattooed half-orc sailor. "He's real feminine and pretty like. It'd almost be like fuckin' a real lady, I reckon."

"Be careful," Cooper warned Julian. "Half-orc dicks are scaly and covered in bumps."

Softy raised his eyebrows at Cooper. "No they ain't."

"Oh, right," said Cooper, looking down at his vomit-covered

feet. "I was... um... I was just joking." He reached under his loincloth to scratch his junk.

The first mate frowned distastefully at Cooper before carrying on. "Mr. Grumm, you're next. Who'll it be?"

"I'm partial to the little guy," said Mr. Grumm, a gangly human sailor with a thick, bushy beard and a voice like throat cancer. "He reminds me of me niece."

Tim hung his head. "That's wrong on so many levels."

"Philo?" the first mate called out. "Where's Philo?"

"Here I am!" A young boy, no older than sixteen by the looks of him, pushed his way through the crowd with a mop.

The first mate smiled at him. "Ah, there you are, Philo. Go on now. It's your turn to choose."

"I'll go with the half-orc," said Philo.

The first mate bunched his eyebrows together. "Really?"

"Father says the ugly ones are easiest."

"Your father is a wise man," said Cooper.

"Shut up, you!" shouted the first mate.

"Listen, boy," Softy said, putting his huge half-orc hand on Philo's shoulder. "One's as easy as another when yous rapin' them."

"He makes a fair point, Philo," said the first mate. "Do you want to take a minute to think about it?"

"Come on!" cried an eager little man in the front row. "He's made his decision. It's my turn!"

"Quiet, Stuart," the first mate said. His voice was pleasant enough, but Stuart knew his place and clamped his mouth shut as if the order had been barked out by a drill sergeant. "This is Philo's first time at sea, and we all want it to be special for him, right?"

The crew all nodded their agreement. Several of the men gave Philo a friendly punch on the shoulder or mussed up his hair. Philo took it all in with a sheepish grin.

"Have you made up your mind?"

"I have," said Philo. "I'm still going to take the half-orc. He's

got big titties."

The crewmen all laughed and wished the boy luck.

No one looked happier at Philo's choice than Stuart. "Ha ha!" he said, rubbing his wiry hands together. He licked his lips as he stared at Dave.

"Hold on a second!" shouted Dave. The sailors stopped their bickering and looked down at him. "I get picked last? After Cooper? This is unacceptable!"

Stuart frowned. "I was gonna pick you."

"Fuck you," Dave shouted at the little man.

Stuart lowered his head.

"Dude," said Cooper. "That was kind of harsh."

"Tim!" Dave called out.

"Uh," said Tim. "Yeah?"

"I'm going to need you to unbuckle my armor."

"What? You want to show off your goods?"

"Just be ready," said Dave. He took a step forward, and Cooper let his arm reach out to allow it. He picked up two of the empty bottles by their necks and held them upside down.

"What do you think you're doing with those?" asked the first mate. He put his hand on his hip and cocked an eyebrow.

"Everybody just back off," said Dave, brandishing the two bottles as if they were swords.

"Seriously though," said Cooper. "What the fuck are you doing?"

Dave backed up until he was against the low wooden wall. "Sorry to spoil your fun, but nobody's getting raped today."

The crewmen looked at one another and laughed.

"Yous gonna just give it up freely then?" said Softy. "Where's the fun in that?" The men laughed harder.

"A bold strategy," said Cooper. "But what's with the bottles?"

"Come on, guys!" said Dave. "This is where we get off!" He hefted himself over the wall with his elbows and let himself fall off the side of the ship.

"Hey!" said Cooper, gripping the wall with his left hand and holding up Dave with his right. "What the fuck are you thinking?"

The pain in Dave's wrist was excruciating as he dangled at Cooper's side, but he dared not let go of the bottle in his hand.

"Come on," Dave cried. "Trust me!"

"Fuck no," said Cooper, struggling to keep his balance as Dave tried to swing himself out to sea. "Quit squirming. You're heavy as fuck."

Dave couldn't take the pain much longer. He concentrated on thoughts of not getting ass-raped until an idea came to him. He let the neck of the bottle in his right hand slide down all the way to the end. With the extra reach that afforded him, he jabbed at Cooper's swollen face with the bulbous end.

"Ow!" shouted Cooper. "That fucking hur—whoa!" He let go of the wall to cover his face and slipped on Julian's vomit. He fell off the side of the ship, taking Julian and Tim with him.

The water was warm up top, but cooled steadily as they sank. The two bottles of air Dave held desperately onto slowed the rate at which they descended, and Dave prayed that Tim's clever mind and nimble fingers would be quick enough to act before they cracked under the ever increasing water pressure.

Dave looked up. Cooper let loose a barrage of bubbles from his mouth, which Dave had no doubt was him shouting "Fuck!"

Beyond that, he saw what he'd hoped to see. Tim was climbing past Julian, then across Cooper, and finally to him.

Tim immediately got to work on the buckles on Dave's armor as Dave began to feel the pressure building in his head. He looked up at the bottles. They were made of thick, sturdy glass, but how much could they take?

The breastplate loosened from the backplate on Dave's left side. If he let go of one bottle, he might be able to wiggle out of the other side. No. That would have to be a last resort. His cheeks were bursting, and a few bubbles forced their way out between his tightly clenched lips. His head felt like an elephant was clenching its asshole around it. Come on, Tim!

Tim got to work on the other side. A few excruciating seconds

later, it was done. The breast and back plates dropped away from each other and continued to fall into the dark depths of the sea, while Dave shot upward like a cork, away from Tim.

Dave let some air out of his mouth as he flew upward toward the light like a stocky, bearded Superman, dragging his three friends behind him.

When he finally popped up from the surface, he sucked in what felt like enough air to fill a zeppelin.

Cooper took in a nice big breath of air as well, but didn't look like he needed it as desperately as Dave had. Tim broke the surface of the water hacking and choking, but awake and alive. Julian, however, merely floated up, not even raising his head out of the water.

"Shit!" cried Dave. "He's drowning! Cooper, help him!"

Ravenus hovered above them, cawing and screeching. It wasn't even words. It was just blind bird panic.

Cooper grabbed Julian by the arms and shook him.

"What the fuck are you doing?" asked Dave. "He's drowning, not sleeping! Do some CPR shit or something!"

"Do I look like a fucking lifeguard to you?"

"Hold these," Dave told Tim. Tim, still hacking and coughing, accepted the bottles. Dave discovered that he was not a strong swimmer. The padding he wore beneath his armor was soaked through, and made movement awkward. He started to sink, but hugged Julian around the waist. "Breathe air into his mouth!"

While Cooper sucked on Julian's face, Dave attempted the Heimlich maneuver, which was, to his limited knowledge, just a matter of hugging someone from behind really hard. Miraculously, their combined efforts worked, and Julian vomited purple-tinted seawater into Cooper's mouth. Cooper made a show of spitting it out, but Dave was pretty sure he swallowed some of it, not wanting to let go of any trace of booze that Julian may have not yet metabolized.

As Julian and Tim hacked and coughed, Dave kept a close eye on the Seventh Serpent, which was pretty far along now and still moving away from them. That was good.

"Good (cough) thinking," said Julian, when he was able to get the words out. "Now what do we do?"

"There's an island over there," said Dave. "We swim."

It was a hard swim. Cooper was the only one of them who could swim worth a damn, and he was hindered by having other people chained to him. Julian's robes and serape dragged through the water like two extra people. Poor Tim was jerked back and forth with every stroke of Cooper's left arm, and Dave severely limited the movement of his right. It was slow going, and that distant little island never seemed to get any closer.

"I wish I could be more help," said Dave, hugging his empty overturned bottle.

"You could heal my face."

"I'm so sorry!" said Dave. "I was going to do that earlier, but I thought I should save it for after we were raped."

Cooper nodded as he swam. "That's good thinking."

Dave took hold of Cooper's wrist. Even bathed in seawater, it was slimy to the touch. "I heal thee." Cooper stopped swimming as his broken face realigned itself. His snout popped out like a crushed plastic soda bottle getting re-inflated. Cooper winced, but after it was done, he let out a long relieved sigh. A train of bubbles rose to the surface, releasing his foul-smelling fart into the salty sea air.

"Is there any way I might be of assistance?" asked Ravenus.

Cooper grimaced. "Jesus. What does that fucking bird want now?"

"He just wanted to know how he could help," said Julian defensively.

"He could start by getting off of my fucking head."

"Ravenus," said Julian. "Why don't you go wait for us on the island?"

"Are you sure, sir?" asked Ravenus. "I don't much like the idea of leaving you out here alone."

Cooper cringed at the sound of the bird's voice. Dave remembered how it had sounded before he picked up the elven tongue, allowing him to understand the bird. Cooper, though he'd leveled up, stubbornly refused to spend any skill points to learn it. To him, the bird's speech sounded like nothing more than screeching and cawing.

"I'm sure," said Julian. "We're okay. We'll catch up with you soon."

Cooper struggled on as the afternoon sun sank down to the empty western horizon, and then below it. Cooper paddled on through the night, and none of the rest of them could do anything but hope they were still swimming in the right direction and that they didn't get eaten by sharks, or krakens, or whatever the hell else might be lurking beneath these waters.

The next morning, by the time the sky grew light enough to see anything, they discovered that they had swum past the island, and were headed away from it. Fortunately, however, it was very close. Cooper changed course, and less than an hour later, found himself able to stand upright on the sandy sea floor. He stood upright and caught his breath.

"You did it!" cried Tim.

Ravenus greeted them with an excited caw as he flew in circles above them.

Cooper looked like he wanted to smile, but didn't have the energy. He and Julian walked the rest of the way, with Tim and Dave bobbing along beside them, hugging their bottles, until their feet could touch the ground as well.

As soon as they reached the beach, Cooper collapsed face-first into the sand. Tim shifted the big guy's head to the side so he could breathe, but other than that, nobody bothered to try and move him. Dave sprawled out on the sand and closed his eyes.

*

Dave woke up to the sensation of water running across his face and someone kicking him through his soggy armor padding.

Remembering that he was chained to Cooper, it occurred to him that it wasn't completely impossible that the stupid asshole was pissing on his face. He quickly shut his mouth and opened his eyes. Just rain. He breathed out a sigh of relief.

"Come on" said Julian, the source of the kicking.

He kicked Cooper as well. "Wake up, guys! It's raining!"

"Knock it off, dude," said Cooper. "We spent the night in the goddam ocean. You're worried about getting wet?"

"No," said Juilan. "I'm worried about dying of dehydration."

"So shut up and stick your fucking tongue out. I'm tired." Cooper tried to roll away from Julian, but Julian yanked on his chain.

"We don't know how long we're going to be here, and we don't know when it's going to rain again. We need to fill these bottles up with fresh water while we can."

"That's not a bad idea," said Dave. He sat up.

Cooper made an effort to get up and walk, but his legs were wobbly. Dave and Julian supported him on their shoulders, dragging a groggy Tim who stumbled along beside them.

"I'll try to make some funnels out of palm leaves," said Julian.

"You do that," said Tim. "I'm going back to sleep." He slipped his hand out of the manacle and sat back against a palm tree.

Julian tugged at his own manacle, but it wasn't going anywhere. "How did you do that?"

Tim yawned. "Seven ranks in the Escape Artist skill."

"So you could have done that at any time," said Julian. "Why wait until now?"

"We were out in the middle of the ocean," said Tim. "It was to my advantage to be chained to the rest of you."

Water turned out not to be a problem. It rained all morning, overflowing their two bottles. Tim used the bones of some long-dead animal to pick the locks of everyone's manacles. Cooper kicked a palm tree until it rewarded him with some coconuts, as well as some nasty lumps and bruises. Cooper reciprocated by climbing up the tree as high as he could and swaying back and forth until the trunk snapped.

Getting into the coconuts proved to be another challenge. The island didn't have any rocks large enough to crack them against, and nobody had any weapons. Cooper soon solved this problem by smashing two of them together. While this proved effective, it only yielded about a third of the fruit available, the other two thirds of which exploded into a pulpy mess in the sand. But there was no shortage of coconut palms on this island, and Cooper only had to fell six more trees until everyone had had their fill. Dave, once again, spent his entire day's allotment of healing spells on Cooper.

Ravenus had no interest in coconuts. He decided to scout the island in search of proper carrion.

"Don't be gone too long," Julian shouted after him as he flew off. "And be careful!"

The four of them sat in silence throughout the afternoon, eating fragmented coconut bits and watching the sun begin to set.

"Any ideas on how we're going to get out of here?" asked Tim.

"I don't know," said Cooper. "It's not so bad here. I could think of worse places to spend the rest of my years."

"I'll forgive your shortsightedness because you're stupid," said Tim.

"That's mighty big of you."

"You're not thinking this through. How much longer are you going to be content living off coconuts? How long is that even going to be an option if you keep ripping the fucking trees down? Julian has already observed that we could run out of drinking water with any prolonged stretch of sunny weather. And unless any of you know how to distill rum, you can forget about booze. Hell, the closest thing we have to a woman here is Julian."

"Hey," Julian objected, and quickly stopped combing his fingers through his hair. "Keep it together, man. We've only been on this island one day."

"Your points are well made," said Cooper. "I have no ideas."

"That comes as no surprise," said Tim.

"We could build a raft," Dave suggested.

"I don't know," said Tim. "Sure, we've got more than enough tree trunks, and we could rummage up some vines or something to lash them together, but that's open sea out there. Would you really trust anything the four of us built to be seaworthy?"

"Of course not," said Dave. "But I can't think of any other—YEOW!" Dave felt like he had just been stabbed in the ankle with a red-hot poker. He looked at his ankle and saw the biggest reasonably-sized ant he'd ever seen, about the size of one of his fat, dwarf fingers. It was light beige, the same color as the sand. He quickly swatted it away, but a closer inspection of the area revealed that it wasn't alone. The place was crawling with ants, greedily munching away on discarded coconut fragments.

"ANTS!" Dave shouted, jumping to his feet. He ran as fast as he could to toward the water, and his friends quickly followed suit. He hadn't made it halfway there when he had the tactile and olfactory sense of being hit by a garbage truck. He and Cooper rolled on the sand.

"What the hell?" said Dave.

"They're all over you, man!" said Cooper.

Dave looked at his armor padding. Sure enough, he was crawling with ants. He must have dribbled a lot of coconut juice on himself.

"Yaaaah!" Dave screamed. "Get them off! Get them off." He ripped his clothes off as fast as he could and jumped naked into the sea, splashing around like a man on fire.

Cooper picked the ants, which had transferred from Dave to him during their tumble, one by one off of his body and ate them. "They're not as bad as you'd think."

Dave's arms and legs were covered in painful welts. It only took three 0-level Heal spells to clear them away, but if they got swarmed during the night while they were sleeping or something, those little bastards might bite them to death. "Okay. Raft it is. We need to get out of here, like pronto."

"Don't be such a pussy," said Cooper, ant guts dribbling down the side of his mouth. "Look, they aren't even biting me."

"They'd probably prefer to starve to death," said Tim. "I can assure you that if it comes to us having to eat one another to survive, you'll be the last man standing."

Cooper farted, and four ants fell off of his back and lay motionless in the sand. "You guys should really get some protein in you."

"I'll gnaw my own hands off, thanks," said Tim.

"Screw you guys," said Cooper, collecting the dead ants and popping them into his mouth. "Go ahead and starve to death. I'm Bear Gryllin this shit."

"Hey!" said Julian, looking up at their ruined picnic site. "How's that for protein?"

Where they had been sitting only a moment ago, two fat, blue peacocks had emerged from the palm trees. They were feasting away on ants.

"If we could bag us one of those," said Tim, "we'd last a lot longer before we inevitably die at sea. Cooper, do you think you could catch one?"

"I don't know. How fast is a peacock? I wouldn't want to lose it in the trees."

"Wait," said Julian. "I can get one, but I want to run it by Ravenus first."

"What the fuck for?" asked Cooper.

"I want to make sure he's cool with us killing and eating a bird."

"If you think I'm going to go hungry to spare the feelings of your fucking crow—"

"He's a raven, and I'm not going to ask his permission. I just want to give him a heads up, so he's not shocked when he comes back."

"I'll give you five minutes," said Cooper. "Then I'm chasing those fat fuckers down."

"How can I get his attention without scaring the peacocks away?"

"Don't you have like a mind-link to him or something?" asked

Tim.

"Yeah, but it's not like telepathy or anything. I can't just will him to go get me a beer or something. It's more like we can feel one another's strong emotions. For example, he'd know if I was in danger."

"I could try to kill you," said Cooper.

"That wouldn't work," said Julian. "I wouldn't really believe it, so I wouldn't be genuinely afraid."

Cooper gave Julian a quick jab in the face, which sent him flying backward to land flat on his back in the sand.

"Jesus, Cooper!" said Tim, trying to keep his exclamation to an excited whisper.

Cooper scanned the sky over the island. It was bereft of big black birds. He shrugged. "It was worth a try." He reached down to help Julian up.

"Fuck, that hurt," said Julian, rising unsteadily to his feet.

"It was subdual damage," said Cooper. "I willed it as I was punching you."

"Thanks a lot," said Julian, rubbing his nose. Then his eyes lit up. "I've got it! Tickle me."

"What?" said Tim.

"I hate being tickled," Julian explained. "If you guys all tickle me, I really will lose my shit and start to panic."

"You really want us to tickle you?" asked Dave.

"Well not necessarily you," said Julian. "No offense, but I'd just rather not get tickled by a naked dwarf."

"You're really that ticklish?" asked Cooper. He poked a probing finger under Julian's ribs. Julian swatted it away with the speed of a ninja.

This brought a wicked grin to Cooper's face. He looked at Tim. Tim shrugged, and the two of them attacked Julian with wiggling fingers.

Julian let out a yelp, but Cooper quickly clamped his giant hand over his face. Julian dropped to the ground and, just as he promised, immediately began to lose his shit. His arms and legs flailed about wildly and uselessly as tears streamed out of his eyes. Tim and Cooper appeared to be having a sadistically good time.

"This is gayer than being fucked by pirates," said Dave, shaking his head and covering his junk.

About a minute later, Ravenus appeared over the trees, homing in on their location like a guided missile. He landed on Cooper's head and started pecking away.

"Ow!" said Cooper, swatting at the bird. His hand made contact, sending Ravenus beak-first into the sand.

"What the devil is going on here?" Ravenus demanded once he righted himself and shook off the sand.

"Don't worry," said Dave. "They're just having some fun." He wanted to cross his arms to demonstrate his annoyance that Cooper and Tim were still tickling Julian, but that would involve him exposing himself. He cleared his throat instead.

"Excuse me," said Ravenus. His tone suggested that he was annoyed as well. "As soon as you three..." Dave just knew the word "idiots" was on the tip of the bird's beak. "...guys are finished this... well, whatever this is, I thought you might like to know that there are two peacocks over there you might be interested in eating."

Tim and Cooper finally released Julian.

Julian wiped tears from the corner of his eyes as he gasped for breath. "You're sure that's okay with you?"

Ravenus cocked his head, staring inquisitively at his master. "Why wouldn't that be okay with me?"

"What's he saying?" asked Cooper impatiently.

"He says it's okay for us to eat the peacocks."

"Ha!" said Cooper. "Birds are dicks."

"Can you reach them from here?" asked Tim.

"No problem," said Julian. "The range on a Magic Missile is incredible." He rolled his wet, sand-covered sleeve up all the way to his shoulder and waved his skinny, bare elf arm around in a circle, making sure he his soaked clothes wouldn't inhibit his movement. He pointed his arm at one of the unsuspecting peacocks,

palm out and fingers spread. "Magic Missile."

Tiny bolts of blue and white lightning crackled down the length of Julian's arm. Even Julian looked surprised at it, although he did not look at all frightened. When the magic reached his hand, it shot out of his palm in a glowing golden bolt of energy, sailed over the sand, and found its mark.

The unfortunate peacock barely saw it coming. One second, it was raising its head to gobble down a fat, juicy ant. The next second, its head was gone. With a quiet splat, the bird's beautiful display of tail feathers was a mess of blood, bone, and brain.

The top of its neck gave a half-hearted squirt of blood into the air, and then flopped forward like a limp dick.

The other peacock let out a loud squawk and disappeared into the trees. Julian let it go. He was massaging his bare arm.

"Are you okay?" asked Dave.

"Yeah," said Julian. "Just tingles is all. I think it was the magic reacting with the salt water."

"Good job," said Tim. "Does anyone know how to make a fire?"

"Not without my tinder box," said Dave.

"Anyway," said Cooper. "We just had a fucking monsoon. There's not going to be so much as a dry stick on this whole god-damn island."

"Well that kind of throws a wrench into our plan," said Julian. "Is it safe to eat raw peacock?"

"I'd wait at least a couple of days until the body's had time to properly start decomposing," suggested Ravenus.

"I'll just stick to coconuts for now," said Tim. "Let's work on building a raft."

Cooper felled a total of two dozen palm trees. Tim found that, if he started it off with his front teeth, he was able to peel away nice long strips of green bark, which Julian and Dave braided into ropes. Hopefully, they would be sturdy enough to hold the trunks together at sea.

The four of them worked all day and through the night. The next morning, the rising sun revealed the fruit of their labor in all its glory.

"We're going to fucking die," said Cooper.

"So it's not the most elegant-looking ship on the ocean," said Tim. "We've tested the wood. It's buoyant. If it keeps our heads out of the water, and we can get it to keep heading west, it'll get us back to Cardinia."

"How much of what you just said do you actually believe?" asked Dave. He frowned at the raft. The largest tree trunks were held together with two sets of manacles. The third set, along with supporting branches that took up nearly half the deck space, held the mast in place. "We don't even have a sail."

"I think we all know what has to be done," said Tim. He and Julian briefly made eye contact, and then both of them looked down at the ground. "We're going to need to use our clothes."

Without a needle or thread, sewing the clothes together proved to be a challenge, even for Tim's nimble halfling fingers. He did his best to align them so that shapes fit together and buttonholes lined up, but it was inevitable that he had to use a stick to punch new holes into places. He wove strands of coconut husk through the holes and tied the garments together. Just before the sun reached the western horizon, he had completed a rather impressive triangular sail.

They carefully tipped the raft on its side to attach the sail to the mast. Dave let out a sigh of relief when they tipped it back upright and it didn't fall apart.

The four of them stood in the last light of the evening, hands over their junk, taking in their creation.

"Well," said Tim. "Who's ready to go?"

"What, now?" asked Julian. "Shouldn't we wait until dawn?"

"What difference does it make?" asked Tim. "It's going to take at least a few days to get back, and that's if we get lucky with the wind. There's no way to avoid traveling at night. I'd rather get this over with as soon as we can than sit on this island and get eaten by ants."

"But you're borderline suicidal," said Dave. "I think we should put it to a vote."

"I'm with Tim," said Cooper. "Let's get the fuck out of here."

"But you're stupid," said Dave. "I'm not sure if your vote should count when our lives are on the line."

"I'm not sure you understand how democracy works," said Tim. "You can't just discount the vote of everyone who disagrees with you."

"I'm just saying maybe we should get a good night's sleep first," said Dave.

"We're going to be four naked dudes adrift on the ocean," said Julian. "I'd think you would want to sleep through as much of that as possible." He sighed. "I wish elves could sleep."

"Don't you see?" pleaded Dave. "This is not a sea-worthy vessel. We are going to die on this piece of shit raft!"

"It's the best we could do," said Tim. "I'd rather die at sea, trying to get home, than spend the rest of my life looking at your dong."

Dave had no counterargument. He didn't want to spend any more time looking at their dongs either. He helped his friends gather what little they had onto the raft. Their provisions included a bottle and a half of fresh water, three dozen coconuts, and one fat peacock carcass. At least Ravenus would eat well when the rest of them shat themselves to death from salmonella poisoning.

They pushed their craft away from the island, following the sun as it disappeared over the horizon. Much to Dave's surprise, the sail actually caught a bit of wind, pushing the raft slowly through the water without ripping it to pieces.

Cooper, who had done most of the heavy lifting during the raft's construction, was the first to tap out. His hand fell away and allowed his big half-orc schlong to flop out into full view. He hadn't been kidding about the scales and bumps. To the best of Dave's knowledge, Cooper hadn't had a chance to pick up any venereal diseases since they'd arrived in this world. It must have just been one more symptom of his horribly low Charisma score. Dave silently cursed his Darkvision and looked away.

Tim didn't last much longer than Cooper. Ripping the bark off of trees with his teeth all day had apparently worn the little guy out. Dave had been so used to picturing Tim as looking like a little kid that he was surprised by just how hairy he was. He had a chest like Tom Selleck, and his crotch looked like a bird's nest with a baby jalapeño growing out of it. Dave looked away, his eyes searching for something to look at other than cock.

Julian was still awake and covering himself. He stared out at the slowly retreating island, as calm as Dave had ever seen a person look.

"So," said Dave. "How long do you think we can last on those two bottles of water?"

Julian said nothing. He just continued to stare, unblinking, into the dark beyond. Shit. He must be in his elf trance.

Feeling a sudden overwhelming loneliness, Dave huddled on the raft, ass to his friends, and fell asleep.

*

He woke up feeling refreshed. He must have had been more tired than he thought. When he opened his eyes, the sunlight was blinking on and off as the raft rocked on the gentle waves. He turned his head to look for the sun, and found a diseased grey serpent in its place.

"WHAT THE FUCK!" Nothing clears away the morning grogginess quite like a half-orc dick dangling right above your face. "Cooper, what are you... what the fuck!"

"Chill out, dude," said Tim. "I told him to stand there because you were starting to burn."

Dave looked down at his arm. It was pink, all right. Dwarves belonged in mountain caves. Their skin was not adapted to prolonged exposure to sunlight. "Sorry, Cooper," he mumbled. "Thank you."

"Oh no," said Cooper. "The pleasure was all mine. There's nothing I'd rather do than stare at your big pale dwarf ass for hours on end."

"Can it, Coop," said Tim. "We've got bigger things to worry about." He looked at the mast. It was empty.

"Where's the sail?" Dave shouted.

"We don't know," said Tim. "It must have been blown loose during the night. Ravenus is out looking for it now, but I wouldn't hold out much hope. It could be anywhere."

Dave turned to Julian. "You don't even sleep! Why didn't you keep an eye on the sail?"

"I was meditating," said Julian. "I'm barely aware of my surroundings when I'm in my trance."

"It's nobody's fault," said Tim. "It is what it is. Now we just have to figure out something else."

"What's there to figure out?" asked Dave. "Take a look at our inventory. Maybe we could stick the dead peacock on the end of the mast, lasso a shark, and hold it out in front of him."

"See there," said Tim. "You've already come up with an idea."

"I was joking!"

"I don't know," said Cooper. "It sounded okay to me. As a potential solution, that is. As a joke, I feel it fell kind of flat."

"Fuck you, Cooper," said Dave. "Do you realize how fucked we are?"

"Losing your shit about it isn't going to help," said Tim. "Just calm down and think."

"Why didn't you make any oars?" asked Dave.

"We didn't need oars," said Tim. "We had a sail."

"Well that's just brilliant."

"How many oars did you make, Captain Cockbeard?"

"Guys!" said Julian. "Less fighting. More thinking."

The four of them sat and thought. No ideas had yet been proposed by the time Ravenus came flying back.

Julian stood up quickly, one hand holding the mast, and the other holding his junk. "Did you find anything?"

"Sorry, sir," said the bird as he perched atop the mast. "Nothing but water for miles around. I couldn't even find the island. I beg your forgiveness."

"It's okay," said Julian. "Thanks for trying."

"I take it that was a no," said Cooper, who couldn't understand Elven.

"Whatever our next move," said Tim, "we have to make sure we survive." He looked up at Ravenus. "Do you think you could catch us some fish?"

"Do I look like waterfowl to you?" the bird snapped back at him.

A brief but awkward silence followed.

"If you want the water foul," said Dave, "why don't you ask Cooper to jump in?"

Julian cringed.

"That was lame," said Tim.

"Oh come on," said Dave. "Don't even tell me you guys weren't thinking of the exact same joke."

Tim looked at his feet. "Okay, so I was still working out the wording in my head."

"Me too," Julian mumbled.

"I don't get it," said Cooper.

"Don't worry about it," said Dave. "Tim was right. It was kind of lame."

"Dude," said Cooper. "Your jokes suck."

Dave crossed his arms over his chest and sulked, not minding that it left his wang hanging out for all to see. He had nothing to be ashamed of after seeing Cooper's leper dick and Tim's tiny sausage. He hadn't yet had the displeasure of seeing what Julian was packing, but if it was anything like the rest of his body, it probably looked like a garden snake.

After half an hour or so of silent, aimless drifting, Tim and Cooper lowered their guard as well. Tim propped his elbows on his knees and cradled his head in his palms. Cooper sprawled out for a nap on the front of the raft, using the peacock carcass as a pillow. Julian kept his privates private, and Dave began to grow concerned about just how much he wanted to confirm his garden snake theory. It's not gay. It's scientific curiosity.

He was on the brink of just flat out asking Julian to let him see his member when a splash from behind interrupted his thoughts.

"Greetings!" sang a voice that nearly sent Dave into the water. He turned around to see a young man and woman standing in the improbably waist-high sea. Each of them offered a friendly wave with one arm while keeping the other hand conspicuously below the water. Closer inspection revealed that the water was not waist-high at all. Everything below their waist was the tail of a fish, sparkling just beneath the surface of the water. The man wore a familiar-looking white silk robe, while the woman was bare-chested, wearing only some sort of strange cotton headpiece, separating her long, flowing hair into two plumes atop her head.

"Mermaids!" said Julian.

"Merfolk," the male one corrected him.

"I'm sorr— Hey, are you wearing my robe?"

"We are grateful for the gifts which you have bestowed upon us," said the female. Her voice was like angel song.

"Excuse me," said Cooper. "Shouldn't you be... um... covering up your nip-nips with clamshells or something?"

"That sounds terribly uncomfortable," said the mermaid. "Does my body upset you gentlemen? You seem unconcerned for your own modesty. Where are your coverings?"

"They're on your fucking head," said Tim.

That's when it hit Dave. That wasn't a headpiece at all. She was wearing Tim's pants upside down on her head. He had to admit, she was making it work.

The merman and mermaid looked at one another briefly, then he spoke up.

"We have come to return the favor with a gift of our own." He pulled a shining silver trident out of the water. Two of the three prongs were impaling a two foot long tuna. "Behold! The marvelous bounty of the sea we bring to—" He stopped short as a coconut bounced off his head.

The mermaid screamed. It was like a thousand wind chimes in a hurricane.

"Jesus, Cooper!" shouted Tim. "What the fuck!"

"He was attacking us!" said Cooper.

"No, he wasn't!" said Tim. "He was — wha!" The three points of the mermaid's trident, and another fish, blurred past Dave's face as she swept Tim over the side of the raft.

Cooper immediately dove headfirst into the water. The mermaid held her arm in a lock around Tim's throat and swam backward away from Cooper. She held her fish-laden trident, ready to strike, in her other hand. She moved through the water with such effortless speed that Cooper didn't stand a chance of catching her.

But as it turned out, he didn't even look at her as he swam. He was going for the unconscious merman. By the time Tim's captor realized what was happening, Cooper was dragging his own hostage aboard the raft.

"You put him back!" the mermaid demanded, swimming back toward the raft. Either she was swimming cautiously slowly, or Tim's ball-fro was causing a lot of drag.

"We can do this the easy way or the hard way, Sebastian!" said Cooper.

"Sebastian was the crab," Julian whispered.

"My name is Fransesca," said the mermaid. "That is my fiancé, Riccardo. You let him go, and I'll give you your friend."

"I've got a better idea," said Cooper. "You give me back my friend, and I'll stop eating your fiancé." He held out one of Riccardo's limp arms and opened his mouth wide.

"Cooper!" Tim shouted. "Stop!"

Fransesca grinned. "Do you know what we do to your kind when they cross us?"

"Which kind is that?" asked Julian.

"The kind with legs," she said. "You're all the same to us. We drag them alive to the bottom of the ocean and pin them to a sunken ship with our tridents."

"She's bluffing!" said Tim. He spoke in a British accent, probably gambling on her not being able to speak Elven. "Make her think you don't give a shit about me. If she thinks her currency is tanking, she'll be eager to spend it."

"What should I say?" asked Julian, also with a British accent.

"Anything," said Tim. "Use your Bluff skill."

"Forget it, loser," Julian shouted at Tim, speaking in his normal accent again. "The bounty for your petty crimes is nothing compared to what the Duke of... um... York, will pay for an addition to his stuffed merfolk collection to mount on his wall."

"But... but..." Tim stammered with a panic that Dave hoped wasn't too obviously fake. "Think of what York will pay for the location of where his daughter's bones are buried. I'm the only man alive who knows that information." His voice cracked at the end. It was a brilliant performance, voluntarily blowing a Bluff skill check in order to make his own position look weaker than it already was.

"What the fuck are you guys talking about?" said Cooper, who, like Fransesca, had not been privy to the Elven part of the conversation.

"Silence, beast!" Julian bellowed at Cooper. "Mind the prisoner, or suffer the lash!"

"Fuck you, dude."

Tim smiled and winked at Cooper.

"Oh... er..." said Cooper. "I mean, a thousand pardons, master." He lowered his head reverently at Julian.

"I've made up my mind!" said Julian. "The halfling is worthless to us now. Set sail for Cardinia at once!"

"But he knows where the bones are buried!" cried Fransesca. "The bones! What if it was your daughter?" She lowered her trident and swam closer to the raft. "Please!"

"The fish-woman has discovered a pearl of compassion in my oysterous heart!" said Julian, getting perhaps a little too caught up in his improvised emperor-of-Rome persona. "Let it not be said that I was an unjust master. You shall have your fiancé back, fish-woman! But as payment for your insolence, I must demand that you surrender your weapons."

Tim gave Julian a look that spoke as clearly as any language. "Knock it the fuck off already."

"Anything," Fransesca cried. "Just please don't hurt him!" She hefted her trident onto the raft and swam to Cooper for the exchange.

Cooper reached past Tim and grabbed a hold of Fransesca's left wrist.

"What are you — what is this?" she demanded. But the damage was done. Cooper had locked her arm in a manacle.

"Congratulations," said Cooper, lifting the chain to reveal that the manacle on the other end was connected to Riccardo's right arm, and that the chain itself was manacled to the frame of the raft. "I unite you in the bonds of holy wedlock."

"Cooper," said Dave. "What the hell do you think you're doing?"

"Just get over here and heal the dude."

Dave didn't understand where this was headed, and he certainly didn't like it, considering the fact that they had all but settled this fiasco. But he couldn't see how any good would come from refusing to heal the merman. He grabbed hold of the mast, which fell over, nearly taking Dave with it. Of course. Cooper had removed the manacle which had been holding it in place. He crawled on hands and knees to Riccardo and placed a hand on the merman's head. "I heal thee."

The coconut-induced lump on Riccardo's head immediately receded, and his eyes fluttered open.

"That feels wonderful!" said Riccardo. He put his unchained hand on Fransesca's cheek. "Fransesca, my love! What ails thee!"

Fransesca lifted her left arm to show him the chain that connected them. It was only then that he even began to take in his surroundings.

"Who are you people?" he demanded. He shook his manacled wrist. "What is the meaning of this?"

"Shut your blowhole, Flipper," said Cooper. "Start swimming for Cardinia."

"By the gods of sea and sand, I shall do no such thing!"

Cooper picked up one of the tridents, pulled the fish off of the barbed tips, and set the fish carefully on the deck. He held the weapon over his head. "You know what I think looks sexy on a girl?" he asked. Without giving them any time to answer, he continued. "Nipple piercings. Hold still, Love."

"Enough!" said Riccardo. "We shall do as you say."

The two merfolk ducked under the surface of the water, and the raft started moving. It really started moving. Dave lay on his belly, holding on with white-knuckled fingers to the frame of the raft.

"This doesn't feel right," Julian said over the sound of the raft crashing through the waves.

"It's cool," said Tim. "It's still morning, and we're headed away from the sun. That's west.

"I meant morally," said Julian. "This kind of feels like slavery."

"It's not slavery," said Cooper.

"We've got people in chains, and we're forcing them to move our boat across an ocean. I seem to recall reading about something like that before."

"They're prisoners of war. It's different."

"You started the war."

"Look," said Cooper. "Do you want to get back to Cardinia or not?"

"I just don't feel right about it."

"I know why you did what you did, Cooper," said Tim. "But I think Julian's right. I don't want to be a slaver."

"I can't believe you guys," said Dave. "We're headed back to land. Civilization! We've got an actual chance of surviving. It's not like we're going to keep them in an aquarium or anything. We'll let them go once we're on solid ground."

"It's a matter of principle," said Tim. "Think about their dignity. We totally emasculated that dude right in front of his fiancé."

"So what do you propose we do?" asked Cooper. "If we let them go, they'll get every fish fucker in the sea to come back here and harpoon us to death."

"I'll reason with them," said Julian. "Explain that this was all a huge misunderstanding."

Cooper frowned, looking down at the manacle on the front of the raft.

"Don't do it, Cooper," said Dave. "They'll get over it. There' s a big, frosty beer waiting for you at the Whore's Head."

"Fuck," said Cooper. He reached down and tugged on the chain. The raft slowed to a halt.

The two merfolk emerged from the water, only up to their chests. They both kept their head down, and Fransesca covered her breasts with her free arm.

"What would you have us do?" asked Riccardo.

"My friend Cooper has something he'd like to say to you," said Julian. "Cooper?"

"I'm sorry," said Cooper, scratching his armpit. Riccardo and Fransesca looked at one another. Riccardo shrugged.

"What for?" Julian prompted Cooper to continue.

"I'm sorry for hitting you with a coconut."

"And?"

"And I'm sorry for chaining you to our raft."

"Go on."

"And I'm sorry for threatening to stab your girlfriend in the tit."

"You see," said Julian. "My friend here is very stupid."

"Borderline retarded," said Tim. Julian turned and quickly shushed him.

"He acts on impulse," Julian continued. "When he saw you raise your trident, he didn't think twice about defending his friends. That's just who he is."

Riccardo looked at Fransesca. She nodded at the raft, urging him to respond. "We accept you're apologies," he said. "So what happens now?"

"We let you go," said Julian.

"Just like that?" asked Riccardo. His voice was wary.

Tears welled up in Fransesca's eyes, as if she feared Julian was just building up her hopes in order to crush them again.

"Just like that," said Julian. "All we ask is that you seek no retribution."

"You have my word," said Riccardo.

"I only wish we had something to offer," said Julian. "A token of our sincerity. An early wedding present."

Fransesca began to cry. Dave didn't know what she was feeling, but she sounded like jingle bells at the bottom of a well.

Riccardo shuddered as an expression of rage flashed across his face. He looked past Julian. "Those are fine looking bottles you have there," he said.

"Really?" said Julian, looking back at the water bottles.

"Quality glassware is highly valued among our people," said Riccardo.

"We'd have to ration our water more carefully," said Julian. "But I think we could spare one of them." He looked at Cooper, and then at Tim, each of whom nodded their consent.

Julian handed the bottle with less water down to Fransesca. She stopped crying as she cradled it in her arms like a newborn child. She looked at Riccardo with eyes as wide as saucers. You'd think Julian had just offered to buy them their first home.

"You can't know what this means to us," said Riccardo.

"Give them the other one, too," said Dave.

"Huh?" said Cooper.

"We need drinking water," said Tim.

"I'll handle the drinking water," said Dave. He looked down at Riccardo. "Is one more bottle a fair trade for your two tridents?"

"It's worth a thousand tridents!" said Riccardo.

"Two will do," said Dave. He handed the other bottle down to a bewildered Riccardo. "I hope you have a long and happy life together."

"You are most generous!" said Riccardo, accepting the second bottle.

"If there's any way we may repay you," said Fransesca.

"Can I touch your titties?" said Cooper.

"Cooper!" snapped Julian.

"Sorry," said Cooper. He released the merfolk from their chains. They embraced each other, careful not to let the bottles clink together, and disappeared under the water.

"That was big of you," Tim said to Dave. "I'm glad you had a change of heart, but what the hell are we supposed to do about drinking water?"

"Look up and open your mouths," said Dave. He demonstrated. The others followed suit.

"Water," said Dave, and quickly opened his mouth again. Cool, clear water materialized out of the air above their mouths and poured in faster than they could drink it. It dribbled down their faces and chests as they greedily tried to lap up as much as they could. After about half a minute, it stopped.

"It's a zero-level clerical spell," Dave explained. "I can do that four or five times a day."

"Why didn't you mention that before?" asked Julian.

"I didn't want to give you any more reasons to think this stupid raft idea was plausible."

Dave took a big bite out of the side of one of the tuna and passed it to Julian. He grabbed the peacock carcass and began to carefully cut away the skin with one of the sharp prongs of a trident.

"What are you doing?" asked Tim.

"Art project," said Dave.

It was late afternoon when Dave revealed his completed project. Peacock skin wrapped tightly around the business end of one of the tridents. He handed it to Cooper. "Here you go."

"What the fuck am I supposed to do with this?"

"Row."

It was a surprisingly effective oar, and Cooper proved to be a competent oarsman, switching sides whenever they began to steer away from the setting sun.

Tim turned out to be a capable fisherman, given a weapon with which he could employ his Sneak Attack ability. Between his use of the other trident and Julian's Magic Missiles, they pulled in more seafood than they could possibly hope to eat.

Dave even managed to fashion some crude pants for them out of giant squid carcasses. They were slimy and uncomfortable, and they certainly wouldn't win any fashion awards, but they covered his junk. That made a world of difference.

Less than a week later, Ravenus — constantly on scout duty — spotted land.

That same evening, crowds of gawking Cardinians parted for Tim, Dave, Julian, and Cooper as they walked through the solid, cobblestoned streets with their sunburnt, weather-beaten heads held high, dragging a tangled, twenty-foot long trail of tentacles behind them.

The End

Dungeon Crawl

ROBERT BEVAN

DUNGEON CRAWL

(Original Publication Date: July 12, 2013)

Cardinia's city center buzzed with the hustle and bustle of commerce, music, and merrymaking, and Tim's halfling ears seemed to pick up every goddamn sound of it. He could tell you the price of a sack of oranges from five stalls away, or even which of the spice merchants had the most complaints about their scales being improperly balanced. What he couldn't tell you is where to find some decent fucking work.

"We're not interested in shoveling shit or gutting fish," Tim said to the man standing atop a wooden crate. "We're looking more for—"

"Get a load of this," said one nearby half-orc to another. They were dressed in filthy, threadbare overalls, but their hair was even combed and slicked back with what appeared to be some sort of oil, but could just as easily been snot, if Cooper was an accurate gauge with which to measure standard half-orc hygiene. "The halfling thinks he's too good to shovel shit."

"Beggin' Your Majesty's pardon, m'lord," said the other half-orc, taking a knee. This was, Tim expected, both to mock him as well as to speak to him face-to-face. "But some of us ain't so fortunate as you, bein' able to hold out for a job as the queen's personal tit massager. We's got families to feed."

"It's not like that," said Tim. "I just—"

"What sort of work are you two gentlemen looking for?" the employment broker asked the two half-orcs.

The half-orc who had been kneeling in front of Tim stood

up like his legs were spring-loaded. "We ain't particular. If the shit-shoveling job is still available, we'd be happy with that."

The employment broker raised an eyebrow. "Can you provide your own shovels?"

The half-orc lowered his head. His partner spoke up. "We have very big hands." He displayed open hands, palms up. They were, indeed, very big.

"The pay is two coppers per wagonload."

"That's most generous, sir."

"Well," said the broker. "I'm afraid it's going to be up to our little friend here." He looked down his nose at Tim. "You were here first, after all. Fair is fair."

Tim looked at the two half-orcs. "Knock yourselves out."

The speaker for the two half-orcs slapped his partner on the back. Both of them grinned broadly and bowed.

The employment broker ripped off part of a piece of paper and held it out by the corner with the very tips of his thumb and index finger. "Be at this address tomorrow at dawn."

The half-orc grabbed the paper eagerly. "Thank you so much, sir. We won't let you down." He looked down at Tim. "Thank you too, sir. Best of luck with your dreams of becoming the king's whore tester. I'm sure the position will open up any minute now."

The other half-orc laughed. "Try not to stretch them out too much with that monster cock of yours."

The two half-orcs walked away laughing.

"Is everyone in this world a sarcastic prick?"

"What sort of work did you have in mind?" asked the broker.

"I don't know," said Tim. "Maybe something a little more unorthodox. High-risk, high-reward. You know?"

"You might try Zorbane's House of Chance."

Tim rubbed his hands together. "Okay, now we're talking. What is that, like some haunted old mansion?"

"It's a gaming parlor."

"What, like a casino?"

"If you like."

Memories of ringing bells, flashing lights, and cigarette smoke flooded Tim's brain. He had gone through a gambling phase a couple of years ago, and had seen more than one blubbery shell of a human being piss themselves rather than spend two minutes away from their slot machine. Witnessing this — and nearly losing the Chicken Hut — had been a big enough slap in the face to steer him away from casinos for good.

"Dude, are you deliberately wasting my time?"

"I could ask the same of you, sir." The employment broker's tone had evolved from impatient to downright snippy. "I match unskilled laborers with reputable employers. My preferred clients are strong, honest, and hardworking. Not whiny, entitled little shits."

Tim balled up his fists, but couldn't think of anything to say. The broker folded his arms, raised his eyebrows, and stared down at him. The guy was a dick, sure, but he wasn't wrong. Tim had been acting like a whiny, entitled little shit.

There was only one thing to do. Without saying a word, Tim turned around and walked briskly away.

He didn't have to waste much time finding his friends. He only had to look for a crowd of people radiating away from something, and he knew Cooper would be at the epicenter. A guard eyed him suspiciously as he shimmied up a nearby lamp pole. Tim stopped halfway up the pole to make it clear that he was only trying to see over the crowd, and not trying to steal the Light-enchanted stone which lit up the streets at night. The guard kept his eyes on him, but seemed satisfied. Tim only had to scan the crowd for a few second before he found what he was looking for. There was a conspicuous void in the crowd near one of the lesser fountains in the city center, and right in the middle of it sat a dwarf, an elf, a raven, and a half-orc. Tim slid down the pole and scurried off in that direction.

"Any luck?" asked Dave as soon as Tim stepped into the zone of disgust that Cooper's presence inspired.

"Nothing," said Tim. "Just manual labor bullshit. You guys

find anything?"

"More of the same," said Dave.

Julian stroked one of his long elf ears. "Maybe there just aren't any adventures to be had. Can you imagine going to an employment agency back home and asking to be sent on a quest? They'd laugh your dumb ass out the door."

"But we're not back home," said Tim. "This is a Caverns and Creatures world. There are bound to be caves to explore, ruined temples, lost treasures, keeps on borderlands, all that shit. We just haven't been looking in the right places."

Cooper pulled a finger out of his ear. It was distinctly browner up to the second knuckle. "We could always just walk around outside the city walls and hope for a random encounter." He sucked the brown off his finger.

Tim closed his eyes, tried unsuccessfully to un-see that, and suppressed his instinct to vomit. "Too dangerous," he said. "We're not high enough level for that. Without a Cavern Master to keep things level-appropriate, we could just as easily run into a gaggle of dragons as we could a single kobold. I want to have some idea of what we're up against before we—"

"Excuse me, gentle sirs," said a voice from behind Tim.

Tim turned around and backed up. The man who addressed them was human. He wore plate armor, painted dark blue with a bright yellow sun on the breastplate. He smiled kindly at them.

"He looks like a cleric," Tim whispered to Dave, who nodded in agreement. "What god is that the symbol of?"

"How should I know?" Dave whispered back.

"Because you're a fucking cleric, dumbass. Didn't you take any ranks in Knowledge of Religion?"

"No," said Dave. "I was going to, but I picked up Elven instead so I could understand Ravenus."

"Who the fuck are you?" asked Cooper.

Julian bonked Cooper on the head with the tip of his quarterstaff.

"Ow."

"A thousand apologies," said Julian. "My friend has a very low Charisma score."

"I don't know what that—"

"What can we do for you today?" Julian's Charisma score was high enough so that he could cut people off in the middle of asking uncomfortable questions and not sound rude.

The cleric smiled. "My name is Dusty Sheglin. I am a humble cleric at the Temple of Rapha. I have displeased my order, and am on a quest for redemption so that I might once again bask in Rapha's holy light."

"What did you do?" asked Cooper. "Did you fuck a kid? Cause I'll beat your ass down right here and now, Padre."

The cleric stood aghast. You could have driven a truck through his open mouth.

Julian gave Cooper another knock on his giant half-orc forehead.

"Knock it off, man," said Cooper. "That hurts."

"Why in Rapha's holy name," asked the cleric, "would that be your first assumption?"

"I'm sorry," said Cooper. "That's what priests do where we're from." Thonk. "Dude!"

"Just shut your big mouth for a few minutes, will you?" said Julian. He turned to the cleric. "I beg your forgiveness... Mr. Sheglin? Father Sheglin? Brother...?

"Call me Dusty."

"Okay," said Julian. "Dusty it is. Please ignore my friend. He's almost as stupid as he is uncharismatic."

"Of course."

"You were saying?"

"Ah yes," said Dusty. "My offense was that I bought a starving orphan a bowl of broth."

Tim's bullshit detector started tingling. He stepped forward. "That's a very noble crime, Dusty. Why, exactly, did the temple frown on this?"

Dusty lowered his head. "I used unauthorized temple funds.

The order is very strict about how they conduct their charities."

Bureaucracy and hypocrisy. This fell in line with Tim's view of organized religion. He backed off.

"What does this have to do with us?" asked Dave.

Julian turned around to glare at Dave and Tim. He tended to get prickly when other people interrupted his conversations with strangers. He said it interfered with his Diplomacy Check. He tolerated it from Cooper — insofar as repeatedly clobbering him on the head could be considered tolerance — because Cooper couldn't help himself, but he wasn't having it from the rest of the party.

"I overheard you gentlemen are looking for some unconventional work," said Dusty. "We may be able to help one another."

Julian eyed him suspiciously. "What, exactly, did you have in mind?"

"My reconciliation with the order depends upon my retrieval of a sacred relic thought to be hidden in the catacombs beneath Old Cardinia. They have not been used for centuries, and the fallen heroes of ages past may not be alone. I am but one humble servant of Rapha. I seek a party of brave companions to protect me from whatever foul vermin have taken up residence in the ancient tomb."

"What's in it—" Tim started, but Julian gave him a look that sliced right through his question.

"What's in it for us?" asked Julian.

"There are bound to be treasures beyond that which I seek," said Dusty. "Whatever else you find is yours to keep."

Julian pursed his lips thoughtfully for a moment. "Guys, huddle."

The four of them stepped away and formed a square. Julian and Cooper took a knee in order to facilitate private conversation with Dave and Tim. Ravenus perched on Julian's shoulder to get in on the action.

"Do you trust him?" asked Dave.

"I don't know," said Julian."

"What's not to trust?" said Tim. "Think about it. He's asking us to accompany him into a tomb. He was upfront about the danger. It's not like he's trying to lure us into a van with candy."

"That's what it kind of sounded like to me," said Cooper. "What if he just wants to lead us into a room full of priests who want to rape us? Or worse... what if they lock us inside and talk to us about their religion?"

"Listen," said Tim. "As a rogue, it's in my nature to be distrustful. As a halfling, I'm the closest to resembling an altar boy. Having said that, I trust this guy. I think we should give it a shot."

After a moment passed with no objections, Julian stood to face Dusty Sheglin. "When do we leave?"

Dusty smiled. "No time like the present."

"We'll need provisions," said Tim. "How much money have we got?"

Julian removed a small leather pouch from his belt and poured some coins into his hand. "Six gold."

Tim frowned. "We'll have to stretch it out, but it should suffice."

It didn't take them long to find a shop on the edge of the city center. The sign outside read 'General Gore's General Store'.

"Rapha provides me with all I need," said Dusty. "I shall wait here. Be swift."

"Suit yourself," said Tim. He led the others into the shop.

"Welcome!" said an aged and particularly stocky dwarf. "Welcome to General Gore's General Store! I am General Gore. How may I be of assistance today?"

Cooper stepped forward. "I'm looking for a large sack and a ten-foot pole."

"Of course, sir," said General Gore. "Right this way."

"Oh wait," said Cooper. He looked down at his crotch. "Never mind. I found them."

Tim shook his head. "Way to keep it classy, Coop."

Scanning the shelves, Tim recognized most of the items for sale were plucked right out of the equipment list in the Caverns and Creatures Player's Handbook. Fifty-foot lengths of rope, manacles, chains, flasks of oil, candles, sealing wax, pickaxes, shovels, and of course the aforementioned large sacks. Without prior game knowledge, he might have suspected this shop to cater mostly to hosts of debaucherous sex parties or murderers looking to dispose of a body.

"What kind of shop is this?" asked Julian, reminding Tim that he, Julian, had very little in the way of prior game knowledge.

"It's a general store," said Tim. "Standard equipment."

Julian struggled to pick up a five-foot log, capped with iron on both ends and with handles hammered along the length of it. "I can't remember the last time I generally needed a portable ram."

"Put that down before you hurt yourself," said Tim. "What do we need?"

"Food?" suggested Dave.

"Good thinking," said Tim. "Mr. Gore?"

"General Gore, son," said the dwarf. "Retired now, but I fought in six wars back before you was a squirt in yer pappy's small sack."

Cooper snorted. "Sack references never get old."

"I'm sorry," said Tim. "General Gore. Do you carry trail rations here?"

The old dwarf grinned. "Best in Cardinia!" He hobbled around to the other side of the counter and disappeared from view. When he resurfaced, he placed a tin box on the countertop. "The missus prepares these." He removed the lid, revealing an assortment of dry food that genuinely looked appealing. "Five silver pieces each. That gets you raisins, nuts, dates, horse jerky, hardtack, and even a cat bladder full of goat's milk to wash it all down with."

"That's adorable!" said Julian. "Get me one."

"Fine," said Tim. "There's four of us, plus Dusty if Rapha decides not to show up and hand him a sandwich." He turned to General Gore. "We'll take five."

"What about Ravenus?" said Julian. The big black bird cocked its head, staring down at Tim.

Tim stepped away from the counter. "He's a carrion eater.

We're spending the night in a tomb. He'll figure something out. What else do we need?"

"Rope is always useful," said Dave.

"Okay," said Tm. "Grab the hemp stuff. We can't afford silk." A rough leather bag on a high shelf, about the size of a bowling ball, caught his eye. The tag read 'Caltrops'. "Cooper, grab me that bag, would you?"

Cooper started to raise his arm, but Julian beat him to it.

"Allow me," said Julian with a smug and stupid grin on his face. With naught but his mind and a wave of his hand, he telekinetically lifted the bag from the shelf and lowered it into Tim's waiting arms.

Cooper gave him a polite golf clap. "New spell?"

"Mage Hand," said Julian. "I've been practicing with it lately. For a Zero-Level spell, it's pretty cool." He looked down at the bag in Tim's arms. "What are caltrops anyway?"

"Little spiky things," said Dave, returning with fifty feet of hemp rope. "They look like those Jacks that little girls play with, you know?"

"That's kind of gay, isn't it?" said Julian. "I mean, if you're planning for some down time, wouldn't you rather get a deck of cards or something?"

"Weren't you the one who was just queefing about how adorable that lunchbox was?" asked Cooper.

"I... I..." Julian's face went pink. His long ears went bright red. "I appreciate the amount of effort the general's wife put into making it look presentable."

"They're not Jacks," said Tim. "They're useful if we need to make a quick getaway. We dump the caltrops behind us, and whatever is pursuing us will have to either slow down or risk getting a spike through the foot."

"Here are the caltrops," said Dave, picking up a sturdy leather bag about the size of a bowling ball. "Do we need anything else? Or should we just spend the rest on torches and oil?"

"Wait," said Julian. "Why the hell do we need so much oil?"

"It's good for setting shit on fire," said Cooper.

"Can't you just do that with a torch?"

"Not when it's attacking you."

Julian's eyes went wide. "Oh."

"There's one more thing we might need," said Tim. He looked down at his feet. "I can't believe I'm about to say this."

"What?" said Dave.

"If we do happen to come across some treasure, we'd probably do well to have..." He tried to think of a different way to put it.

Cooper grinned like a madman. "Go on, Tim. Say it."

"Fine," Tim huffed. "We should buy a large sack."

Dave laughed so hard that he had to steady himself against one of the building's support beams. Cooper's face was slick with tears and snot.

"You guys are like fucking six-year-olds," said Tim, stomping off to grab the large sack himself.

"What's so funny?" Ravenus asked Julian.

"Not sure," said Julian, matching the bird's British accent. "I'm pretty sure it's a scrotum joke, but I don't get why it's as funny as all that."

"What's a scrotum?" asked Ravenus.

If Julian answered, it was drowned out by Cooper and Dave's idiotic cackling. Only when Tim was safely out of the others' fields of vision did he allow himself to crack a smile. He grabbed a burlap sack off the top of the pile. Large sack.

When the shopping was done, Dusty Sheglin was waiting for them outside.

"All ready to go?" he said chirpily.

"What?" said Dave. "Like, right now?"

"How many opportunities pass us by with each passing second we don't spend living life to the fullest, my fine furry friend? By the way, you must tell me what happened to your arm there."

Dave quickly crossed his arms, hiding his leopard-furred left forearm under his right. "I don't want to talk about it."

Old Cardinia, as it turned out, was just beyond the part of town the Whore's Head Inn was located in. They could have popped in for a drink if they'd had a mind to, but Tim thought better of making the suggestion. This Dusty Sheglin character seemed pretty eager to get on with his redemption. The terrain transitioned from slummy shithole to lush grassland surprisingly quickly. The grass was thick and green, punctuated here and there by smooth, sun-bleached white stones, and the soil felt moist and rich beneath Tim's bare halfling feet. It was hard to believe that they were still within the borders of the city.

Dusty Sheglin stopped at the edge of a two-foot-high stone wall. Whatever purpose this wall had served was likely long forgotten. It was maybe one hundred feet long, and neither end seemed to mark anything special. "Here we are."

"This is the spooky abandoned tomb?" asked Tim. "I've got to admit, I was prepared for something a bit worse."

"This is only the entrance," said Dusty.

"Where?" said Dave. "Behind the wall?"

"We're still inside the city walls," said Julian. "If there's an entrance to a catacomb full of monsters around here, what's keeping them from getting loose in the city?"

"The main entrance to the catacombs are miles beyond the city walls," said Dusty. "This is a secret entrance, hidden well on both sides, unknown to man or beast except for me... and soon you as well."

"I'm sorry," said Tim. He looked over his shoulder, panic rising inside him. Something was wrong about this. "This feels like bullshit. There's no entrance to a catacomb here. There's just grass, some rocks, and a wall. What's your game, dude? What do you want with us? Why have you brought us here?" He loaded a bolt into his crossbow, making sure not to point it directly at Dusty. Hopefully the gesture would convey the message that the time for fucking around had come and gone.

"Relax, little friend," said Dusty, flashing his warm smile. "There is no game here. My vows forbid me to bear false witness. Lying to you now would only negate this quest for redemption

that I'm on."

"So where's this secret entrance?" Tim demanded.

"I'm sitting on it."

"The wall?"

"That's right."

"Show me."

Dusty stood up on the very edge of the wall and pointed at Cooper. "You there, big fellow. Would you kindly stand on that rock for me?"

Cooper looked down quizzically at the large white stone he was standing next to. Tim's mistrust of this cleric had apparently gained some traction, because Cooper looked to Tim for approval before acting. Tim nodded, and Cooper stepped on the stone.

"There's a good lad" said Dusty. "Now if the dwarf may be allowed to come over to the other side of the wall and stand on this stone over here." He pointed down, presumably at a stone, but the wall blocked Tim's view.

"Stay where we can see you," cautioned Tim.

"The wall is not that high," said Dusty. "I assure you, he will never leave your sight."

Dave walked around to the other side of the wall until he found the place Dusty had been pointing to. "Hey, it moved."

"Very observant of you," said Dusty. "Most people could step on that stone all day and never notice it. Ready, halfling?"

"Ready for what?" said Tim.

"It's your turn. There's a very small stone buried in the grass somewhere about five feet behind you. See if you can find it."

Tim dragged his feet as he walked, hoping to catch the stone with his feet if he missed it with his eyes. He only spent a minute or two searching before he found it. "Am I supposed to stand on it?"

Dusty nodded.

Against his better judgment, Tim stepped onto the stone. If he hadn't been anticipating it, he never would have noticed the stone sink into the ground about a quarter of an inch.

"Very good," said Dusty. "Now mind none of you move. This won't work unless everyone is playing their part. Elf, I need you to run over to the other end of the wall. There, right on the edge, you'll find one stone which is just a shade darker than the rest. I need you to push that in and hold it. Can you do that?"

"Sure," said Julian. He ran enthusiastically to the other side of the wall. Ravenus flew along beside him. "Found it!" he called back.

"Give it a push!" Dusty shouted. "And remember to hold it down!"

Julian was too far away for Tim to see what he was doing, but whatever it was must have worked. Dusty smiled and waved bye-bye to Tim as the section of wall he was standing on,, about a foot long, began to sink slowly into the earth. When it was halfway down, the next pat of the wall started to descend. When Dusty's feet reached ground level, the third bit started. It was forming a staircase. It didn't make all of the noise of stone scraping against mortar that Tim would have expected. It was no noisier than an elevator.

"When you hear it stop," said Dusty as his waist sank out of view, "you'll want to be quick on your feet. As soon as one of you leaves your position, it'll start to rise again. It's faster than it looks."

Tim watched impatiently as, section by section, the wall sank into the ground. He started working on a game plan in his head. "Okay guys," he called out. "Here's what we're going to do. On three, we're all going to book it to the top stair. Dave, you're the slowest, so you do the count."

"One!" shouted Dave.

"No!" said Tim. "You have to wait for the goddamn wall to stop first."

"Oh right," said Dave. "Sorry, I'm a little nervous."

"Cooper," said Tim. "You're the fastest, so you're going to carry me."

"Got it," said Cooper.

"Anything for me?" asked Julian.

"Just run like a son of a bitch."

After another minute or two, the whirring stopped.

"It's finished!" Julian called out.

"Come on down!" shouted Dusty. His voice echoed out of the ground like he was in a subway tunnel. A really really deep subway tunnel.

Dave rubbed his hands together. "Okay, here we go. One! Two!" He jumped off his rock and set off for the staircase as quickly as he could. "Three!" He walked like a man trying to look dignified while trying to make it to the bathroom before he shits himself.

Dusty hadn't been lying about the stairs rising again. Tim heard the whirring before he even started running, his eyes on that first step. He just barely glimpsed the tips of Julian's ears disappear below the surface with Ravenus flapping right behind him.

Cooper stood at the edge of the stairwell, frantically waving his arm at Tim. "Come on, man! Hurry the fuck up!"

"I'm going as fast as I can!" Tim shouted back. "Cut me some slack. I'm only three fucking feet tall!"

Dave made it to the stairs and hopped down. Cooper ran toward Tim, scooped him up, and ran toward the middle of the hundred-foot-long hole in the ground.

"What the hell are you doing?" cried Tim.

"Shortcut!" said Cooper.

"Are you out of your fucking mind?"

"I'm very angry!"

"I don't give a fu—"

Tim's breath was cut off suddenly by Cooper's expanding bicep and pectoral muscle squeezing the air out of him.

"Brace yourself," said Cooper. His voice was several octaves lower than normal. The big idiot had gone into Barbarian Rage.

"Cooper," Tim was barely able to squeak the words out. "What are you doing?"

"We've got to get ahead of Dave, or he'll slow us down."

Tim wanted to make one last effort to talk some sense into Cooper, but was distracted by his body being jerked around. One second he was facing forward with a clear view of the pain that undoubtedly lay ahead of him, and the next his vision was completely obscured by a face full of half-orc nipple. And then the bouncing of Cooper's stride stopped. They were airborne. Cooper roared like a drunk grizzly doing a cannonball off the high dive. Tim had heard once that the last thing a person sees before they die is imprinted on their retina. He didn't want to leave this body behind, his eyes scarred forever with the image of a huge and hairy nipple.

"What the fu—"

Dave's voice disappeared beneath a cacophony of armor against stone against weapon against rolling bodies, mixed together with a healthy dose of swearing from Cooper. Tim was happy to note that there was surprisingly little pain. At least, not for him. For all his idiocy, the big brute had managed to keep him protectively cradled during the fall. As they tumbled down the stairs, Tim also reflected thankfully that Dusty had been chosen to carry the oil flasks and Julian the food. Cooper, being the strongest, could easily have carried everything, but nobody trusted him with the oil or wanted to eat anything that had been in his bag.

The last leg of the fall was a drop that couldn't have been any higher than seven or eight feet. Cooper released Tim from his sweaty embrace. The dank, musty air of the catacombs smelled like a spring meadow by comparison.

Julian kicked Cooper lightly in the ribs.

"Ow," Cooper groaned. The rage had left him.

"Get up, you crazy bastard," Julian demanded. "What was that all about?"

"I thought the extra Hit Points I got from raging would absorb the fall," said Cooper.

"Those go away as soon as the rage ends," said Tim. "Any damage you sustain remains afterward."

"I know that now," said Cooper. "I think I broke my ass."

Dave rolled onto his back. "I think you broke my ass too."

Dusty Sheglin put his hands on his hips and looked down at Cooper. "Do you think it's wise to alert the entire labyrinth of catacombs to our presence all at once?"

"You did say we should hurry," said Tim.

"I meant that you shouldn't dilly dally," said Dusty. "I didn't mean for you to free fall all the way down."

"Quit your moaning and dole out some healing, cleric," said Cooper. "My ass hurts."

Dusty looked away and crossed his arms over his breastplate. "The order has stripped me of all my clerical powers. They shan't be restored until my quest for redemption is complete."

"What a bunch of dicks," said Cooper. "How about it, Dave?"

"Yeah sure," said Dave. He and Cooper touched fingers. "I heal thee." He touched himself on the temple. "I heal me."

"That's just great," said Tim. "We haven't been here five minutes, and we're already down two Heal spells and one Barbarian Rage. Oh, and our other cleric is useless." He looked up. It was too late to turn back. The stairs had ascended beyond any of their reach and were now starting to block out the sunlight from outside. "Someone light up a torch."

After a few false starts, Dave managed to catch a spark from his tinderbox on the tallow-soaked flax atop one of their torches just as the last step sealed away the sunlight. He held the lit torch over his head. The room they were currently standing in was made of the same kind of stones as the wall outside had been. The effect for someone discovering this room from within the catacombs, once the stairs had ascended again, would be that they had just run into a dead end, albeit one with a curiously high ceiling. Dave held out his torch to Tim. "Here you go."

"Keep it," said Tim.

"I don't need it. I have Darkvision."

"I'm a rogue," said Tim. "I need to stay out of sight if I'm going to get my Sneak Attack bonus."

Dusty smiled and shook his head. "I must say, you gentlemen have a peculiar way of talking."

The ceiling sloped down sharply as they walked down the corridor until it evened out around the twelve foot mark, about half as tall again as Cooper. The ceiling was featureless but for two small stalactites.

"That's odd," said Dave. "This isn't a natural tunnel. There shouldn't be any stalactites."

"Complain to the manager," said Tim, looking up at the stalactites as he and Cooper passed under them. Without warning, the stalactite above Tim let go of the ceiling and fell. Halfway down, it opened up like a tentacle umbrella. Tim barely managed to jump out of its way.

"The fuck?" said Cooper. And then his face was covered by a black squid-like creature wrapping its leathery tentacles around his neck and shoulders.

"Cooper!" shouted Julian.

"Grrmblfrrkbrr!" Cooper responded.

The black squid-thing which had failed to land on Tim's face waved its circumference of webbed tentacles in a fast clockwise motion that caught air beneath it. It flew back up to the ceiling. It would have been a remarkable thing to behold if its friend wasn't suffocating the life out of Cooper.

Julian tried to beat the creature off of Cooper's face with his quarterstaff, but Cooper was thrashing around so wildly that most of Julian's blows struck him instead.

Tim loaded a bolt into his hand crossbow, all the while keeping a careful eye on the strange creature which had once again taken the form of a stalactite on the ceiling. When it dropped again, Tim was ready for it. He easily rolled out of the way. When the twice-foiled creature tried to retreat upward again, Tim unloaded his bolt into the membrane between its tentacles. It's flight pattern interrupted, it spiraled out of control, crashed into the wall, and fell to the floor.

It immediately started trying to fly again, but Tim was having

none of it. He pulled out the dagger he kept hidden in his boot and jumped the little black squid-bitch. It was dead long before he stopped stabbing it. When he finally ran out of breath, he took a break and turned to the others.

Ravenus was pecking at the discarded remains of the other creature, which Dave, Dusty, and Julian had apparently managed to remove from Cooper's face. They were all staring at Tim in wide-eyed wonder.

"Sorry," said Tim. He felt the warm blood rushing into his cheeks. "It was like a bat fucked a squid. It freaked me out, that's all."

"What are those?" asked Julian.

"Darkmantles," said Dusty. "More of a nuisance than anything. Shall we move along?"

Another forty feet down the passage, they met another stone wall. Dead end.

"Well I guess that's that," said Cooper. "It's been real."

"This has to be a secret door," said Tim. "There's got to be some stone you push to open it or something."

"I think I know where it is," said Dave. "Cooper, hold this." He handed Cooper his torch and touched the end of a second torch to the flame. The fire glowed bright for a moment, and then relaxed again as Dave waddled back the way they'd come from. "I'll be right back!"

When the glow of each torch were barely still touching, Dave stopped. A second later, the stone wall blocking their way began to slide upward.

"He did it!" said Tim.

"Shh!" hissed Dusty.

"He did it!" Tim whispered it this time.

Dusty poked his head into a corridor running perpendicular to the passage they were in. "Come on," he said, stepping through the secret doorway.

Tim, Julian and Cooper followed him, and the stone wall began to slide back down again.

"Hey guys!" said Dave. "Wait for me!"

"Julian, quick!" said Tim. "Your quarterstaff!"

Julian propped his staff under the doorway. The stone door didn't even stutter as it smashed the stick into splinters. "Well, shit."

The secret door was completely closed again before Dave was able to get anywhere near it. Cooper tried to push up on it, but it wasn't budging.

"Well, shit," Julian repeated. "Now what do we do?"

"Maybe there's a button on this side too," said Tim. The stones were much smoother in this corridor. Even the stones on this side of the secret door were polished. When the door shut, the stones lined up perfectly with the rest of the wall. He thought that if he looked away, he might not even be able to find the door again. It was a fruitless pursuit. None of the stones looked unique. Everyone fanned out to push on random parts of the walls, but it had no effect. A moment later, the door slid upward once again.

"Dave!" Tim called out. "You okay?"

"I'm fine, but there's no way I'm going to make it under that door in time."

"Let me try," said Cooper. "I'm the fastest one here."

"Okay," said Tim. "Go ask Dave to show you which stone to push, and then wait for him to get all the way out before you let go."

"Right," said Cooper. He jogged down the secret passage. Shortly after that, Dave emerged into the light of the torch that Julian was holding.

"Ready!" said Tim.

"Do try to keep your voices down," said Dusty, repeatedly looking down either side of the corridor.

The door began to slide back down, and the light from Cooper's torch bolted toward them with impressive speed, but it just wasn't enough. On his hands and knees, Tim watched Cooper skid to a halt just beyond the closing door.

"Damn," said Tim. "That was a lot closer, but he just isn't fast

enough. Even if he was, he's too big to make it under the gap."

"Hmm... " said Julian. "Faster. Smaller." His face lit up. "A horse!"

"You're one for two there, buddy," said Tim. "Nice try, though."

"No," said Julian. "You don't understand. I'll summon a horse out here. We'll tie one end of the rope to it, and the other end to you."

"I'm not sure I like where this is going."

"I'll ride the horse at full gallop. It'll be plenty fast enough to get you under that gap."

"Can anyone think of a plan that doesn't involve me being dragged by a horse?" Tim only received blank stares. "Please?" No response. "Shit. Dave, you better make sure you have a Heal spell ready to go."

"You got it."

"Hey Dave," asked Julian. "How did you know where the right stone to push was?"

"It's part of being a dwarf, I guess. I pick up on irregularities in stonework. I noticed that stone poking out a bit more than the others before we knew the way was blocked. It actually kind of annoyed me."

"Shit," said Tim. "It's going to take Cooper forever to find—" The secret doorway slid open. "I stand corrected." He called into the passage. "Cooper, stay where you are!"

"Horse," said Julian. A brown riding horse popped into existence next to him, complete with saddle, bit, and bridle. Julian tied one end of their recently purchased rope around the saddle horn. "Okay, that should hold."

Tim took the other end of the rope, Dave's torch, and the large sack. "I'm really not looking forward to this." He trudged down the secret passage until he came to Cooper waiting with his hand on the wall.

Tim held out the torch for Cooper. "Hold this." He tied the end of the rope to the drawstring of the large sack. He pulled the bag up over his head so that only one arm was poking out.

"Dude," said Cooper. "What the fuck are you doing?"

Tim felt along the wall until he found Cooper's hand. "Okay, I've got it from here. Go back to the others. Tell them I'm ready."

"Ready for what?" said Cooper. "You look like a testicle."

"Go!" shouted Tim from inside the sack.

As Cooper walked away, Tim stood alone. Alone in the dark, in a strange world, in a strange body, in a burlap sack. He should have finished college, met a nice girl, settled down. There wasn't any future in the Chicken Hut. He really should sell that dump. He had a lot more to offer the world than stuffing rednecks full of fried chicken. How had his life turned so shitty? He was creative, better-than-average-looking, intelligent. Hell, even here in the game he had an Intelligence Score of 17. He should have been smart enough to figure out a better plan than this. A smart person would have just led the horse in here to lean against the..." Hey guys! Wait! I've got an—"

The drawstring pulled tight around Tim's exposed arm and he was yanked off his feet. Being dragged by a horse wasn't as bad as he had anticipated. The sack kept the stone floor from tearing his skin off. It wasn't completely unlike water-skiing. It was actually kind of — Thunk! Fuck, that hurt. Thunk! He bounced off of another wall, and he was still sliding. That could only mean the plan had worked.

Eventually, the bag stopped moving, but Tim's stomach did not. He threw up. He was pretty sure he had a broken collarbone and a concussion. He didn't know if he could move or not. He guessed not, but he wasn't going to try and find out. He'd just lie in this dark, vomit-soaked sack and wait for death to release him.

It was a close race, but Dave got to him before death could. It wasn't until Dave pulled the bag open that Tim realized he could only see out of his left eye. What he saw with his monocular vision was Dave wincing at the sight of him. He must have been in worse shape than he thought.

Dave laid his pudgy dwarf hand on Tim's forehead. "I heal

thee."

"Yeeeooowww!" Tim howled as his skull restructured itself and his shoulders realigned. The healing magic surged down his right arm. He hadn't even had time to register that his wrist was broken before he felt the searing pain of bones fusing back together. He lost control of his bladder. The warmth of fresh urine spread across his crotch and upper thighs.

It took Dave two more healing spells to bring Tim back up to full Hit Points. Who knew that bouncing off of a stone wall at the speed of a galloping horse would hurt so much? They don't teach you that shit in school.

By the time the healing was done, Julian had returned on his horse. "You okay?" he asked Tim.

"Never better," said Tim.

"He's all patched up," said Dave. "But I'm all out of healing spells."

"This was such a stupid idea," said Julian, dismounting his horse. "We're going to die in here."

"Quit your moaning," Tim snapped at Julian. In his little halfling heart, however, Tim knew that Julian was right. Death was a frighteningly real possibility, and with each step they took down here, it was looking more like a probability. "Look, I'm sorry Julian. I'm just in a lousy mood. And to be perfectly honest, I'm scared as shit right now."

"I know," said Julian, looking at the ground next to Tim. "Me too."

"Help me out of this bag, would you?" Dave grabbed Tim by one arm and Julian took the other. Cooper slid the wet sack out from under him. "Hey... where's Dusty?"

"Who are you?" a raspy voice demanded. "How did you get here?"

When Dave and Julian turned around and stepped to the side, Tim saw a striking figure shielding its pale eyes from Dave's torchlight. He was tall and slender like Julian, with the same ridiculously long ears. But unlike Julian, his face was black as pitch and his long hair was as white as freshly fallen snow. He looked like a photo negative of Marilyn Manson. He wore leather armor as black as his skin and held a dagger defensively, but not threateningly before him.

"Um..." said Julian. "We're lost. We were on our way to the um... Forest of um... Dreams, when—"

"I don't believe you," said the dark elf. "The Forest of Dreams is leagues away from here."

"There's actually a Forest of Dreams?"

"Julian!" snapped Tim.

"Oh shit." Julian clapped his hand over his mouth. "Did I say that out loud?"

"And how in the Abyss did you get a horse down here?" asked the elf. "I demand you state your true business here at once, or else I'll have to—"

The dark elf's pale eyes widened as the business end of a short sword sprouted upward out of his chest. His arms dropped to his sides. His dagger clattered onto the stone floor. The tip of the blade turned downward as Dusty Sheglin stood up behind the lifeless elf, shoving the hilt of his sword up his victim's back.

The cleric's face betrayed no emotion as he let the dead elf slide off of his blade onto the cold stone floor.

Julian's horse whinnied.

"What the fuck was that for?" cried Julian.

"Keep your voice down," said Dusty. "There may be more of them. And for Rapha's sake, get rid of that damned horse!"

Julian's face looked like it was about to explode, but he whisked the horse out of existence with a flick of the wrist. "What kind of cleric are you?" he asked, barely keeping his voice to an excited whisper.

"The kind who stamps out evil wherever he finds it," said Dusty.

"You're supposed to stamp out evil by being an example of goodness and kindness," said Julian. "Love thy neighbor and all that shit."

"That sounds like a very inefficient means of stamping out evil," said Dusty, sheathing his short sword into a scabbard hidden beneath his cloak. "I prefer to stab it."

"How do you even know that guy was evil?"

"He's a drow. They're all evil."

"What the fuck is a drow?"

Dusty looked at Julian as if he'd just asked him how many nipples he had.

"Drow are an evil race of elves," said Tim. "They have black skin and white hair."

"And that makes them evil?" asked Julian. "You could just as easily be describing Morgan Freeman."

Dusty laughed. "I thought I'd seen everything when I witnessed a dwarf healing a half-orc. I never thought I'd live to see the day when a halfling has to explain to an elf what a drow is. Who are you people?"

"Never mind who we are," said Tim. "This whole thing stinks of bullshit. What aren't you telling us? We're stuck in a dungeon with two healers who are all out of healing, there are drow walking around, and you don't seem the least bit concerned. Why is that?" He crossed his arms and offered up his most demanding facial expression.

Dusty smiled kindly down at Tim. "Now now, child. We have nothing to fear. We are on a mission to serve holy Rapha. His grace will shield us from those who would do us harm."

Shit. It made sense. He was a full-blown religious nutter, like those people who don't take their kids to the hospital when they're sick. Dusty was going to lead them into a nest of drow, blindly depending on the protection of some god who he'd already admitted he was on the outs with. They were all going to die.

"We need to hole up somewhere and talk this thing through," said Tim. "I need to know that you have some sort of plan."

"Rapha has a plan for us all."

"Not good enough," said Tim. His voice was firm, but he managed to hold himself back from saying 'Fuck that,' which had been the first response to come to mind. He needed time. "Maybe break for lunch?"

"But we've only just arrived," said Dusty.

"I could eat," said Cooper.

Julian pointed down the corridor. "I passed a door down that way. If there's a room we could hide out in, it would be safer than picnicking out here in the hallway."

Dusty rolled his eyes and sighed. "Fine. Would someone kindly pick up the drow's body?"

Julian glared at Dusty. "Why don't you pick him up? You're the one who put him down."

"I'll pick him up," said Cooper. "Let's just get moving, huh? I'm hungry." Cooper scooped up the dead elf and slung him over his shoulder.

Tim snagged the dagger the drow had left behind. It was long and sleek, and looked to be well made. The blade was shiny black, and the hilt looked like it might be silver. It could be worth a coin or two. He tucked it under his belt for now though. Whatever he met down here, he didn't want to get close enough to fight with a dagger. He readied a bolt in his hand crossbow.

When he raised his eyes to look ahead, they came in contact with two pink eyes staring back at him. A fat white rat sat upright on its hind legs, just staring, like it was scrutinizing him. Tim raised his crossbow. "Fuck off, you fat little bas—"

"No!" Dusty called out, jumping into the line of fire just as Tim pulled the trigger. The bolt caught him high in his breastplate, up near his left shoulder. The rat disappeared into the darkness of the corridor beyond.

"Jesus Christ!" said Tim, trying his best not to shout. He brought his voice back down to an angry whisper. "Are you okay? What the fuck were you thinking?"

"I'm fine," Dusty said, smiling. He sat back against the wall and wrapped his right hand around the bolt. He winced briefly as he plucked it out of his chest. A small piece of his armor flaked

onto the floor. "Barely nicked me."

"You just murdered an elf in cold blood," said Julian. "And then you risk your life to save a rat?"

"The drow," said Dusty, "was evil. His kind have turned their faces from the light of Rapha. A rat is innocent. Whether you like them or not, they are one of Rapha's creatures, and should not be harmed unnecessarily."

Tim picked up the chip of armor that had fallen to the floor. "Tell me that again after the fuckers gnaw your foot off." Tim looked up to find Dusty staring curiously back at him. "Sorry. I've got a bad history with rats."

"I see," said Dusty.

"What kind of shitty armor are you wearing anyway?" asked Tim, fingering the broken bit he'd picked up. It was much lighter than steel. Hell, it was lighter than most wood. It crumbled when he pinched his fingers together. "Is this papier-mâché?" He knocked on Dusty's breastplate. His knuckles made a hollow thud on the armor. "It is! Why the fuck are you wearing armor made out of papier-mâché?"

For the first time, Tim thought he saw a look of doubt flash across Dusty's eyes. It was gone in an instant though, and may have only been Tim's imagination.

"The order reclaimed my armor when I was sent away. It's temple property, after all." Dusty stood up and tested the mobility of his left arm. It appeared to be in full working order. "So I made this set of false armor, so that mine enemies shall know that they face a devoted servant of Rapha!"

"Why didn't you talk like a crazy asshole before you lead us into this dungeon?"

"Tim!" Julian snapped at him. "Not cool, man."

"I'm sorry," said Tim. "I get cranky when I'm hungry."

"Let us waste no more time bickering amongst ourselves," said Dusty. "If you men are so insistent that we consume our provisions right now, we should make haste in finding a suitable place to do so."

Cooper and Tim led the way. The small sphere of visibility that Cooper's torch provided revealed nothing but identical stone walls passing slowly by on either side of them, interrupted every twenty feet or so by columns of darker, rougher stone, structural support by the looks of them. Tim held his crossbow ready for the slightest provocation.

Eventually, they reached the closed wooden doorway that Julian had spotted. Tim put his ear to the wood.

"I can't hear anything," he said. "I'd better check it for traps."

Dusty laughed. "Traps? That's preposterous. Look at it. It's a blank wooden door. What kind of traps are you hoping to find?"

"I'm hoping I don't find any," said Tim. "But I want to be safe."

"Why would they trap a door way back here?" asked Dusty. "Remember, nobody knows about that secret passage we came in through. It would make more sense to concentrate their defensive efforts closer to the main entrance."

"I'm a rogue," said Tim. "Checking for traps is what I do."

"Suit yourself," said Dusty. Tim kept his eyes fixed on the door, but he knew that crazy cleric was looking down on him with a condescending smile.

As it turned out, the cleric had made a good point. There wasn't much to check for. Tim ran a finger down the gap between the door and frame, but it merely came away a little dirtier for his efforts.

"Okay," he said. "This door's clear."

"Thank heavens!" said Dusty. "The suspense was killing me!"

Tim tried the handle. "It's locked."

"So pick the lock, Mr. Rogue," said Dusty. "That's what rogues do, right?"

Tim looked at the floor. "I couldn't afford Thieves' Tools when I rolled my character."

"I'm sorry," said Dusty. "What are you talking about?"

"I don't have any thieves' tools."

"Some rogue you are. Shall we carry on then?"

"Fuck that," said Cooper. "Let me try." He kicked the door

hard with his right foot. The door didn't budge. Cooper fell on his ass, piledriving the dead elf's head into the stone floor. "Ow."

"The hinges are on this side," said Dusty. "Perhaps the door opens out this way."

"Oh yeah," said Cooper. He stood up, leaving the dead elf on the floor. "That's true." He grabbed the handle and yanked it. It broke off in his hand, leaving the door freely swinging. Cooper pulled it open, and the already musty air of the corridor mingled with the air escaping this room for what must have been the first time in centuries. It was thick with rot and decay, stinging Tim's eyes and forcing itself down his throat like the tentacle of a dead octopus. This place would not do for lunch.

When everyone's coughing, gagging, and (in Cooper's case) shitting had subsided, Tim thrust his torch into the room, trying to penetrate the thick, putrid air. The light revealed three figures, wrapped from head to toe in ancient, decomposing strips of fabric. They stared at Tim through gaps in their wrappings. The stare was like being stabbed in the soul.

Tim stood paralyzed with fear as the three mummies started shambling toward the door. Tim knew in his heart that this was the place he was going to die. He reflected on all the places he'd never visit, the family he would never have, the apologies he would never make. His friends would die down here too, and it was all his fault. He was a cancer in everyone's life he ever came in contact with. His death would make the world a brighter place. He dropped his torch, fell to his knees, and began to weep.

The next thing he knew, he was yanked by the back of his shirt and sent crashing into Julian, who was sitting on the floor sobbing. Tim wrapped his arms around Julian and hugged him tightly. "I'm sorry, man."

Julian sniffed and hugged Tim back. "Me too."

Ravenus was squished in between them, his wings pinned to his sides in their embrace. "What the devil?"

"Would you two fags get up and help us?" shouted Cooper. He had his back pressed up against the door, his thighs straining to

keep it closed. Dave sat under him, adding what support he could with his bulk. But the mummies were pounding the crap out of it on the other side, each hit pushing Cooper and Dave forward, widening the gap between door and frame.

"Don't let them touch you!" said Dusty, standing a cautious distance away. "They'll curse you with mummy rot!"

As the pounding at the door moved to the forefront of Tim's mind, his crippling despair began to fade. He became suddenly aware that his mind had been fucked with and that he was hugging Julian. "What the shit?" He let go, and Julian covered his face and broke down into heavier fits of sobbing.

"Julian," said Tim. "Snap out of it, dude!" He grabbed one of Julian's long ears. "Wake up, man! Give me some oil!"

"Take it!" Julian cried. "Why don't you take my heart while you're at it?"

"What the fuck is going on with those two?" asked Dave.

"I'm sure I don't know," said Ravenus.

Tim took a flask of oil out of Julian's bag. Those dusty old rag-walkers would soak this shit up like a Bounty paper towel ad. He stood to the right of the door, waiting to time his throw so as to make it through the gap.

Kachung! The pounding on the door echoed through the dark corridor. Tim threw the flask. His aim was true and his timing spot on. It smashed the floor on the other side of the door.

"Hang on guys!" Tim said to Cooper and Dave. "Just give it some time to—"

Kachung! The next time a mummy beat on the door, the gap was considerably more illuminated. It worked. The oil had found its way to his dropped torch.

"Ha ha!" said Tim. "We've got them now!"

"We do?" said Cooper. His massive half-orc feet were beginning to lose ground.

"Just hold them for a few more minutes," said Tim. "The fuckers are on fire."

"Aren't you forgetting something?" asked Dusty.

"I wouldn't put it past him!" Julian cried out between sobs. "He forgot about me quickly enough!" He squeezed Ravenus. "You're my only friend!"

"Julian," said Tim. "What the fuck are... never mind. Sheglin, what are you talking about?"

The cleric pointed at Dave.

"Huh?" said Dave. "Ooh ohh! Ow! Fuck!" He sprang to his feet. His ass was on fire. "Water water water water water!" he said, gesturing at the floor. A puddle began to form as if it were seeping up out of the dry stone. He quickly plunked his ass down in the water, and the fire hissed out.

"Could use some fucking help over here!" shouted Cooper. He was straining against the door, which now had flames licking up this side of it. The flaming puddle of oil was spreading out under the bottom gap, and would reach his feet soon.

"Fuck!" said Tim. "The door's on fire!"

"Shit!" said Cooper. "What do we do now?"

"Get ready to run," said Tim. "On three. One—"

"Fuck that!" said Dave. "Just go!" He jumped up out of his puddle and bolted down the corridor. At least, it started off as a bolt, but soon relaxed into the steady clunk, chunk, clunk, chunk that was Dave's top movement speed in his armor.

Tim grabbed Julian by the ear and pulled hard. "Get up, damn you! We have to go!"

"Just let me die!" Julian cried. "What do you care?"

Cooper abandoned the door, took a step back, and unbuckled his greataxe.

Ka-swoosh! An inferno of blazing undead exploded out of the doorway behind Cooper. There were more than three. In fact, those initial three just fell forward dead dead, charcoal corpses still on fire, but having had all the undeath burnt out of them several rounds ago. They collapsed into the corridor to be trampled by the next wave. The first mummy to stumble out was flaming away nicely, reaching a burning arm out toward Cooper.

"Fuck you!" said Cooper. "And fuck Brendan Fraser!" He

caught the mummy under its right arm with his axe, and cleaved up through its left shoulder, neatly removing its arm and head.

Tim aimed his crossbow at the next mummy to come through. This one was also completely engulfed in flames, but Tim's bolt to the face was still not enough to put it down.

"Magic Missile!" Julian cried from behind Tim. A golden bolt of light whizzed by Tim's head, and exploded in the mummy's crotch. It collapsed onto the pile of flaming corpses. That was good. The more flames those fuckers had to walk through, the more likely they'd ignite themselves.

"Let's move!" said Tim as two more mummies emerged from the doorway. These two weren't quite as fiery as the others had been. Just some flames creeping up their legs. Julian and Tim ran together. Cooper jogged backwards after them, keeping an eye on the pursuing mummies. The bastards were strong, but they were slow as crap. "We'll be okay if we keep moving."

"Feeling better, Julian," said Dave. He and Dusty had stopped running when the fighting broke out.

"I don't know what came over me," said Julian.

"It happened to me too," said Tim. "Some kind of mummy fear attack or something."

"More like Crybaby Bitch Syndrome," said Cooper.

"Hurry along," said Dusty. "There's a secret passage around the next corner. We can lose them in there."

Sure enough, after another hundred feet of running, the corridor turned right. Dusty and Julian were the first to turn the corner. Dave had fallen behind everyone else, but was still moving at least as fast as the mummies.

"Hey Sheglin," said Cooper as he rounded the corner. "How do you know so much about—" He stopped talking and running as he stared at the fletching of an arrow poking out of his chest.

"The fuck?" Tim shouted.

"Drow!" Dusty called out. He ducked behind one of the corridor's support pillars. Julian mirrored him on the other side of the corridor. It wasn't much cover, but it was better than nothing.

But while Julian was merely hiding, Dusty was frantically pawing at random stones along the wall.

"Fuck!" said Tim. "Cooper, get down!" Cooper didn't need to be told twice. His eyes rolled up and he fell forward, slamming his face into the floor.

An arrow struck the wall near Tim's face, chipping some dust into his eye. He ducked back around the corner. Dave was still clunking and chunking forward, no doubt more concerned with the horde of flaming mummies that was chasing him than with the unseen enemy ahead of him.

Tim poked his head back around the corner. "Julian! Toss me some oil." A couple of arrows clattered off the wall behind him.

Julian reached in his bag, found a flask of oil, and tossed it toward Tim. It was a poor throw, and smashed on the floor about halfway between them. "Sorry!"

"Come on," said Tim. "Hurry up!"

"Better idea!" said Julian. "Take cover!"

A few seconds later, Ravenus flew around the corner, clutching an oil flask in his talon. "Master Julian says you requested this, sir."

"Brilliant!" said Tim. "Go drop it on those mummies."

Ravenus flew off, his black form disappearing into the darkness. A moment later, the barely visible mummy flames burst into raging human-shaped infernos, giving Tim a clear target to shoot at.

"Would you mind," Dusty's tone was distinctly less polite than his words, "providing me with some cover fire?" He was still searching the wall, while at the same time trying to cling as closely to it as possible.

Tim poked his head around the corner. "I can't even see them!" said Tim.

"Just shoot in that direction!"

"Okay," said Tim. He fired off a bolt into the hostile darkness. If anyone caught it, they kept that information to themselves.

"Just a second, Tim!" said Julian. And just a second later, he shouted "Light!" The entire corridor lit up. With a flick of his forearm, he sent the light bouncing down the stone hallway. When it stopped, they were left back in the dim light of their one remaining torch, but where the light shone, it revealed the faces of five very surprised-looking drow.

By the time Tim had loaded his next bolt, he spotted one of the drow making a go for the light-enchanted stone Julian had sent their way. Fuck that guy. He fired, catching the drow in the gut. It wasn't fatal, but it wasn't a wound that fucker would soon forget.

Whatever Dusty had been doing with that wall had finally paid off. A section of wall slid to the side, revealing another secret passage. Dusty slipped inside, and Julian was right behind him, narrowly avoiding two more drow arrows.

"Tim!" cried Dave. "The mummies are getting closer. Should I try turning them?"

Tim joined Dave around the corner. "No. Fuck them. Let them come. We need to drag Cooper over to that secret door." He called out, "Julian! We need a distraction!"

"I've got just the thing," Julian called back. "Horse!"

"Let's go," said Tim. He grabbed one of Cooper's arms, and Dave grabbed the other. Together, they dragged the huge half-orc through the entrance of the secret passage while some poor bastard of a horse whinnied and screamed as it was shot and stabbed to death.

"Unbelievable," said Dusty. "You should be ashamed of yourselves, using a Mount spell in such a manner."

"Screw you, Sheglin," said Tim. "I didn't hear you coming up with any ideas."

"Time's wasting," Dusty said Curtly. "We must hurry."

"No," said Tim. "We need to buy some time to see what's wrong with Cooper."

"I'm sorry, my boy," said Dusty, "but it would appear that your friend is dead."

"Fuck that," said Tim. "No way he died from a single arrow to

the chest. Julian. Give me some oil and summon another horse out there."

"Um... okay," said Julian. He cautiously poked his head out from the relative safety of the secret passage, and then yelped as an arrow clattered off the wall right next to his head. "Horse!" he said, quickly pointing a finger.

Tim used the equine obstruction to move about freely, pouring oil on the floor, splashing it all over an area about twenty feet in the direction of the elves, all the way back to the entrance to the secret passage, and a small trail leading to the puddle resulting from Julian's inept throw, and from there another trail around the corner toward the oncoming mummies. All of this he did to the sound of yet another noble steed screaming and whinnying whilst unwillingly giving its brief life for his and his friends' survival.

By the time he was finished, Dave had dragged Cooper into the secret passage. When the horse had taken all of the arrows it was going to take, the equine screams went silent, replaced by approaching footsteps and incomprehensible whispers.

Julian started to lower the torch to the oil, but Tim stopped him.

"What did you go and waste all of that oil for if you're not going to light it?" asked Julian. "I thought we were trying to buy some time."

"Sh!" said Tim.

"There's a secret passage in the wall, Master Natel," said one of the drow. "They went in there."

"They can't move very fast dragging that half-orc with them," said another, probably Master Natel. "Vinn, Nightshade, find out the source of that light coming from around the corner and follow in after us."

"Of course, sir," said a third voice, oozing with lusty pleasure. Tim guessed that was Nightshade. It sounded like the voice of someone named Nightshade.

"Go!" Tim whispered excitedly. "Hurry!" The dirt walls of the secret passage were barely wide enough apart to drag Cooper's massive body through. Tim hung behind, leveling his crossbow at the secret doorway.

"Come on, Tim!" said Dave.

"Keep going,"said Tim. "I'll catch up."

The mummies were getting closer. The light from their flaming bodies was growing stronger outside. It was just enough light for Tim to make out the first drow shadow creeping up near the secret entrance. Tim fired. He didn't have a target, but he was successful in making that shadow jump back. Just a little more time. He loaded another bolt.

"Who are you?" Master Natel's voice called in from just outside the tunnel entrance. "What is it you seek here?"

"Um..." said Tim. "We... uh... we seek an item of great religious importance to my friend here."

"I can assure you," said the drow. "We have nothing like that in our possession. Now be a good lad and come out of there. We promise to escort you out peacefully and—"

WHOOSH!

Tim smiled to himself as the corridor lit up. The mummies had arrived.

The dank air echoed with drow screams and the clatter of weapons falling to the floor. Apparently, suddenly being on fire came as a great surprise to them.

"What the fuck?" said Cooper. "Where are we?"

Tim ran back to the group. "Cooper, you're awake!"

"Yeah," said Cooper, sitting up on the dirt floor. "Why wasn't I awake before?"

"You got hit with a drow arrow." said Tim. "Knocked you right out."

"What happened to the drow?"

"They're on fire," said Tim, pointing a thumb over his shoulder. "That's them screaming out there."

"Sweet."

"Let's go!" Dusty urged.

The rest of the group followed him single file through the cramped secret passage. Tim was last in line. He scattered caltrops in his wake until he had emptied almost half the bag. His little fire stunt wasn't likely to kill his pursuers, and neither were the mummies. The best he could hope to do was weaken them, slow them down, and piss them off.

"That was kind of a dick move," said Julian as they trudged through the tunnel. "That guy was trying to make peace with us, and you lit him on fire."

"Have you forgotten," said Tim, "that your peace-loving friend back there was just trying to murder us? For fuck's sake, they poisoned Cooper!"

"We're invading their home," said Julian. "And have you forgotten that our kind cleric friend up there just up and murdered one for no reason."

"E-vil!" said Dusty in a singsong voice.

"Oh right," said Julian. "I forgot. Because they're black. Maybe we should have bought a pick-up truck to go with that rope."

"Look," said Tim. "This isn't like refusing to fly on a plane because another passenger is wearing a turban. This isn't real life. We're in the manifestation of a game world. The game's rulebook explicitly states that drow are evil. It's the same reason why Cooper can't read or understand a British accent. That's just the way it is."

"Fine," said Julian. "I'm still not comfortable with setting people on fire because they're black, though. It just feels wrong."

Dusty Sheglin stopped in his tracks and turned around. "Okay. I simply must know what it is you fellows are talking about."

"It doesn't concern you," said Tim.

"Yeah," said Cooper. "Let's find your stupid fucking relic and get out of here. I'm hungry and my chest hurts."

"Yeow!" a voice screamed from behind them.

"They're right behind us!" said Dusty. "We must hurry!" He scrambled down the passage, and the others followed close behind him. They stumbled along the dark and dirty path for another five minutes or so before it came to an abrupt end.

"Well shit," said Julian.

"What are we going to do?" asked Dave.

"The only thing we can do," said Cooper. He unstrapped his axe and tried to maneuver his body in such a way that he would be able to swing it in such tight quarters.

"Nonsense," said Dusty. "We'd be sitting ducks for those drow poison arrows. He reached up and pressed his palm against a part of the dirt wall which looked exactly like every other part of the dirt wall. A section of floor slid open under the wall, revealing a hidden staircase. "Hurry," he said. "Go down there."

Without hesitation, Juilan, Cooper, and Dave hurried down the stairs. Tim took a single step down and stopped. He was descending further into complete darkness, and he didn't like it one little bit. "What's down there?"

"Eternity!" said Dusty.

Tim didn't even have time to voice the 'Huh?' in his head. Before he knew what hit him, his crossbow was swiped right out of his hand, and a sudden jolt to the back sent him tumbling head over feet down the stairs.

When he finally hit the packed dirt floor at the bottom, he opened his eyes and waited for his vision to stop swirling. As it turned out, swirled vision wasn't a problem. He had no vision. He had to close and open his eyes a few more times just to make sure they were indeed open. They were, but there was nothing to see. He was in an inky black void. "Where are we?"

"In a cell, by the looks of it," said Dave.

"You can see?" said Julian.

"Yeah."

"I can't."

"You've got low-light vision," said Dave. "I've got darkvision. Your eyes can function with a small amount of light. Mine function even with no light at all."

Tim felt around in the dark for the bottom stair and sat on it. "That's really fucking interesting, Dave. Would you mind giving

us some kind of idea about the situation we're in?"

"Why don't you ask Dusty?"

"Because he just kicked me down the stairs like a redneck abortion."

"Speak of the devil," said Dave.

Suddenly Tim could see again. The room was lit with torchlight as Dusty Sheglin walked in. Unfortunately, he was on the other side of a partition of iron bars. A quick observation of the lock to the cell door told Tim he was going to need more than his dick to pick it.

"It's a pleasure to see you gentlemen again," said Dusty, affixing his torch to an empty sconce on the wall. "Have you met my friend Gimble?"

"What's going on, Sheglin?" demanded Tim.

Dusty ignored the question. He tapped quietly on one of two wooden doors in the cramped little room. "Gimble?"

"Out in a minute!" said a voice from within.

Dusty simply stood in the middle of the room and the awkward silence.

Beside the door this Gimble character was behind, there sat a wooden desk piled high with books, papers, quills, and jars of various colored ink. In front of the opposite wall stood a bookcase filled with books, vials, scrolls, and assorted knick-knacks. Some of them looked decorative. If any of them had a function, Tim didn't know what it was.

Finally, Gimble's door opened, and a drow emerged. His hair was as white as any other drow they'd encountered down here, but it was wild, haphazardly braided in some places, tied off with beads here and there. It was as disheveled as his desk. He rubbed his black hands on his filthy robe and squinted at his prisoners. Unsatisfied, he produced a pair of glasses from an inside pocket. They were huge and round, and made his already wild red eyes even more unsettling, as did his yellow-toothed grin when he finally got a good look at his captives.

"Well done, friend," he said to Dusty. His voice was like silk

rubbing against sandpaper. "Fine specimens, all of them. But you'll recall that I needed the blood of five different sapient creatures." He grinned his wicked grin at Dusty. "Are you volunteering yourself as the fifth?"

"The elf has a bird tucked under his robes."

"Sapient creatures, you fool!" said Gimble. "A bird is not sapient. You barely qualify yourself."

"It's his familiar," said Dusty. "It can talk, and it's a notch more intelligent than any of these others here."

Gimble raised his white bushy eyebrows. "Stupid bunch, are they?"

Dusty looked at the prisoners, shook his head, and laughed. "Don't get me started. They blew all their money on one day's worth of food, which they wanted to gobble up as soon as we entered the catacombs, and more than a dozen torches. Tell me, what do you need so many torches for if you're only planning to be gone a single day?" He threw his hands in the air. "And they didn't even buy a ten-foot pole! Who goes exploring underground tombs without a ten-foot pole? I ask you that!"

"A grievous oversight indeed," said Gimble.

"The barbarian," Dusty continued his rant, "unquestionably the dumbest of the lot, flew into a rage just to increase the ferocity with which he fell down the stairs. Don't even get me started about the halfling and the horse. Can you believe he fancies himself a rogue, and he doesn't even own a set of Thieve's Tools? It's insulting really."

Gimble put his slender black hand on Dusty's shoulder. "There, there, friend. Calm down."

"I don't get it," said Julian. "Why are they friends? He's black."

This drew blank looks from everyone on either side of the prison bars.

"Dude," said Cooper. "Not cool, man."

"For the last time!" Dusty said. "He's a drow!" He pulled at the hair above his temples. "Would you believe me if I told you that this elf over here has literally never heard of drow before?"

Gimble pursed his lips and furrowed his brow. "I would find that most unlikely."

"Fuck this," said Cooper. "I'm hungry. Let's break out the food."

"I tell you, Gimble," said Dusty. "These past couple of hours have been mental torture. I didn't think I could—"

Someone from outside rapped loudly on the door. Dusty put a finger over his lips and gave the prisoners a warning glare. He retreated into the room Gimble had come from. Gimble waved his hand at the cell, and a rough grey curtain slid across a rod, blocking their view.

The door creaked open.

"What is it?" snapped Gimble.

"There have been," a second voice began, and then stopped. "Why do you have a torch lit in here?"

"I came down with a chill," said Gimble. "I wanted to warm my hands. Is there a reason you disturb my study?"

"There have been reports of intruders at the back of the catacombs. Two of our number have been slain. Your brother requests that you —"

"My brother," snarled Gimble, "cares not what ills may befall me. I'm just an incompetent wizard. He said so himself."

"I have been ordered to —"

"Stuff your orders!" snapped Gimble. "If my brother requires my counsel, he can pay me the respect of coming here in person. Now go away before I feed you to Oliver!"

The door slammed shut. A second later the curtain flew open. Gimble paced as much as one could in such a tiny space. He was lucky to get a second step in before he had to turn around. "My brother requests my presence!" he said to the prisoners. "Like he's the high priest of Meb-Gar'shur."

"Older siblings can be a pain in the ass," said Tim, leaning face first against the bars.

Gimble pulled down on his long black ears. "I know, right?"

"Don't listen to him," said Dusty, who had just re-entered the room. "He is trying to establish a friendly rapport with you. Make you feel empathy with him, so that you don't kill him."

"Ha!" said Gimble. "Fat chance of that. But I have a bone to pick with you, old friend." His index finger thunked against Dusty's fake armor. "I just got word that two of my kin are dead. We had an arrangement. No one was supposed to get killed."

"The first one caught us by surprise," Dusty explained. "We didn't have a choice. I dispatched him quickly and quietly."

"And the other?"

"I don't know," said Dusty. "Your little halfling friend there shot one of them, and set a group of them on fire. One of them must not have survived."

"Mercy of darkness!" said Gimble, glaring at Tim. "How am I supposed to enslave and rule over my people if you go and burn them all to death? Answer me that!"

Tim put his palms up in the universal 'What the fuck?' stance. "What was I supposed to do? They were —"

"He even tried to kill Oliver," said Dusty.

Gimble gasped. "No!"

"Who the fuck is Oliver?" said Tim.

Gimble pulled open the bottom right drawer of his desk. It was twice as large as any of the desks other drawers. The smile across the drow's face was met with excited squeaking from within the drawer. The dark elf pulled out and cradled a fat white rat.

"Shit," said Tim.

"I nearly blew my cover trying to save him." Dusty smiled at Tim. "Fortunately, this group will believe anything you tell them, so long as it comes with vague promises of treasure. They are as greedy as they are stupid."

"Hey!" said Tim. "Fuck you, Sheglin!"

"Yeah," said Julian. "For a priest, you're kind of a dick."

Tim and Dusty simultaneously palmed their foreheads.

"What?" said Julian.

"He's not a priest," Dave explained patiently. "He's a rogue, just like Tim."

"Hey now," said Dusty. "I'm a far better rogue than your idiot friend there."

Julian didn't look like he had quite put it together yet, so Dave explained further. "The whole thing was an act. The fake armor, the quest for redemption. His inability to perform even one minor clerical act."

"Ooohhh..." said Julian, the light of understanding finally sparking in his eyes. "So he's like a con-man, or a criminal?"

Dave shrugged. "Sure, something like that."

"Which explains why he's cool with black people."

"Jesus fuck, dude!" said Cooper. "Cool it with the black people already. He's a fucking drow! This is a fantasy game world. There are no black people."

"Cooper!" said Dave.

"Oh wait. That didn't come out right. What I meant was —"

"Shut up!" cried Dusty. "All of you just shut up!" He turned to Gimble. "Give me my reward so that I may get out of here... away from these cretins for good!"

"Go back to sleep now," Gimble whispered to his rat, covering its face in little kisses. He lowered the rat back into the drawer and slid it ever so gently closed.

He opened the top left drawer and pulled out a flat, square box, only about an inch thick. He opened the box and reverently picked up a braided cord — too big to be a bracelet and too small to be a necklace — with a single green gemstone at the front.

"The Headband of Intellect," he whispered. "What do you plan to do with the gift of such higher intellect?"

"Nothing," said Dusty. He licked his lips and stared at the headband. "This is my big score. I'm gonna sell it for a fortune, and retire in the Southern Islands."

"You humans disgust me sometimes," said Gimble, making sure to hold the headband a safe distance from Dusty's reach. "Always after some next big score, a quick fix to all your problems. You lack patience and forethought. It took me years of careful planning to steal this from my brother. Years more to construct tunnels and secret entrances so that I might hire someone to smuggle in volunteers for the blood ritual which, in turn, took years to research." He looked down at the headband in his hands. "Clever as I am, I lack the brain power to complete this ritual on my own. I need the extra intellect which this headband will provide. Only once I have completed the blood ritual, and have successfully enslaved my people, may you take this and sail off to whatever island you like."

"Very well," said Dusty. "How long will this take?"

Gimble placed the headband on his head. The green stone glowed bright on his forehead. His eyes rolled back into his head and he trembled for a moment, and then it was done. He snapped back into focus and his cunning eyes looked sharper than ever.

"I have most of the preliminary work completed," he said. "It will just be a matter of setting things, up, drawing a few runes on the floor, and exsanguinating our guests."

"Sweet!" said Cooper. Everyone looked at him.

"What the fuck is sweet about that?" said Tim.

"He's going to set us free," said Cooper. "You know, like Lincoln?"

"That's emancipate, fucktard," said Tim. "Exanguinate means he's going to drain out all of our blood."

"Oh," said Cooper. "That sucks."

"You see what I've had to deal with all day?" said Dusty. "Half the time I don't even know what they're talking about."

Gimble opened the door he had first appeared through. "Stop moaning and help me get these boxes out of the closet."

"Well why don't we just kill them first?" suggested Dusty. "Their blood isn't going to go anywhere."

"For the spell to take effect," Gimble explained, "I need to be consuming their blood at the precise moment they pass from life to death." He handed Dusty a wooden box about as large as two adult-sized shoe boxes side by side.

"Something's moving inside here," said Dusty.

"Of course they're moving," said Gimble. "They're snakes." He opened the middle drawer of his desk and pulled out a black dagger, similar to the one Tim had taken from the drow Dusty had killed.

How could Tim have been so blind. He should have recognized Dusty for what he was right then and there. That had been a classic rogue Sneak Attack. A cleric couldn't have pulled off a move like that.

Dusty held out the box at arm's length. "Are they poisonous?"

Gimble scoffed. "Of course not, stupid human. Don't be ridiculous." He sliced his thumb open with the dagger, got on his knees, and began to rub a circle of his own blood on the floor. "It hurts my brain to hear such silly babble."

"Ah well," said Dusty, smiling. "You can never be too careful." He pulled the box in closer so that he could hold it with one arm. With his other arm, he carefully lifted the lid to look inside.

Gimble continued scooting backward and counter-clockwise, letting his thumb bleed a circle on the ground. "Poison has to be inhaled or ingested. Snakes are venomous."

"Huh?" said Dusty. He was quickly answered with a hiss and a snake to the face. He screamed and dropped the box. It landed upright, but with the top wide open. "Fuck! Help me!"

It was a tiny black snake with yellow stripes, maybe six inches long. But it scared the shit out of Dusty as it hung from his nose by its fangs.

"You cursed fool!" said Gimble. He pinched the snake gently on its neck. "Hold still, you sniveling little... huh? What's..." The drow looked confused. Even more interesting, however, was the headband levitating above his head.

"My prize!" Dusty screamed, jerking his head up and tearing a gash in the left lobe of his nose where the snake had been hanging on. He pushed away Gimble, who stepped in the box of snakes. After a brief chorus of hissing, Gimble's red eyes went as wide as 3-balls, and he collapsed to the floor.

"What the fuck is going on?" said Tim.

"Mage Hand," said Julian. "Can you believe it's a zero-level spell?"

Tim looked over. Julian had his arm extended, pointing at the floating headband. It was just out of Dusty's reach and floating toward the torch on the wall.

"No!" cried Tim and Dusty at the same time. Dusty ran to the wall. Just as he was about to reach it, the headband suddenly switched course, flying straight up to the ceiling, away from both the flame and Dusty's grasp.

Cooper reached into Julian's bag. "Huh huh," he grunted. "Watch this."

As Dusty jumped again and again, trying to catch the floating headband, the party's last remaining flask of oil smashed into the wall right next to him, splashing his face and upper body with the highly flammable liquid. It took less than a second for his hair to catch. But the real damage came when a stray spark touched his fake armor, which burst into flames like it was made out of... well, papier-mâché.

Tim shrugged. "When in Rome." He tossed out the rest of his caltrops toward Dusty. The false cleric screamed and tore at his fiery costume, stumbling around until his left foot found one of Tim's caltrops. He shrieked and fell over, landing on a couple more caltrops in the process. He was just close enough for Cooper to grab his arm and pull him toward the bars of their cell.

Dave lit a torch off of Dusty and threw it onto Gimble's desk. The drow's books and papers started to go up in flames.

"What was that for?" said Julian, still concentrating on the Headband of Intellect, bringing it back toward him.

"Because fuck that guy," said Dave.

Tim found a piece of Dusty's cloak that wasn't on fire and ripped the entire garment off of him. He folded and flipped and stomped on it until the fire was out. In the meantime, Cooper took a nice long leak on Dusty until he had that fire under control as well.

It didn't take long for Tim to find what he was looking for. Every self-respecting rogue should have a quality set of Thieve's

Tools on his person. And the set Tim found in a secret pocket of Dusty's cloak looked to be very high quality indeed. He had the cell door open in no time.

Miraculously, both Dusty and Gimble appeared to still be alive. They'd probably be skipping the gym today, but with a few days rest or a bit of clerical healing, they'd probably pull through, even if half of Dusty's body was covered in third-degree burns and Gimble's foot was the size of a basketball. Dave shooed the snakes away with a torch, and Cooper dragged both of the semi-conscious bodies into the cell. Tim tied the two together back to back, and put the large sack over their heads and upper bodies, because fuck them.

Julian tucked the Headband of Intellect into his pocket. "We should get out of here while everyone's looking for us in the back of the catacombs."

"Good idea," said Tim. "Follow me, and try to be as quiet as you can." He opened the door. At least a dozen drow spearmen looked down at him. "Fuck."

"You lot need to come with us," said the drow in front. His voice was not angry or threatening. It was the calm and confident voice of someone who would welcome a bit of resistance.

The corridors here were more along the lines of what Tim had expected in a catacomb. Great cavities were carved into the walls, perfect for housing coffins. If there were ever any coffins in here, they were gone now. Most of the cavities were empty. But in a few of them, Tim spotted young drow, reading a book or playing cards. They would stop whatever they were doing and look at the sad group of prisoners as they passed.

The corridors here were also much bigger than the ones in the back of the catacombs. There was plenty of room for a line of guards to flank the four prisoners on either side. They didn't even bother disarming Cooper or Dave, but most of the spears were concentrated in Cooper's direction.

"Where are we going?" Tim dared to ask.

Much to Tim's surprise, he was answered. "We're taking you

to Lord Silverwind." The voice that spoke up was female. Tim was very curious as to what a female drow looked like, but he didn't want to push his luck.

Thunk! "Ow!" said Cooper.

"Eyes straight ahead," commanded an assertive male voice. Tim felt he had made the right decision.

Tim whispered to Julian, who was marching beside him. "If ever there was a time to pull a good Diplomacy roll out of your ass —"

"Enough chatter up front!"

"Why didn't you hit him on the head?" asked Cooper. Thunk! "Ow! Fuck, man!"

"No more talking!"

They only walked for a few more minutes before the drow in charge called them to halt in front of a large set of polished wooden double doors.

The doors opened inward into a dark room which felt large, despite the fact that Tim couldn't see more than five feet into it. Their footsteps echoed as if they were walking through an empty cathedral. Tim and Julian held on to one another as they shuffled slowly forward.

"Forgive me," a deep voice echoed out of the darkness. "It has been so long since I've had light-dwellers visit me down here. Lights please."

And so it was done. The light in the room rose suddenly from complete darkness to eerily dim as drow along the perimeter of the circular chamber placed light-enchanted stones into sconces along the wall. Two more stones were placed to either side of the leader's chair.

The chair was an impressive sight. It looked to be made entirely of human bones. Five feet wide at the skull-lined base, and the back of it rose at least eight feet high, constructed mostly of femurs. The large arms of the chair were just a line of ribs running down each side, until they gave way to an explosion of finger bones running down the front, as if the chair itself was

constantly trying to grab whoever was looking at it.

Depending on how structurally sound the chair was, it could easily have sat a giant. A drow should look silly in such a large piece of furniture. But the drow who sat in it now, presumably Silverwind, did not look silly in the slightest. His legs didn't dangle over the front like a child's. Instead he sat cross-legged. The effect made it seem like he was sitting atop an altar.

"Nightshadow, Duskblade," said the drow on the bone throne. "Fetch my brother to bear witness. Drag him here against his will if you must." He looked directly at Tim. "And the gods help this sorry band of scoundrels if any harm has come to him."

"About that," said Dave.

"Silence!"

The spearman directly in front of Dave swirled his weapon overhead, around his back, and brought the bottom end of the shaft up right into Dave's nuts. Dave groaned and dropped to his knees.

"My name," the leader continued in a civil tone while Dave writhed on the ground, "is Lord Silverwind. You stand accused of trespassing, murder, and the destruction of property. Have you anything to say for yourselves?'

Tim looked for an out. There were none. The group of guards who had escorted them in remained behind them, and now they were sandwiched between an equal force of guards in front of them.

"We plead not guilty on all counts, your honor," said Julian.

Silverwind looked curiously at the drow standing directly below him. He merely shrugged.

Dave finally managed to struggle back up to his feet.

Silverwind leaned forward. "Surely you don't deny standing before me right now. Is that not proof enough of your trespassing at least?"

Julian took a step forward, and was immediately met by the tips of half a dozen spears. He bowed his head. "Apologies, my lord. We were coaxed here by a human who was in league with your brother to enslave you all."

A soft murmur of laughter rumbled through the guards and bystanders. Even Silverwind himself had a laugh. He lowered his feet over the edge of the bone throne, and actually did look like more of a child now.

"This human you speak of," said Silverwind. "Do you propose that he was the one who stabbed one of my men through the back, and then proceeded to shoot and set fire to another one?"

"Absolutely," said Julian without blinking an eye. Tim was impressed. If you're going to lie, you might as well go all out.

Silverwind raised a hand, and the laughter ceased at once. "I must say, that is the boldest and most desperate defense I've ever been presented with. You have made me laugh, young elf, but I'm afraid that will not be enough to save you."

"What if I offer you proof that my testimony is genuine?" asked Julian.

Silverwind hopped down from the bone throne. "Listen, light-dweller. I appreciate the lengths you are going to in order to spare you and your friends' lives. But let's be honest. This is an embarrassing display. Would you not prefer to die an honorable death?"

"I speak the truth!" Julian insisted. "We stopped your brother from performing a blood ritual which would have turned you all into his slaves!"

The chamber erupted with laughter again. Silverwind raised his hand and the laughter eventually quieted down.

"So you say," said Silverwind, smiling sympathetically. "Here's the problem, though. My brother, for all his passion and ambition, is an idiot. He lacks the charisma to be a leader and the intelligence to cast such a powerful spell. The poor bastard can barely throw together a Magic Missile."

Julian crossed his arms defiantly. "And therein lies my proof."

"We are not pressed for time," said Silverwind. "And you have no chance of escape. Since my men find you so entertaining, I shall allow you to carry on with your nonsensical blathering until such time as I grow bored with it. Do tell, what is this proof you keep insisting you have?"

"I want your word that you will set us free if you are satisfied with my testimony," said Julian.

"You have it," said Silverwind curtly. "Now say what you have to say."

"Can we trust him?" Julian whispered. "I mean, he is black after all."

"I beg your pardon," said Silverwind.

"I really wish you'd learn to say the word drow," said Tim. "It's not hard."

"Whatever," said Julian. "He's evil, right? How do we know we can trust him?"

Tim thought for a moment before speaking. "If he's Lawful Evil, he'll stay true to his word."

"What the hell is Lawful Evil?"

"It doesn't matter," said Tim. "We can discuss it later. Right now, I don't think we have any choice but to trust him."

That's when Cooper farted. It was a quiet squeal at first, like a kettle letting you know the water's beginning to boil. But when all eyes turned to him, he let it rip like an untied balloon. The two guards directly behind him dropped their spears, fell to their knees, and vomited.

"Sorry," said Cooper. "I've been holding that in since we got here."

"Enough!" shouted Silverwind. "You make a mockery of these proceedings! My patience is exhausted. Either provide sufficient evidence to support your wild accusations, or suffer a slow and agonizing death!"

"Here it is!" said Julian. He reached into his pocket and produced the Headband of Intellect. "If my understanding is correct, this went missing some years ago."

Silverwind pushed his way through the guards. "Give it here!" He put out his hand.

Julian nervously dropped the headband into Silverwind's

hand. "We had a deal."

Silverwind donned the headband. His eyes rolled back in his head and his body trembled. When he came to again, he addressed his people.

"What the elf says is true!"

"It can't be," said his second in command. "Blackfeather is an idiot and a coward to be sure... but a traitor?"

"There can be no other explanation."

Tim heard the double doors open behind him, but dared not turn around. A moment later, a drow in sleek black plate armor approached Silverwind and whispered in his ear. It was a prolonged whisper, and the longer it went on, the wider the grin grew across the drow leader's face.

"How delightful," said Silverwind when his messenger had finished his report. "Do bring them in."

The armored drow dashed away like an evil gazelle. When he re-entered, the chamber was filled with Blackfeather's moans, Dusty Sheglin's raspy, shallow breathing, and gasps from all the drow who looked upon them.

When they came into view, Tim couldn't believe either of them were still alive. Dusty looked to be more char than man, and Blackfeather's right leg looked like it belonged to someone who lived at a Sizzler buffet.

"Yeee!" Blackfeather cried out as an accompanying drow tossed the burnt, blackened corpse of a rat onto his swollen leg.

"Oliver," Julian whispered, taking Ravenus from his shoulder and hugging him tightly against his chest.

Dave lowered his head. "Oops."

"Duskblade," said Silverwind. "Escort these men to the surface." He looked at Tim. "With the understanding that they will forget all about this place and never return."

Tim nodded enthusiastically.

"My lord," the second in command spoke up. "What of the deaths of Stormsong and Cloudwhisper? Surely, that cannot go unpunished."

Julian bit his lower lip and pointed at the charred, wheezing figure of Dusty Sheglin.

Silverwind paused in thought. He looked at his second. "I am no fool. The truth of exactly what transpired here today may never be known. It is a certainty that these men are less innocent than they claim. By how much, who can say? What I do know is that if it were not for them, you and I both might currently be under the spell of this sniveling buffoon here. But aside from that, I am a drow of my word."

The second bowed his head. "You are wise and just, my lord."

"If you gentlemen would follow me," said Duskblade.

The guards aligned themselves into two columns leading toward the double doors and held their spears vertically.

Before they left, Cooper knelt down next to Dusty. "I'm going to eat your share of the rations, cockbag. And later when I shit it out, I'm going to keep it in a jar and call it Dusty."

Duskblade led them through a short labyrinth of subterranean passages, through doors, up and down stairs. Every now and again, he'd stop to point out a trip wire, a weight-sensitive stone in the floor, or even an entirely illusory section of floor masking a thirty foot drop into a spike pit.

Some of the traps Tim was confident that he would have discovered himself before falling prey to them. Others he gave himself fifty/fifty odds on. A few of them he recognized to be beyond his meager Trapfinding ability.

He finally stopped in front of a large granite entryway. "Beyond this door lies your freedom. Use it wisely and never return to this place." It occurred to him that this was the first time the drow had spoken since they left Silverwind's chamber.

"Don't worry about that," said Tim. "We've already forgotten it. Right, guys?"

"Forgotten what?" asked Dave with a desperate laugh.

If Duskblade was amused, he did not show it. He scowled at Tim, and then at Dave. Only his red eyes moved on his black stony face. Then he nodded. "Sleep."

"Huh?" said Tim. He thought maybe he heard a shout, but he might have just dreamt it.

*

Tim woke up bathed in sunlight and surrounded by tall, green grass, looking straight up into the bluest sky he'd ever seen. Something nearby was grunting and smacking, and Tim hoped that it wasn't some wild beast feasting away on one of his friends. As quietly as he could, Tim stood up and tiptoed toward the noise.

Even if he had made a successful Move Silently check, anyone paying the slightest bit of attention would have seen him coming from a considerable distance, his movement given away by a green explosion of grasshoppers making way for him whenever he stepped.

Cooper, however, was not paying the slightest bit of attention. With his mouth slurping up the contents of one of their lunchboxes, as it was, he probably wouldn't have noticed a stampede of rhinoceroses if Tim had sent one bounding his way.

"Hey," said Tim.

Cooper stopped eating and turned around. "Hey Tim," he said. "What's up?"

"You're really going to town on that lunchbox."

"It's my second one," said Cooper. "I had a promise to keep, after all. I'll tell you what, though. General Gore did not overestimate his wife's cooking prowess. Bitch knows how to pack a lunch. Julian's over there." He pointed to a flattened out trail of grass. "Go grab one for yourself."

Tim found Dave and Julian lying face down next to one another. Dave was snoring like a motherfucker, and Julian had his arm around Ravenus (also sleeping) like he was a teddy bear. Julian's bag was wide open, so Tim grabbed a lunchbox and joined Cooper again.

"Where are we?" asked Tim, nibbling a bit of hard tack. Much to his surprise, it was tastier than hard tack had any right to be.

There was a hint of ginger in it.

"Fuck if I know," Cooper said, puzzling over how he was meant to consume the goat milk from the cat bladder. It didn't come with a straw. Tim was about to suggest poking a small hole in it when Cooper just popped the whole thing in his mouth, bit down, gulped down the liquid, and spat out the bladder. After a moment's pause, he picked up the bladder and popped it in his mouth again. "It's meat, right?"

Tim was halfway through his lunchbox when Dave and Julian finally shambled out of the grass like a couple of zombies. Julian had been lying face down earlier, so Tim hadn't noticed his shiner and swollen jaw.

"Dude," said Tim. "What the hell happened to you?"

"Fucker hit me," said Julian, rubbing the side of his face. "I really wish elves weren't immune to Sleep spells."

Dave yawned and stretched his thick, stubby arms out. "Does anyone know where we are?"

Tim put his palms up, gesturing to the grass surrounding him. "You and I are in the same boat."

Cooper stood up and scanned the horizon. "I don't know," he said. "There looks to be a break in the grass over there." He pointed in what, as far as Tim was concerned, an arbitrary direction. "Maybe a river or a road?"

"Ravenus," said Julian. "Go find Cardinia. Come back and lead us."

"At once, sir," said the bird. He flapped his big black wings and took off into the air.

Ravenus returned after only a few minutes, reporting that the break in the grass Cooper had spotted was indeed a road, and that Cardinia would only be a couple hours march from their current position.

"Let's take this meal to go, guys," said Tim. "It'll taste better behind the safety of the city walls."

"It really is good," said Dave through a mouth full of something.

"Maybe we could stop at the general store and pick up some more when we get back," said Julian.

"Good idea," said Cooper. "I need to buy a jar. I only hope I make it in time."

The End

The Creep on the Borderlands

ROBERT BEVAN

THE CREEP ON THE BORDERLANDS

(Original Publication Date: August 24, 2013)

"Come on," Tim said to the anthropomorphic lizard creature across the counter. "That's a perfectly functional dagger. It's in pristine condition."

The lizard monster looked up at Tim through the monocle strapped to its head, magnifying its scaly-lidded eye as well as Julian's discomfort. "It's ordinary. Nothing special about it." It was surprisingly articulate for someone speaking through a mouth full of pointed teeth and a forked tongue. "I'll give you five silver pieces for it."

"Julian," said Tim. "Would you please talk some sense into him?"

Julian waved an open hand in front of the creature's face. "You'll give us more than five silver pieces."

The creature's lower eyelids swept up over its eyes and back down again. The highly magnified left eye allowed Julian to experience this blink in stunning detail. It freaked him the hell out.

"No," the creature said curtly. "I will not."

"What the hell was that?" asked Tim.

"Diplomacy?"

"Bullshit. You were trying to use the Jedi mind trick on him."

Julian shrugged. "I had to know."

"Oh, fuck!" said Cooper, who sounded as if he were either impossibly far away while still inside this weapon shop, or behind some kind of concealment.

"Shit," said Tim. "What is it now?"

"It sounds like it's coming from my office," said the lizard creature, removing the monocle from its face. "Why is the door closed?" Its body swayed when it walked, its spine swerving back and forth in a serpentine manner.

"Dave!" shouted Tim.

"Huh?" said Dave from the other side of the store.

"Where's Cooper? You were supposed to be keeping an eye on him?"

Dave stroked his thick, bushy beard. "Oh, I guess he slipped away while I was checking out these mace heads."

"Slipped away?" said Tim. "He's a seven foot tall half-orc barbarian! How could he —"

"Great mother of Sobek!" shrieked the lizard creature, standing in front of his now open office door.

"What happened?" said Tim, rushing toward him. "What did he do?"

Julian followed. A foul and familiar smell filled the air. He was reminded of the Porta Potties at the Hancock County Annual Chili Cook-Off.

The lizard creature stepped aside, fuming. "See for yourself."

The office was a tiny room, furnished only with a rough wooden desk and chair. Cooper stood, scratching an armpit, to the side of the chair. The wall behind the chair was coated in a splatter of half-orc shit. It was a medley of browns and greens, with a touch of yellow here and there. It had the consistency of pudding... and corn. It might have been mistaken for a work of abstract art by someone lacking both a nose and personal acquaintance with the artist.

"Dude!" cried Tim. "What the fuck, man!"

"Sorry," said Cooper. "I thought this was a bathroom." He stuck out a pouty lower lip.

"What could possibly have led you to believe this was a bathroom?" the lizard creature hissed. "The door is clearly marked OFFICE!"

"I can't read your lizard language," said Cooper.

"Oh come off it, shit brain," said Tim. "It's written in the common tongue." He turned to the lizard monster and clasped his hands together pleadingly. "He can't read at all. He's illiterate."

Cooper hung his head. "You don't need to go and tell the whole world."

"This is no excuse!" said the store owner. "Does that look like a bathroom to you?"

"It kind of does now," said Dave, having just arrived on the scene with his short dwarf legs.

"Shut up, Dave!" said Tim. "Cooper, how could you think this was a bathroom?"

"I thought this was a toilet," said Cooper, pointing down at the chair. "It has a hole in it."

"The hole is in the back of the chair!" said Tim. "Not on the seat!"

"I'll admit, I had to sit at a very awkward angle, which accounts for some of the height." Cooper looked up at the highest point of shit-stain on the wall, partially covering an intricately hand-drawn map. "I was going to complain."

"That hole," snapped the lizard creature, "is for my tail."

"Since when do you even seek out a bathroom anyway?" asked Dave. "Why didn't you just go outside and shit down your leg like you always do?"

"Fuck you, Dave!" said Cooper. "Pardon me for trying to act civilized."

"Civilized!" screamed Tim. "You sprayed your shit all over the wall of a man's place of business!"

"It makes sense," said Julian.

"What's that?" asked Dave.

"Cooper's low Charisma score is what makes him so offensive, right? I mean that's why he's always pissing and shitting everywhere."

"Yeah, so?"

"So it only makes sense that if he goes out of his way to be non-offensive, the results are only going to be worse."

"There's a certain logic at play there," admitted Dave.

"We have to get out of here," said Tim.

"Nobody is going anywhere until justice has been served," snarled the shop owner, back behind the counter, removing what appeared to be a Samurai sword from an ornate wooden case and placing it casually on the counter as if he was displaying it for a customer. That done, he removed a shiny black pebble from a tiny sconce on the wall. When the stone was removed, a quiet buzz filled the air, like an invisible bee constantly hovering two feet away from wherever you were standing.

"Julian," said Tim. "Now would be a good time to try Diplomacy again."

"Come on," Julian said to the shop owner. "He's our friend. It was an honest mistake. Surely you don't mean to kill him for it, do you?"

"Kill him?" said the lizard monster. "Of course not. What do you take me for?"

"Honestly, sir," said Julian. "I don't know. I've been trying to work that out since we got here. Dire iguana?"

"Lizardman," grumbled the shopkeeper, his scaly lips curving down at the sides.

"Well," said Tim. "So much for Diplomacy. I'm really very sorry sir, but we really have to go now. You can keep the dagger. Come on, guys." He rushed toward the open entrance of the shop.

A brilliant blue flash of electricity sent him flying backwards through the shop like he'd just bounced off the front of a moving bus. He hit the rear wall of the shop, which Julian now noticed was bereft of weapons, or any sort of decoration at all, save for a drab rectangular leather mat, about an inch thick, hanging from butcher's hooks on the ceiling about two inches away from the wall. The mat absorbed Tim's impact like a catcher's mitt, and he fell gracelessly to the rough wooden floor, where he lay face down sizzling and smoking. His fingernails and toenails were black. His formerly curly hair now spiked straight out, still crackling with residual electricity.

"What the hell was that?" asked Julian.

"Security," said the shop owner, leaning back and crossing his scaly arms across his chest. "I run a weapons store. A would-be robber could arm himself to the teeth with the very items he intends to steal. It's important to have adequate security measures in place."

"Is he dead?" asked Julian, joining Dave and Cooper, who were standing over Tim.

"I doubt it," said the shop owner, as if the question was whether or not he thought it was going to rain this evening.

"What are you waiting for, shithead?" Cooper said to Dave. "Heal him!"

Dave took a knee and placed his hand on Tim's. Tiny blue bolts jumped from Tim's hand to Dave's. "Yeaow!" cried Dave, pulling his hand back.

"Come on," said Cooper. "Don't be such a pussy. Hurry up."

Dave cautiously placed his index finger near Tim's hand. He closed his eyes and gritted his teeth as he inched it closer and closer. When they finally touched, Dave sighed with relief. "I heal thee."

A puddle of piss began to spread from beneath Tim's crotch area. He groaned as he sat up. "Where am I?"

"Sorry about that," said the lizardman. "I recommend you all just sit tight until the authorities arrive. I just happen to be close personal friends with —"

"Razorback!" called a voice from outside the shop. "Is it safe to come in?"

"Ah, there he is now." The lizardman grinned. "Just a moment, Esteban." He placed the black pebble in the sconce once again and the buzzing stopped. "Please, come in."

A member of the Kingsguard walked in. That much was evident by his red cloak, silver-plated pauldrons, and matching breastplate, more ornamental than functional. These guys were less common than the regularly patrolling city watch, but well more common than the Elite Kingsguard, who stuck mainly to the palace grounds.

One piece of the uniform that was, to Julian's best recollection, unique to Esteban was the shiny black pebble hanging from a steel chain around his neck. He tucked it under his breastplate when he caught Julian staring.

"Is there a problem here?" asked Esteban, placing his hands on his hips. "Would-be thieves, is it? Don't tell me. The elf with the hungry eyes?"

"I was just curious," said Julian. "I wouldn't —"

"The dwarf then?" said Esteban. "With the furry arm. Good gods, man! Is that leopard fur? However did you manage —"

Dave crossed his arms, hiding the furry part. "There's more to me than that, you know."

"Ah ha!" said Esteban. "It must be the halfling. He looks to have just lost a fight with your security system."

"What's going on?" asked Tim. "Who are you?"

"It was the half-orc," said Razorback.

Esteban rolled his eyes. "It's always the half-orc, isn't it."

"Hey man," said Cooper. "That's racial profiling. I could have your badge."

"What is this giant cretin blathering about?"

"Not a clue," said Razorback. His forked tongue darted out of his mouth three times in rapid succession. "There's something peculiar about this group."

"So," said Esteban. "What did the half-orc attempt to make off with?"

"This wasn't a robbery," said Razorback. "Go have a look inside my office."

"Stand aside!" For once, the Kingsguard spoke with an authority befitting his rank. Tim, Dave, Julian, and Cooper took a step back.

Esteban opened the office door and quickly shut it again. "Rapha's light!" he cried. "What foul depths of depravity would possess you to... why, man?"

"It was an honest mistake," said Cooper.

"Sir?" said Tim.

Esteban turned around and stared at him, his mouth still hanging open in disgust.

"What, exactly, is the penalty for this sort of crime?"

"I honestly have no idea," said Esteban. "Theft is simple. We remove the offenders hand, or claw, or tentacle, or whatever. This..." He pointed at the office door. "This isn't even an offense that anyone has thought to put on the books yet, much less think up an appropriate punishment for."

"Does that mean we're free to go?" asked Cooper.

"Shut up, Cooper," said Tim.

"It will be up to the district magistrate," said Esteban, frowning thoughtfully. "I suppose he may cut off a buttock?"

"Can I choose which one?" asked Cooper. "If it's got to happen, I've got this nasty growth I wouldn't mind getting —"

"Shut the fuck up, man!" said Tim.

"Esteban," said Razorback. "A word?"

"Of course, old friend," said the Kingsguard. He stepped behind the counter.

Razorback spoke in a hushed tone, but not so much so that he could reasonably expect even a pair of human ears not to hear him. "I thought this lot might be right to assist us with our little problem on the borderlands. Hmm?"

Esteban scowled at the group. "Them?" he said to Razorback. "This is a situation which requires delicacy. These men just defecated all over your office."

"Sir," said Dave. "That wasn't all of us."

"Do shut up, lad," said Esteban. "The grown-ups are talking."

"Delicacy is only but one of many possible strategies," said Razorback. "One might even consider the complete opposite of delicacy as an alternative solution."

"You have my ear for now, friend," said Esteban. "But I like not where your words lead. Make haste toward your point."

The lizardman put his arm around the Kingsguard's shoulder and led him a step further behind the counter. He whispered something into the man's ear, his forked tongue flickering about. Tim looked to Julian to see if his huge elf ears were picking any of this up, but Julian shook his head.

Esteban drummed his fingers on the counter. "Intriguing."

After a little more whispering, Esteban gave the group a gleaming, used-car-salesman grin.

"Gentlemen," he said. The word slithered out of his mouth like he was vomiting snakes. "How would you like to put this whole messy business behind us?"

Cooper smiled a big, stupid half-orc smile. "I'd like that a lot. Thank you very much."

"Hang on," said Tim. "What do you have in mind?"

Esteban sat on the countertop, crossed one knee over the other, and steepled his fingers. "Think of it as a diplomatic mission. It's a trifle really. Take care of this little job for us, and I think I can convince my reptilian friend here to drop the charges against all of you. What do you say? Hmmm?"

"All of us?" asked Dave. "Cooper was the one who shat on the wall. What would you charge the rest of us with?"

Esteban raised his eyebrows, as if surprised by the question. "You'd be charged as accessories, of course."

"He shat on the wall!" said Dave. "How could we possibly have accessified... uh... accessorated?"

"Accessorized," said Julian.

"Thanks," said Dave. "We didn't accessorize anything!"

"The halfling pissed on the floor," said Razorback.

"That wasn't my fault!" said Tim, stretching his tunic down to hide the wet spot on his pants.

The lizardman grinned, baring his pointed teeth as he casually picked up his very expensive looking sword. "And let's not forget how the dwarf spilled blood all over my prized Zhou Shin blade.

"I did no such thing!" said Dave. "Have you lost your —"

"Shut up, Dave!" said Julian. Dave gawked at him angrily. "Sorry Dave. But I want you to calm down and replay that last accusation in your head very slowly. See if there are any lines you can read between."

Dave's beady little dwarf eyes moved from left to right and back again while he mumbled Razorback's words to himself. He looked up wide-eyed at Julian, and then at Razorback. "Hey, not cool."

"I'm beginning to take a liking to the elf," said Esteban. "Clever chap. I may not charge him with anything. If things go according to plan, I may even be in a position to hire a personal assistant."

"Just tell us what you want us to do," said Tim.

"I've got this," said Julian.

"Oh, sure. See if you can negotiate a dental plan into your new job while the rest of us are hanged and skewered."

Dave stood next to Tim, a line of solidarity. He crossed his arms and glared at Julian.

"You should also ask for a high starting salary," said Cooper. "That way they can talk you down to something that's still reasonable."

Tim and Dave glared up at Cooper.

"What?" said Cooper. "That's just good business sense."

"I'm not looking for a job!" said Julian. "And I'm not selling you guys out. I want to get out of this game as much as you guys do." He spun around to face Esteban. "Now what do you want from us?"

"We have a situation," said Esteban. "Razorback and I run a small operation out on the borderlands."

"Are we really that close to a border?" asked Tim. "Who is the neighboring realm?"

Esteban stared confusedly at Tim for a moment. "Did you just fall out of the sky, my lad? What kind of question is that? His Majesty's realm extends across this entire continent. I'm not referring to a political border. I speak of the line where civilization ends and wilderness begins."

"Okay, fine," said Julian, waving his index and middle fingers in a circular motion. "Get on with it."

Esteban leaned in. "Our little enterprise, so to speak, is what you might call off-the-books, if you get my meaning."

"So you're corrupt," said Julian. "We'd already guessed that. It's not a massive surprise that you'd be involved in some illegal smuggling operation."

"Oh, it's not illegal, so to speak," said Esteban. "Much like your friend's offense in the office, there hasn't actually been any specific legislation written explicitly forbidding what we do, but it's not the sort of thing a man in my position would be well served to have it known that he was a part of, if you get my meaning."

Julian wondered which of their tongues was the most serpent-like. "What do you do exactly?"

"We run a small import/export business with the lizardfolk colony in the Swamp of Shadows, the same clan which Razorback here hails from." He smiled and pointed an open palm at the lizardman. Razorback nodded.

"What do you provide the lizardfolk with?" asked Julian. He looked around the shop. "Weapons?"

"Heavens no!" said Esteban. "Why, if word leaked that I've been arming the savages on the border—"

"Hey," said Cooper. "Try to show a little decency, man. One of those savages is right behind you."

"Savage!" hissed Razorback, slamming a fist on the counter.

"Hang on, man," said Cooper. I didn't mean to say —"

"I run a legitimate place of business here, one which you decided to spray with your shit. And you have the nerve to call me a savage?"

"You misunderstood what —"

"Cooper!" snapped Tim. "Shut the fuck up!"

"Sorry."

"Please continue," said Julian. "You were saying?"

"We provide them with freshly deceased bodies." Esteban's words betrayed not even the slightest trace of regret or disgust. "They enjoy feasting on the flesh of creatures they feel view them as a lesser race."

"That should turn some hearts and minds," said Tim.

"And stomachs," said Dave.

"Where do you get all these dead bodies?" asked Julian.

"Bodies are easy enough to come by," said Esteban. "This is a crowded city. Vagrants die in the street all the time."

"And you're okay with just feeding those poor folks to savages?"

"If it doesn't bother them," reasoned Esteban, "why should it bother me? I'm doing a public service, if you think about it."

Julian raised his eyebrows, challenging the Kingsguard to elaborate on his claim.

"A conventional burial costs time and money, not to mention a bit of real estate, which could be better spent on any number of public works projects."

"Do you honestly believe that outweighs the dignity you're denying the deceased?"

"Well how about this?" argued Esteban. "Suppose a secret order of necromancers up and decided to raise all of the bodies in the public cemeteries and wreak havoc on the city? The fewer bodies they had to work with the better, wouldn't you say?"

Julian folded his arms. "Are you listening to yourself?"

Esteban hopped down from the countertop. "Why are we even arguing about this?" He pointed a shaky finger at Julian. "You are the criminals! You will do as I say, or I'll have all your asses chopped off!"

"I could sew them together and make a cushion for my office chair," said Razorback. "A punishment befitting the crime."

"Well get on with it then," said Julian. "Is it really necessary for us to know every last detail of your business in order for us to do you this favor? Just tell us what you want us to do."

Esteban eased himself back up onto the counter. "Very well. As you may expect, running an operation such as this one requires the cooperation, discretion, and services of quite a number of people. Expenses add up. And then every now and again, an unexpected nuisance rears its ugly head, and drives those ex-

penses up, to the point where we're barely making a profit anymore."

"And the nuisance in this case would be..."

"On the trail leading from the main northern road to the Swamp of Shadows, there lives a mad old hermit. A most unpleasant fellow, by all accounts. He's been harassing my couriers to the point where they're demanding a higher fee for their services."

Julian frowned. "And you want us to go kill this old guy."

Esteban jumped like he'd just had a cattle prod shoved up his ass. "Hold your tongue, man!" He craned his neck to look down the aisles of the shop. There were no customers. "I am a member of the Kingsguard. We do not sanction murder."

"Then what do you want?"

Esteban smiled and reached an arm around Julian's shoulder. His crawling fingers felt like a tip-toeing spider. "You're a clever lad. All I want is for you to come up with a solution to our little problem."

"I guess we could ask him to relocate," said Julian. "I mean, one stretch of swamp is just as good as any other, right?"

"Ha ha," said Esteban. "I don't think you'll find him very receptive to conversation. He's madder than a bag of squirrels, you see." He turned around and ran a finger down the sleek, shiny blade of Razorback's prized sword. "I had hoped that you fellows might find a more permanent means of persuading him."

Julian maneuvered out from Esteban's arm. "I'm not so good with innuendo, but it sounds to me like you want us to go murder some old man in a swamp."

Esteban pursed his lips and lowered his head. "Let's see... How can I put this in a way that you'll understand?" He looked Julian squarely in the eye. "How about this? I want you to go murder this old man in the swamp."

"Esteban!" said Razorback.

Esteban waved a hand dismissively at the lizardman. "Oh don't worry. Nobody's going to believe this lot."

"Why don't you just go kill him yourself?" said Tim. "Or have your couriers do it for you?"

"Because I've got you," said Esteban.

"Well yeah," said Tim. "That makes sense now, but what about before you met us? You've had this problem for a while, right?"

"The couriers I employ are respected tradesmen with reputations to protect. They are not hired thugs. And as for me, well I am a —"

"Yeah yeah," said Tim. "You're a Kingsguard. So fucking honorable. We know. What about the lizardfolk in the swamp? If they're as savage as you say, then why don't they just go and eat him?"

"The lizardfolk won't touch him," said Esteban. "They like to have the crazy old bastard around so they can teach their young what humans are like."

"May I have a moment to consult my friends?"

Esteban grinned. "Why of course."

"Feel free to use my office," said Razorback.

"That's all right, thanks." Julian joined his friends at the back of the shop. "Options?"

"I don't see that we have any," said Dave.

"Nonsense," said Tim. "There are always options. Here's what we'll do." He gestured for them all to huddle closer together, which they did. Cooper's stench was nigh-unbearable. "We'll accept his terms, walk out the door, and just fuck off to the bar."

"I wouldn't recommend that," Esteban called out.

Tim nearly jumped out of his skin. "You dick!" he said to the Kingsguard. "This is supposed to be a private consultation."

"You aren't the first group of outsiders we've asked favors of," said Esteban, sauntering around to the other side of the counter. "And despite what you may believe, you are far from the cleverest." He bent down behind the counter. When he resurfaced, he heaved a heavy wrought-iron frame onto the countertop. Where normally there would be a photograph, there was nothing but a blank, shimmering surface. It looked like a mirror, but cast no reflection of anything. "Come here, little one."

Tim raised his eyebrows and pointed to his own chest.

"That's right," said Esteban. "Come here and have a look. Razorback, fetch our little friend here a cool beverage."

The lizardman trudged toward his office door like he was walking the green mile. He snarled at Cooper before opening the door and slipping inside. After about a minute, he sprang out of the door, slammed it behind him, and let out a long exhalation. He carried a flask of dark blue, bubbling liquid.

"Have a drink," said Esteban, placing the flask on the counter in front of Tim.

"No thanks," said Tim. "I'm not thirsty."

"You should mind your dwarf friend, and stop pretending that you have any choice."

Tim looked back at his friends.

"If he wanted to kill us," said Julian, "he would have done it already."

Tim picked up the flask and sniffed it. His face didn't betray any opinion of what it smelled like. He tilted his head back and necked the whole thing in one go.

As soon as the liquid touched Tim's mouth, an image appeared on the shiny surface inside the frame. A bright pink, seemingly shapeless blob sprouted a line that grew down out of it, until it ballooned out into a larger blob in the middle of the frame.

Julian realized suddenly what he was seeing. It was a 3D rendering of Tim's oral cavity, esophagus, and stomach. When the pink image seeped into his intestines, the borders expanded and became fuzzy like a magic marker on a paper towel. It was entering his bloodstream. A pink haze swirled around the central image until it coalesced into veins and arteries, mapping Tim's entire body. Arms and legs sprouted out, which moved when Tim moved his own arms and legs. Other organs, starting with his heart and lungs, began to take shape. His brain, eyes, and kidneys soon became recognizable. And there were still other organs which Julian, who hadn't studied enough human anatomy, was unable to properly identify.

Shortly after Tim's insides were more or less fully exposed, the picture grew hazy again, as veins and arteries gave way to capillaries. Muscles obscured the internal organs, and skin finally materialized on the outside, leaving an image of a bald, naked halfling standing there gawking back at a gawking Tim. When he came to his senses, he quickly put his hands over his little halfling junk.

"Fucking awesome," said Cooper. "Me next!"

"I'm afraid not," said Esteban. "Regrettably, the Ink of Location is too costly for me to give you each a dose. I'll have to trust the rest of you to not abandon your little friend here."

"Ink of Location?" said Tim. "I've never heard of that."

"I'm not surprised," said Esteban. "I may have invented it for all I know. I commissioned it from a group of students at His Majesty's Royal Institute of Magic. You can't earn a post-graduate degree without inventing some new spell, potion, or magical item. Most of them fritter the opportunity away on some new cantrip or useless piece of —"

"What does it do?" asked Tim.

"Ah! Of course," said Esteban. "When you leave here, the image of you on this Magic Mirror will grow smaller, giving me a constant, real-time view of your position in relation to the mirror. The ink will stay in your system for five days. Just to be safe, I'll allow you three days to complete your mission. If you fail, or attempt to run, I'll name you as prime suspects in the murder of an adorable human child. You'll be hunted down by every Kingsguard, city watchman, vigilante, and bounty hunter in Cardinia."

"You'd never see that kind of response if a lizard child got killed," grumbled Razorback.

"Wait," said Tim. "What adorable human child?"

"One will turn up."

"Fuck," said Tim. His shoulders slumped as he let out a resigned sigh. "Let's go, guys."

After Esteban drew them a simple map, circling a wide area in which he expected they would have the best chance of encountering the crazy hermit, Tim, Julian, Dave, and Cooper stepped out of the shop and into the drizzly gray afternoon.

"Ravenus!" Julian called out as soon as they'd left the shop.

Ravenus flew out of the alley next to the shop, a huge flapping mass of black feathers, and perched atop Julian's quarterstaff. "Here I am, sir. There's a dead dog in the alley. Tastes like it's been there close to a week. I can't remember the last time I've eaten so well." He let out a deep, guttural belch. By the smell of it, Julian judged Ravenus's assessment of the dog's time of death to be correct.

"Jesus, Ravenus!" said Julian, coughing and waving the putrid bird belch out of his face.

"Beggin' your pardon, sir," said Ravenus. "It just slipped out."

"It's all right," said Julian.

Ravenus cocked his head to the side and looked down at the group. "If you don't mind me saying so, sir, the lot of you appear to be in rather a sad state. Why so glum, chums?"

"We've just been coerced into murdering an old man."

Ravenus flapped his wings excitedly. "Another adventure? Jolly good! Dibs on the eyes."

By the time they got to the city's northern gate, the drizzle had turned into a full-on downpour. Muddy puddles grew and connected to one another, forming gulfs for horses to clop through and shit in.

Julian wondered if he just hadn't noticed how much horses shit before, or if there was something about the rain that really put their bowels in motion. It seemed that everywhere he looked, horses were carpet-bombing the area, like they were all trotting home from Taco Bell.

He tried to step carefully, but there was hardly any point. He couldn't see through the murky brown water. At least he and Dave were wearing boots. Poor Tim and Cooper were walking through this barefoot. Cooper probably didn't mind. If anything, horse shit would only be doing him the favor of masking some of his own natural funk. But Tim, with his small strides and big,

hairy feet... he must be squishing his way through horsey bombs with every other step. He was soaked up to the knees with filthy brown water, but his face didn't betray anything in the way of disgust. It looked more exhausted and depressed than anything, like he was carrying the weight of the world on his tiny halfling shoulders.

"It's a nice time to be leaving the city," said Julian, trying to spark up some conversation with Tim.

"Lovely time," said a guard who had apparently overheard him. "That is, if you're looking to die." Julian turned around to look at him. The guard speaking to them stood a head above the other two guards manning the gate. He wore a black, waterproof cloak, but Julian spotted the glint of his silver decorative breastplate beneath it. Kingsguard. He hoped Tim failed to notice it.

"The road is less traveled on rainy days, and the forest creatures grow more bold in the cover of heavy rain. A small band of ill-equipped men like yourselves may become a prime target for a group of goblins, or an owlbear, or worse yet even."

"Yeah?" said Tim. "Well if we see your mom out there, we'll tell her you said hi."

"Tim!" Dave shrieked.

The glint of silver had apparently not gone unnoticed by Tim.

"I beg your pardon!" said the Kingsguard, placing his hand conspicuously on his sword hilt. The two city watchmen behind him looked at one another with their mouths hanging open.

Cooper made a fist and conked Tim lightly on the top of the head. A light conking from Cooper was still enough to send Tim face first into a horse shit puddle.

"I'm sorry," Cooper said to the Kingsguard. "He's my son. He's a retard." He wagged a finger down at Tim, who had just pushed himself up out of the puddle. "One more outburst like that, Billy, and I'll knock that extra chromosome right out of you!"

"Cooper!" Dave shrieked.

"Dude," said Julian. "Do you have any idea how offensive that is?"

"Huh?" said Cooper.

"You apologize to this nice man right now."

"No!" said Dave. "That's not —"

Julian cut him off with an open palm. "Cooper, you apologize right this instant."

Cooper lowered his giant half-orc head. "I'm very sorry, sir. I didn't know you were retarded."

Julian buried his face in his hands. "My fault. Good call, Dave." It was Diplomacy time. Julian lowered his hands and looked up at the Kingsguard, who looked more confused than angry, with sad puppy-dog eyes. "On behalf of our group, I offer you our most humble apologies. My friends mean no offense. We simply —"

Cooper let out a thunderous fart. "My bad. That one's been brewing for a while."

For all the rain pounding the ground, there was precious little wind. The toxic gas cloud radiated from Cooper's ass like slow-motion video footage of a nuclear weapon leveling a city.

"By gods, king, and country!" shouted the Kingsguard. He steadied himself against the gate with his free hand and moved his sword hand up to cover his mouth and nose.

Desperate times. Julian took a knee. "Once again, I sincerely wish to —"

"Just go already!" demanded the Kingsguard. "The lot of you, be gone from my sight at once!"

Dave didn't need to be told twice. He was clunking down the road as fast as his short, armored legs could take him.

"Thank you, sir," said Cooper. "If there's —"

"Shut up, Cooper," said Julian.

"But I —"

"Not another fucking word. Grab Tim and let's go."

When they had put a couple of miles between themselves and the city walls, Dave spoke up. His voice shook a bit, as if he had been building up the courage to say what he wanted to say for a while.

"You know what, Tim? I think that was a dick move, what you

did back there."

Tim patted his hips and chest. "Well let me see if I can find you one of my Fucks-to-Give. Oh shit. Looks like I'm fresh out."

"That's what I'm talking about," said Dave, his voice more confident now. "I know you're not happy here. None of us are. But death isn't the way I want to leave. I want to go home."

"How do you know death isn't the ticket home?" said Tim. "What if, when our characters die, we wake up back in the Chicken Hut, back in our own bodies, and it was all a dream or some shit?"

"Those aren't dice I want to roll," said Dave. "And it's not your decision to make."

"I'm sorry," said Tim. "I always get a little cranky after I've been electrocuted to the point of pissing myself."

"It's cool," said Dave. "Just try to think of all of us when you lose your shit."

"I'll admit I stepped over the line," said Tim. "But I won't accept all of the blame. Cooper is the one who shat in the lizardman's office and called the Kingsguard a retard."

"I was just trying to be helpful," said Cooper.

"Well that's the thing," said Dave. "Julian got me thinking back at the weapon shop. You're not supposed to be helpful. Not with words anyway. If a monster attacks us, you can be helpful by beating the shit out of it with your axe. But don't try to be helpful in a social setting. It will only backfire. You have a Charisma score of 4. If you need to shit, just go outside and shit down your leg like you always do. If you want to say something helpful, just keep your mouth shut."

Cooper pursed his lips and furrowed his brow. Julian waited for a 'Fuck you, Dave', but it never came.

"I must say," said Ravenus, perched on Julian's shoulder. "The mood here has grown quite grim. Might I take my leave and hunt for worms? This wet ground should be crawling with them."

"Why don't you go scout the area?" said Julian.

"With all of this rain, sir, I can barely see ten feet in front of

me."

"Well go fly around anyway," Julian snapped. "You're putting on weight."

"Why I...!" Ravenus lowered his head and hunched his wings. "Right away, sir." He flapped off into the rain.

Julian felt bad. He wanted to call Ravenus back and apologize, but he didn't. He needed some time to sort out his thoughts alone. And, if he was honest, Ravenus had been getting a bit heavier. Some exercise would do him good.

His silent contemplation didn't last long. The meditative patter of the rain beating the ground was broken by a bovine scream.

"What the fuck was that?" asked Cooper.

"Sounded like a cow," said Tim.

"That was no 'Moo'," said Dave.

They stood around looking dumbly at one another for about ten seconds before Ravenus returned.

"Hey listen," said Julian. "I'm sorry for what I said about you putting on weight. You know I love you just the way you are, right?"

"Sir, now is perhaps not the best time for —"

"I don't say it enough," said Julian. "I appreciate you. You've saved my life more than once."

"I'm afraid we have a situation."

"I mean, you can fly. And here I am calling you fat."

"You make a good point, sir, but —"

"What the fuck is going on?" asked Cooper.

"I'm not sure," said Tim. "I think Julian may be about to pop the question to Ravenus."

"There's an owlbear not fifty yards away from here!" cried Ravenus.

"A what?" asked Julian.

"An owlbear!" said Ravenus.

"The Kingsguard back at the gate mentioned owlbears. I meant to ask what they were."

"Not much to it," said Cooper. "Pretty self-explanatory really.

Just imagine what you get when a bear fucks an owl."

"You get a bear dick covered in blood and feathers," said Julian. "A mammal can't mate with a bird."

"Why don't you go over and explain that to him?" said Cooper.

"Well I'm definitely going to go and have a look," said Julian, taking a step in the direction Ravenus had flown in from. "I mean, how many times in your life are you going to get to see a real live owlbear?"

Ravenus grabbed the back of Julian's serape with his talons and started flapping backwards. "Sir, I really don't think that's a good idea. Owlbears are terribly vicious creatures."

Julian pulled his serape free of the bird's grasp. "Don't worry. I'll keep my head down. The grass is plenty tall enough to hide in. Who's coming?"

Dave and Tim shook their heads.

"I'm suddenly feeling a lot less suicidal," said Tim.

"Someone should go with him," said Dave. "Just in case." He and Tim looked up at Cooper.

"I don't want to see an owlbear," said Cooper.

"Then just follow behind him," said Dave. "Keep him in your sight."

"Fine," Cooper grumbled. "Lead the way, Ranger Dick."

Julian stepped off the road and into the muddy grassland. Grasshoppers exploded out of his way with each step he took.

"For the record, sir," said Ravenus, flying in tight circles around him, "I'd like to repeat my objection just one more time. This is unnecessarily dangerous."

"Your objection is noted, Ravenus. I want to see the owlbear."

"Very good, sir." Ravenus flew ahead and disappeared into the rain.

When he was about twenty yards away from the road, Julian heard Cooper's massive footsteps squishing into the mud after him.

Julian stayed low as he pushed aside the tall grass. He'd stop occasionally to poke his head up over it and look ahead, and to glance backwards to make sure he could still see Cooper. On one such occasion, Cooper squatted down when Julian turned back.

Julian immediately followed Cooper's example and ducked down. He put his hands out to his sides, palms up, and mouthed the words 'What's wrong?"

"I've got to take a shit," said Cooper. "If you want to watch, it's gonna cost you a gold piece."

Even with Julian's giant elf ears, Cooper's words were barely audible through the relentless patter of the rain. He turned around and started creeping forward again, when Ravenus flapped into view and scared the shit out of him.

"Jesus, Ravenus!"

"A thousand pardons, sir," said the bird. "I felt I should warn you. The owlbear is just up ahead. Must we really go through with this?"

"I just want to take a peek," said Julian. "Then we'll sneak away." He crept forward carefully, trying to disturb the grass as little as he possibly could.

Finally, he reached his quarry. Even though it was less than thirty yards away, the beast was barely more than a silhouette through the rain. It was bigger than he had expected, standing about eight feet tall. Its body was covered in brown feathers, but it was no true bird. It was more like a gorilla in a chicken suit. Julian wanted to get a good look at its face before he left, but it was buried in the mangled remains of an extremely dead cow.

The straight vertical pattern of the rain stirred as a gentle breeze blew past, providing some relief from the oppressive summer air. The relief was short lived, as it carried with it the scent of Cooper's shit. Julian gagged. How many times in a single day must one's nose be subjected to Cooper's rectal emissions?

The owlbear jerked its head up suddenly, threw away the shredded cow corpse, and sniffed the air. Its beak was a sharp, pointy horror, soaked red with blood that ran down its feathered neck and chest. Its eyes were not like anything Julian had ever seen on a mammal or a bird, or any other creature for that mat-

ter. They were two swirling whirlwinds of madness.

Julian ducked down behind the grass, relatively confident that the owlbear hadn't spotted him, but not so much so that it offered him any sense of comfort. Ravenus was right. This was a stupid thing to do. What the hell was he –

The air shook with a sound that was something between a screech and a roar, like a T-Rex just got kicked in the nuts. Julian crouched as low as he could.

Cooper, having apparently finished his business, stood up. "Holy shit!" He ducked back down.

The owlbear must have spotted at least one of them. The squelch and slurp of its footsteps through the mud grew closer with each step. They were too far apart to be a charge. It felt more like it was investigating something it thought it might have seen. There was only one thing to do. Give it something to see.

"Horse," Julian whispered. After a small crackling of magic in the air, a gorgeous white stallion stood looking down at him. It blinked as the rain splashed onto its beautiful coat and streamed through its flowing white mane. It let out a small whinny, which Julian guessed was probably horse-speak for 'The fuck?'.

The pace of the squishy footsteps picked up considerably as the approaching owlbear bellowed its horrible screeching roar.

"Run!" Julian commanded the horse. The horse obeyed, bolting away as fast as it could, cutting a straight path through the tall grass.

Two seconds later, the owlbear stepped into the path of grass the horse had left flattened behind it. Julian held his breath. The owlbear didn't even turn his way. It ran after the horse, waving its huge feathery arms in a mad rage, like the horse had violated its daughter or something.

When the owlbear was finally lost to the rain, Julian exhaled. Cooper was standing right over him, extending a hand to help him to his feet.

"Thanks," said Julian.

"Not bad," said Cooper. "But just so you know... People have

been known to use the Mount spell in ways other than finding new and creative methods to murder horses. Hell, some crazy fuckers even ride them."

"Har har," said Julian. "That horse is going to be just fine. I'll admit that owlbear was a lot scarier than I thought it was going to be, but it wasn't particularly fast. There's no way it's going to be able to catch a horse at full gall—"

A horse scream pierced through the rain. It started in high and slowly began to fade. A second later, instead of continuing to fade, it just went completely silent all of a sudden.

"That was weird," said Julian. "Why did it just cut off like that?"

"The magic horses disappear when they die," said Cooper. "The owlbear must have bit its head off."

"That's impossible," said Julian. "I saw that thing run. It wasn't even close to the speed of a horse."

An owlbear roar thundered through the air, deeper and louder than the one they heard before.

"Fuck," said Cooper. "He's pissed."

"Why?" asked Julian.

"Think about it," said Cooper. "His lunch just winked out of existence while he was eating it."

"Is everyone okay?" asked Ravenus, flapping down to perch on Julian's quarterstaff.

"We're fine," said Julian. "How did that owlbear catch the horse?"

Ravenus shook the water out of his feathers. "It didn't, sir. That was another owlbear. A big one at that."

"What's the bird saying?" asked Cooper, who couldn't understand the Elven tongue.

"He said we'd better get the hell out of here right now."

Julian and Cooper backtracked down the path of flattened grass they had created. The rain let up just enough so that Ravenus was visible flying above and ahead of them. As briskly as they walked, the presence of wandering owlbears in the vicinity made

it feel like forever. Finally, Ravenus maintained a tight, circular holding pattern just ahead of them, and Julian knew they were close to the road.

"So," said Tim when they finally reunited. "Have you scratched 'owlbear gazing' off of your bucket list?"

"This place is crawling with them," said Julian. "We should get moving."

The party continued northward through the rain, encountering neither traveler nor owlbear, until they reached a trail veering west off the main road, composed of sun-bleached mollusk shells.

"This is probably the road that leads to the Swamp of Shadows," said Dave.

Tim pulled out the map Esteban had drawn for them. It was soggy and smeared almost to the point of uselessness. "Good enough for me."

They followed the shell trail for an hour before the clouds had finally blown their collective load. The patter of rain gave way to the croaks of frogs and the chirps of crickets as afternoon grew into evening. It was only when Dave demanded a five-minute rest that Julian realized how low the temperature had dropped since they began their journey. He actually began to shiver in his rain-and-sweat-soaked serape.

Dave must have felt the sudden chill inside his armor as well, as he was ready to move again in less than five minutes.

Evening turned into night, and the billowy grey clouds allowed a crescent moon to peek through, along with a couple of stars. After another hour's crunching along the shell path, the grassland gave way to a sparse forest of cypress trees. Twenty minutes later it became evident that the path they walked on was now the only solid ground around, rising above stagnant black water on both sides. As they walked further into the swamp, Julian began to pick up a sound that was neither cricket nor frog. It sounded more like... zydeco?

Sure enough, half a mile up the road, the music drowned out

the creepy-crawlies of the landscape, which had become thicker with trees. The accordions and harmonicas playing to a fast, washboard rhythm were unmistakable to Julian's stupidly long ears.

After a series of confused glances, raised eyebrows, and shrugs, the group marched on in the direction of the music. Ten minutes later, they spotted a light shining through the looming cypress trees.

Distracted by the music, Julian nearly ran into an old wooden signpost poking out of the water next to the path. He read the sign aloud. "Bon Temps Tavern."

"Wouldn't hurt to pop in for a drink," said Cooper.

"Maybe we could even stay the night," said Dave. "I don't know how much I like traveling further into an unfamiliar swamp in the dark."

"It sounds like a friendly enough place," said Julian.

"One drink," said Tim. "And we'll talk about where to go from there."

A bridge of rough wooden planks led from the trail to the tavern. The building itself was raised about fifteen feet out of the water on a series of posts. If Julian had to guess the style of architecture, he would have said unsupervised eight-year-olds building a tree fort. It looked like a mosquito fart could send the whole thing toppling into the marsh. The most impressive feature was the awning over the entrance. The top half of an alligator skull about the size of a compact car. It boasted teeth as long as Tim's forearms. It might not have been the most inviting entrance in a different setting, but here it worked. It said that you should come in and have a drink, because you never know what you could run into if you hang around outside too long.

The planks creaked as they walked single file up the wooden stairs toward the huge skeletal alligator maw. The music coming from inside was in full swing, accompanied by a lively din of conversation and raucous laughter.

Julian reached the door first, but was hesitant to open it.

Cooper pushed past him. "This place sounds great!" He opened the door, and they all spilled inside.

All conversation in the tavern stopped almost immediately as the accordion whined to a halt. The lizardmen on harmonica and washboard played on a bit, lost in the rhythm of the song they were playing, until they got a nudge from the accordionist.

More than half the congregation was made up of lizardfolk. The rest were a mix of human, half-orc, half-elf, and a few humanoids that Julian couldn't identify. Whatever their race, they were all clearly working-class people. Their clothes were filthy, their fingernails were grimy, and their teeth were discolored. Every bloodshot eye in the house was on them.

"Evenin', strangers," said the lizardman on accordion. His tone was suspicious, completely at odds with the frivolity of the music he had just stopped playing. "Now what it is bring you fine folks out here in the middle of the night?"

The truth wouldn't do, so Julian thought up the best lie he could on a second's notice. "We're um... We're ecologists," he said. "We've come to check the salinity of the marsh."

"What he say?" asked the harmonica player.

"I think he done said he come to check the senility of Big Marsha," said the lizardman on the washboard.

Nearly all of the lizardfolk in the place stood up at once, along with a fair number of humans and half-orcs.

A particularly large half-orc, dressed in mud-stained overalls frayed below the knees, wiped his forearm across his beer-foamed mouth and stepped forward. "You folks got some big ol' hickory nuts come in here insult Miss Marsha like that."

"Wait, no," Julian said. "We didn't mean..." Words failed him. "What just happened?" he said under his breath.

"Critical Fumble," said Tim. "It doesn't matter how high your Charisma score is. Every now and again, you're bound to roll a 1."

A long, extended note shrieked out of the accordion, gaining the musician the tavern's attention. "Now settle down, folks." He grinned a sharp-toothed lizard grin. "If these folks wanna come round here an' pick a fight with Big Marsha, well hell... That be mo' entertainment than we can provide."

The crowd laughed, murmured words of agreement to one another, and went back about their business. Now that was a successful Diplomacy check.

"Who the fuck is Big Marsha?" said Cooper.

The accordionist, still grinning, nodded his reptilian head toward the bar. Of the two lizardfolk tending the bar, it wasn't hard to guess which one had earned the moniker 'Big Marsha'. The bartender on the left was as normal-looking as any anthropomorphic lizard Julian had seen all day. He crossed his arms over his chest and took the universal tough-guy pose as he stared at the group of newcomers. The one on the right looked like it — she, Julian supposed — lived on a diet composed exclusively of deep-fried Snickers bars. As she stared back at them, she disproved Julian's diet theory by lashing her tongue out of her wide, Jabba-like mouth, and snatching a passing mosquito out of the air.

"Go on, Randy, Germaine," Big Marsha said to two humans sitting at the bar. "You go grab youselves a table. Miss Marsha gotta have a word wit' her new guests."

The two men obediently picked up their drinks and moved to an empty table.

The obese lizardwoman slapped four shot-glasses and one normal-sized glass on the bar. "Well come on now!" she said. "You got somethin' to say to Miss Marsha. Here I am. Come on over n' sit down a spell. First shot's on the house."

Julian, Tim, Dave, and Cooper walked slowly across the room, trying to avoid the distrustful stares of mammalian and reptilian eyes. With each step Julian took toward the bar, the entrance — and, more importantly, exit — to the tavern felt a mile further away.

When they finally made it to the bar, Big Marsha uncorked a bottled and filled all of their glasses. She placed a shot in front of Julian, Tim, and Cooper, and the larger glass she placed in front of Dave. Then she frowned and looked over at the band. "Go on

now, you good-fo'-nothin' hacks. I don't pay you to stand there and ogle me. Get to playin'!"

The lizardman on the washboard bobbed his head up and down as he scraped a bone across his instrument in a fast rhythm. The harmonica player joined in, followed finally by the accordionist. The party was in full swing again.

Big Marsha picked up the remaining shot glass. "Welcome to Bon Temps." Her whole body jiggled as she tilted her head back and swallowed the drink.

Julian couldn't quite put his finger on what it was. Definitely some bottom-shelf liquor. But it went down nicely enough and warmed his insides.

"Now let's see if I can rustle up somethin' fo' you friend here," Big Marsha said to Julian.

"Huh?"

"Boudreaux," she said to the other bartender. "Run out back and check the possum traps."

The bartender snapped to attention, the tough-guy look completely abandoned. "Yes, ma'am!" He scuttled through the swinging doors behind the bar like he was on a mission from God.

Big Marsha stomped her foot down behind the bar, and all four of them jumped. She bent down, and reappeared with a flattened cockroach in her hand. "Here you go, big fella," she said, bringing the dead bug way too close to Julian's face. He wanted to scream or run, but was frozen in fear and panicked confusion. What the fuck was she doing?

Just when he was about to lose his shit, Ravenus plucked the bug out of her hand. Of course! Ravenus was on his shoulder! He'd completely forgotten that. She wasn't trying to rub cockroach guts on his face after all.

"Ravenus," said Julian. "Why don't you go sit on the bar?" The sound of crunching cockroach next to his ear was making him queasy.

Ravenus hopped down onto the bar and greedily swallowed the big bug.

"Oh, you's a hungry one, ain't you," said Big Marsha. "Well don't worry none, honey. Boudreux's out fetchin' you a special treat."

Big Marsha poured another round of drinks. Julian noticed that she failed to wash her cockroach-touched hand, but kept the observation to himself.

"Now tell Miss Marsha true," she said. "What bring you folks all the way to Groulet at this time of night?"

"What's Groulet?" asked Dave.

"Why that's the name of our fine little community."

"I thought you said it was called Bon Temps."

"Bon Temps is the name of the tavern," Big Marsha snapped. "Groulet is the name of the town. Squeeze the wax outta those fat little dwarf ears of yours and pay attention!"

Dave sat wide-eyed and silent.

Big Marsha chuckled to herself. Her leathery skin rippled down in waves as she laughed. "Miss Marsha just messin' with you." She stopped laughing. "But really now. What you folks be doin' here?"

"We're just passing through," said Julian.

"Don't nobody pass through Groulet," said Big Marsha. Ain't nothin' beyond here but the Swamp of Shadows. You folks got no business up in there. Miss Marsha tell you that much fo' free."

Boudreaux re-entered through the swinging doors holding a dead possum up by the tail. "This one been dead a while by the look of him."

Big Marsha grabbed the soggy dead creature with both hands and plopped it down on the bar in front of Ravenus. "Here you go, Sugar."

Julian felt a strange swirl of emotions unlike anything he'd ever felt before. His own disgust and revulsion seemed to be battling for dominance with Ravenus's excited gratitude, which he could feel due to the empathic link they shared. "Thank you," he managed to croak out to Big Marsha without throwing up.

Ravenus hopped up on the dead animal, ripped open a big

hole in the skin, and buried his beak in the creature's guts.

"Now that's a good boy," Big Marsha said with a broad smile. "You poor thing must be 'bout starved to death." She reached under the bar and pulled up a small burlap sack and a wooden bowl. "How 'bout you boys? You hungry?" She bare-handedly scooped out some shelled peanuts and dumped them in the bowl, placing it before them.

"No, thank you," said Julian, Tim, and Dave in one voice. Julian was apparently not the only one who had taken note of Big Marsha's sanitary practices.

"Sure," said Cooper, popping a few peanuts into his mouth. "Thanks!"

"Pardon me for asking," said Julian. "But do your patrons not find it at all off-putting to have a dead rodent on the bar?"

"Ha!" said Big Marsha. "These ain't city folk like you. This is Groulet folk. Fur trapper, gator hunters, fisherfolk. Everyone you see here handle the insides of animals every blessed day. The Swamp of Shadows ain't no place for the squeamish."

"Are you going to try to stop us?"

Big Marsha bellowed out a laugh that shook the rickety foundations of the whole building. Boudreaux joined in with her.

"He wanna know if I gonna try to stop 'em. You hear that, Boudreaux?"

"Oh, I heard him all right, Miss Marsha," said Boudreaux.

"Boy, iffin I wanted to stop you, all four of you would be chopped up an' on gator hooks by now. I ain't yo mamma. You go on an' die in the swamp iffin that's what you wanna do. All's I was tryin' to do was offer some friendly advice."

"If at all possible," said Tim. "We'd like to leave in the morning. Do you have lodging available for the night?" He placed two gold coins on the bar.

"Well I'll be," said Big Marsha, picking up one of the coins and holding it close to her eye. "The king's own currency. We don't usually see much of that 'round these parts. Folks 'round here mostly pay in furs an' fish." She put the coin back on the bar.

"Boudreaux, go on an' clean out your room. These folks gonna stay in there tonight."

"But Miss Marsha!"

Big Marsha picked up a broom leaning against the wall behind her and thwacked Boudreaux repeatedly on the head with it. "Don't you sass me, boy!"

Boudreaux held up his arms defensively and cowered under the attack. "Yes, Miss Marsha. I'm sorry, Miss Marsha!" He hurried back through the swinging door again.

Big Marsha scooped up the two gold coins and slipped them under the bar. "Boudreaux's getting' yo' accommodations ready now." She poured another round.

About half an hour later, the first of the patrons began to head out into the darkness. The rest of the night Julian could only remember in flashes, and only vaguely.

The band left at some point.

Ravenus vomited possum guts all over the bar, perhaps intentionally, so that he could continue eating.

Tim fell asleep.

Big Marsha had Dave and Cooper in stitches with some story that Julian couldn't stay conscious long enough to follow. It might have had something to do with frogs.

The next time he blacked out, his face hit the bar hard, and he didn't wake up again...

*

...until the next morning. The sunshine was bright in his face, and the air smelled like rotten eggs and old fish. But he was dry, and that was a vast improvement over... He had to take a moment to remember where he was. Bon Temps. Boudreaux's room. Okay, that much was settled.

Next item on the agenda. Why was he naked? He and Big Marsha didn't... No, there wasn't enough booze in the world. Was there? He shuddered and sat up. His friends were still sleeping.

And not one of them was wearing a stitch of clothing. Dave's armor was piled up in the corner of the room, but nobody else's clothes were anywhere to be seen. Cooper yawned and rolled over onto his back, allowing his huge, scaly, disease-ridden monster dick to flop into view.

Julian couldn't stomach the sight of it. Not this morning. Not with the hangover he was suffering. He scanned the room in a panic, looking for a good place to throw up. The window! He ran to the open window, poked his head out, and spilled the contents of his stomach — fuck — right onto his own shirt. All of their clothes had been washed, and were hanging out to dry in the sun on a line below the building.

Laughter roared out from below. Julian spotted Boudreaux and a human, who may or may not have been at the bar the previous night, pointing up at him and laughing their asses off. They were standing on a bit of reedy land, gutting an alligator as long as a bus.

"Now look what you gone an' done!"

Julian peeked his head further out of the window to see Big Marsha standing under the building, reeling in the laundry. "Sorry," he croaked.

"S'alright," said Big Marsha. "Won't make no difference anyway once you gone ten minutes through the swamp. Sho' I can't change yo' mind? Y'all is nice folks. I hate to see you die is all."

Julian didn't have the strength to continue this conversation. He brought himself back inside, shielded his eyes from the sight of Cooper's junk, and sat back against the wall.

Five minutes later, there was a light tap on the door just before it began to swing open. Julian hurriedly covered his own junk just as Big Marsha walked in with a pile full of folded laundry in one hand, and a wet, vomit-covered shirt dangling from the other hand.

"Ain't no need to be shy," she said. "Y'all ain't got nothin' Miss Marsha ain't seen before."

"Thank you," said Julian.

"Time to rouse yo' friends, boy. Breakfast be ready in ten minutes, and then it's time for y'all to go."

Julian shook what chunks of vomit he could from his shirt out of the window. It was still wet and sticky going on. His serape was clean and dry, though. So even if he felt disgusting, he at least looked presentable.

He threw everyone's clothes over their junk before nudging them all awake with his foot. "Come on, guys. Rise and shine. We've got a swamp to go die in. Let's go."

Dave, Cooper, and Tim moaned and groaned, but eventually gave up the notion that Julian would stop kicking them if they just ignored him long enough.

"What time is it?' asked Tim.

"What's that smell?" asked Dave.

"Why are we naked?" asked Cooper.

Cooper's question hastened Dave and Tim in shaking off the grogginess.

"Wow," said Tim, smiling for the first time since Julian could remember. "It really feels good to be in some clean, dry clothes."

"Yeah," said Julian. "Couldn't agree more."

Breakfast consisted of fried eggs, fried oysters, and fried frog. Big Marsha shook her head as Tim, Dave, and Julian picked off the hind legs of the frogs and left the rest behind. She and Cooper happily gobbled up what was left. Ravenus feasted on the possum that was still rotting on the bar, waiting for him. As big a bird as he was, it was more dead rodent than he could hope to eat in a week. Still, when they parted ways, Big Marsha packed it up in a bag for him.

"We appreciate your kind hospitality," said Julian.

"Aw, ain't you a sweet thing," she said, beaming back at him. Then her face turned serious. "I don't know what you boys reckon you gonna find in the Swamp of Shadows, but I reckon it's only gonna be trouble an' death. Now y'all go on and do what you gotta do. But Miss Marsha gonna send y'all off with some words of wisdom."

"We would appreciate that," said Dave.

"Hmph," said Big Marsha, putting her fleshy hands against her wide hips. "Iffin y'all be willin' to listen to some true wisdom, you'd scoot yo' cute little asses back on home to Cardinia. But I done said my piece about that."

"What further wisdom do you wish to bestow upon us?" asked Julian.

Big Marsha shook her head and smiled. The grey-green skin of her cheeks actually turned a little pink. "Boy, you could charm the skin off a snake talkin' like that."

Julian looked at Tim for a clue as to what he should infer from that.

Tim shrugged. "Maybe you rolled a 20 this time."

Big Marsha wore her serious face again. "Here's what I gots to tell you." She raised a finger. "One, don't start no shit with the lizardfolk up in there. They ain't so used to outsiders as we are here." She raised a second finger. "Two. There's a crazy old man out there. I don't know how he live or what he do, but he been out there since before my mamma hatched. You stay away from him. He won't hurt you if you leave him be. Now, he may try to provoke you, but whatever he do, you just ignore him and go on about yo' business."

Dave, Tim, and Cooper lowered their heads and averted their eyes.

"Thank you for your advice," said Julian.

"Y'all stop by on yo' way back, iffin you's still alive, hear?"

As they continued down the shell path, they spotted a house here and there. Some were raised on posts, as Bon Temps had been, and others just floated freely in the water on pontoons. The few people they saw mostly pretended not to see them. Those who did acknowledge them simply shook their heads.

The air was hot and humid. Julian's shirt was soon soaked in enough sweat to neutralize the stickiness of his vomit. It was no less sticky, but it just felt better to be sticky with sweat. Eventually the path faded to dirt, then mud, then nothing but stagnant

black water.

"What do we do now?" asked Dave.

"We keep going," said Tim.

"What? Walk through the swamp?" said Dave. "We don't know what's in that water. Couldn't we build a raft, or a skiff, or something?"

"We don't have that kind of time," said Tim.

"But we don't even know how deep it is," said Dave.

Cooper pushed Dave off the edge of the trail. For a moment, he was completely submerged, but he quickly found his footing and stood up. The water came up to his neck.

"Fuck you, Cooper!" Dave shouted, reaching up his hand.

Cooper grinned and pulled him out of the water. "Now we know."

"Dave and I are too short to walk through that," said Tim.

"I can carry you," said Cooper. "But Dave's heavy as a motherfucker in that armor."

"Julian?" said Tim.

"What?" said Julian. "I can't carry Dave. Look at me!"

Cooper slapped his forehead. "Goddamnit, Julian! The one time you could use your stupid Mount spell for its intended purpose, and it doesn't even occur to you."

"Oh right!" said Julian. "Horse!"

The horse popped into existence, saddled and ready to serve. This one was brown, with a white underbelly and a white stripe down the front of his face.

"Oh, you're a pretty one," said Julian, running his hand down the horse's mane. "I'm going to call you 'Stripe'."

"I'm going to call him 'Two hours and counting'," said Tim. "Let's get moving."

With a little bit of a struggle, Cooper managed to heft Dave onto the horse. Tim sat up on top of Cooper's shoulders, as if they really were father and son. Cooper, Julian, and Stripe stepped into the black water.

They hadn't been traveling twenty minutes when Dave started complaining.

"Are you guys tired?" asked Dave through a yawn. "I'm exhausted."

"Quit your moaning, you pussy," said Cooper. "You're riding a fucking horse."

Dave's heavy dwarven eyelids sank gradually until they closed completely. He didn't look right. He was pale. He looked older somehow.

"Is Dave all right?" asked Julian.

"He's probably just overheated because of his armor," said Tim.

Dave let out a loud snore and fell off of the horse into the water.

"Oh, for fuck's sake," said Cooper. He placed Tim on a nearby spot of ground above the water, and sloshed through the marsh to the place where Dave had fallen. He dragged Dave onto the high ground.

Dave choked up a bit of water, and then went right on snoring.

"Something's wrong," said Tim. "He looks like shit."

It was true. Dave's eyes and cheeks were sunken. He looked like he had just aged fifty years.

"Cooper," said Tim. "Hold still. You've got something on your leg." He pulled out a dagger.

Cooper froze at the sight of Tim's dagger. "What is it?"

"Nothing to worry about," said Tim. "Just a second." A quick poke and it was done. The black spot on Cooper's leg popped like a balloon filled with blood and fell off. "Just a leech."

It took a moment for Julian to consider some ramifications. "Leeches!" He tore his serape off and began to unbutton his shirt. He'd stripped completely naked before he discovered two leeches on each of his ankles. "Get them off! Get them off!"

Tim plucked off the little blood-suckers with his dagger.

Julian sat down against a cypress knee and caught his breath. A though occurred to him. "Dave!" he shouted.

"What?" said Tim.

"Leeches!" cried Julian. "Take off his armor!"

At once, Julian, Tim, and Cooper went to work on Dave's armor. Tim slapped Julian and Cooper's hands away, as he was the only one nimble enough to unfasten the buckles in a timely manner.

As Tim unfastened the buckles, Cooper removed the plates, revealing huge, bloated leeches all over Dave's body. Julian frantically ripped them away as they were revealed. He hesitated at the sight of a leech on Dave's scrotum, and at least twice the size of it. Tim made short work of it with his dagger.

"Wake him up!" said Julian.

Tim slapped Dave on the face a couple of times. "Come on, man. Wake up!"

"Five more minutes, mom," said Dave.

Julian splashed water on Dave's face.

"I don't want to go to school, mom!" said Dave. "Coach Dickerson watches me in the shower!"

Julian, Tim, and Cooper stared silently at one another for a moment.

"I told you there was something off about Dickerson," said Cooper.

Tim slapped Dave in the face again. "Come on, Dave. You've got to heal yourself!"

"I told you that twelve years ago," said Cooper.

"Okay!" said Tim. "So you were right about Coach Dickerson. Focus on Dave. He's lost a shitload of blood and he's slipping away."

"Oh my god," said Julian. "He's emaciated."

Cooper cupped his hands underwater and held it over Dave's genitals. "Frost me."

"What?" said Julian.

"Ray of Frost!" shouted Cooper. "Hurry the fuck up!"

"Frost," said Julian, pointing a finger at the water cupped in Cooper's hands. The water turned into a solid chunk of ice.

"Motherfucker!" shouted Cooper, ripping his hands away. The

ice chunk fell into the water. Cooper rubbed his hands together a few times, grabbed the ice chunk, and rubbed it on Dave's balls.

Dave's eyes went wide. "The fuck!" He screamed. "Cooper, what are you doing? Get off of my nuts!"

"Heal yourself," said Tim.

"Huh?" said Dave.

"Hurry up!" said Tim. "Before you pass out again. Just do it!"

"I heal me," said Dave. With some effort, he brought his finger to his nose. At once, he became more focused, and some color returned to his face.

Tim sighed with relief. "Good job. I thought we'd lost you. Better have one more go."

"I heal me," said Dave. His face and body expanded with fresh blood like a balloon. His dwarf dick stood up at attention, and Tim, Cooper, and Julian looked away.

"What's that squirting out of him?" asked Ravenus.

"Ew, Ravenus!" said Julian. "Just let it go, huh?"

Once Dave had covered his essentials, the rest of the group helped him strap his armor back on.

Stripe gave a small whinny. When Julian turned to look at the horse, he was shocked by how thin it was. Its formerly white underbelly was black and bloated with a nest of fat leeches.

"Stripe!" Julian cried.

The horse's eyes rolled up and it fell over, blinking out of existence when it hit the ground. A hundred or more fat leeches squirmed on the ground, confused at having suddenly lost their host.

"You bastards!" Julian screamed jumping up and down on the leeches, spraying horse blood all over the ground.

"Congratulations," said Cooper. "You've murdered another horse."

"I didn't —" Something warm and pasty splashed onto the side of Julian's face. "What the...?" He wiped his face and looked at his hand. The substance was thick and brown, specked with bits of red. It smelled like... "Is this shit?"

A laugh wheezed out from a nearby cypress tree. Julian looked up and saw a naked old man in a fit of laughter. He had long, matted white hair and a beard that hung down to his navel. His pubes were also matted and white, hanging down to his knees like a second beard.

"It's him!" said Dave. "That's the old man we're supposed to —" Splat. Dave got a faceful of old man shit. He spat and spat. "Fuck! That went in my mouth!"

Cooper had readied his greataxe for a fight, but it fell by his side as he laughed at Dave. When his own chest was suddenly splattered with shit, he barely seemed to notice. He just kept laughing at Dave.

Tim was less amused. He furrowed his brow as he cocked back his hand crossbow. "Let's do what we came here to do and get the hell out of here." He leveled the weapon at the old man and fired.

The crazy old bastard made no move to dodge or even flinch. He snatched the bolt right out of the air, rubbed the shaft up and down his ass-crack, and threw it back at Tim, laughing his foul, wheezy laugh. The bolt landed short of Tim, still in usable condition, but Tim opted to load a fresh bolt.

"I'll admit that was pretty impressive," said Tim. "But I'm starting to think 'unpleasant' was a bit of an understate—" Splat. Tim's shirt and vest were soaked in shit. "Oh come on, man! I just had these cleaned, you dick!" He tried to wipe it off with his hand, but only managed to smear it around.

"Let's see him try to catch this," said Julian. "Magic Missile!" A golden bolt of magic shot toward the old man. He opened his shit-caked palms and hissed an inarticulate word. The Magic Missile was absorbed by a shimmering force field in front of him.

"Shit," said Julian. "He's a sorcerer."

"Double shit," said Tim. "I think I just found his familiar."

"Oh my God!" cried Dave, genuine terror in his voice. He stroked the leopard fur on his forearm.

Julian turned his attention from the old man in the tree to see what they were looking at. A panther stalked out of the shadows, snarling aggressively, but not yet making a move to attack.

"Go," the old man rasped.

"He can talk," Tim said to Julian. "Maybe he's having a lucid moment. Try to reason with him. Use your Diplomacy."

"What's the Difficulty Check for convincing a person to let us murder him?"

Tim sighed. "No, dumbass. See if you can convince him to move to a different part of the swamp or something. We can tell Esteban and Razorback we killed him, and no one will be the — Ow!"

A plume of black feathers was suddenly poking out of Tim's neck. His eyes rolled back and he fell forward into the mud.

"Tim?" said Cooper. A black dart, just like the one which had struck Tim, suddenly appeared on Cooper's chest. "The fuck?" He said, looking down at it. Fwop. Fwop. Fwop. Three more darts flew from out of the shadows to pierce Cooper from every direction.

"What's going on?" said Julian. He looked up in the tree. The old man was gone. The panther had disappeared as well.

A dart clinked off of Dave's armor. He picked it up. The needle was coated in some kind of sticky orange paste.

Julian resisted the urge to summon a horse to hide behind. Whoever was out there lurking in the shadows had them outclassed and outnumbered. A horse wasn't going to save him this time.

He felt a prick in the back of the neck and fell swiftly into darkness.

When Julian woke up, the left side of his face burned and itched, and his left eye was swollen shut. Looking up with his good eye, he discovered that his arms and legs were constrained by living vines holding him spread-eagle between two trees. Desperately wanting to scratch his itchy face, he struggled against the vines, but they were too strong and thick. He rubbed his face on his shoulder.

"Now don't go and scratch it," said a familiar reptilian voice.

"You only make it worse."

Julian turned to the source. "Boudreaux?"

"Don't go lookin' all surprised," said Boudreaux, crossing his arms and shaking his head. "Miss Marsha done told you don't be messin' with the old man."

Looking beyond Boudreaux, Julian spotted Dave. He was also restrained with vines, and his whole face was swollen and red. He breathed frantically through his nose, as his tongue filled his whole mouth, poking out like a big pink tomato.

Tim was to Dave's left, his right hand beet red and as large as his head. His eyes were closed and he was moaning, as if in some sort of delirium.

Cooper was wrapped in a thicker tangle of vines than everyone else, an obvious precaution against his great strength. He didn't appear to have been affected by the strange rash the rest of them were suffering from, but he didn't look happy to be restrained at all. He squirmed and struggled and swore at the vines. When they wouldn't budge, he said "I'm really angry."

"Wait, Cooper!" said Julian. "Let's see what they —"

"Rrrwwwaaauuurrrggghhh!" roared Cooper, his body hulking out. He wrapped his giant hands around his constraints and ripped them right out of the trees. The vines around his legs suffered a similar fate. He beat his massive chest, raised his hands, and bellowed out a victory roar.

Fwop. Fwop. Fwop. Fwop. Fwop. Fwop. Cooper's victory was cut short by half a dozen darts in the chest. He collapsed into the mud.

Cooper's assailants emerged from behind trees. Six lizardmen, each armed with naught but a reed tube.

They picked up Cooper and plucked the darts out of his chest.

A seventh lizardman waddled onto the scene. He was a great deal fatter than the other ones. Not Big Marsha fat, but still a great deal fatter than what Julian judged was the norm for lizardfolk. This one wore a necklace and skirt made of alligator teeth. The former looked to be made of normal alligator teeth, the latter from something akin to what greeted customers at Bon Temps.

The six lizardmen holding Cooper raised him off the ground, spreading his arms and legs out as they had been before. The fat lizardman stood facing Cooper. He began to wave his arms and chant in a language that Julian didn't understand. Boudreaux stepped back, keeping well out of their way.

"What are they doing to him?" asked Julian.

"They just putting him back up where he belong," said Boudreaux. "Make sho' he don't hurt himself."

As the fat lizardman chanted, new vines crept down out of the treetops and up out of the tangled roots and cypress knees, wrapping themselves tightly around Cooper's wrists and calves. When Cooper was sufficiently secure, the fat lizardman stopped chanting.

He turned his attention from Cooper to Julian and waddled over in his direction. He looked up at Julian with one good eye, and one not-so-good. The off eye was milky white and didn't look to be functional.

"Um..." Julian could feel his voice shaking. "Hello."

The lizardman grunted and looked down. He plucked a leech from his inner thigh and popped it right into his mouth.

Julian supposed you didn't earn a body like that being finicky. His heart was pounding and his face was burning. "My name is Julian." He had to start with something.

The lizardman spoke through a series of what sounded like burps, slurps, and gargles.

"I, uh..."

"He want to know if you gots any questions," said Boudreaux."

"Questions?" repeated Julian incredulously. "Okay. Here's one. What do they plan to do with us?"

The lizardman dressed in teeth spoke to Boudreaux without having had Julian's words translated. Julian took this to mean that he understood the Common tongue, but refused to speak it.

"He say the chief wanna have y'all fo' supper."

Julian swallowed. "That could be interpreted two entirely different ways. Which one did he mean?"

"He didn't specify," said Boudreaux. "Any mo' questions?"

"What's wrong with my face?" asked Julian. "Hell, what the fuck is wrong with Dave?" He looked across to Dave, whose face was swollen like a hairy red balloon.

"Well I can answer that," said Boudreaux. "The old man done flung his shit at you."

The six lizardmen with the blow-darts, who had been standing around silently until now, quietly laughed. Even the fat one smiled.

"Yeah," said Julian. "I seem to recall that. So what? Does he shit acid or something?"

"There's berries grow wild out here in the swamp," said Boudreaux. "Deadberries we call them. Bright red, and poisonous as devil sperm. No joke, one of those deadberries be enough to kill a grown man, iffin he be stupid enough to eat it. But that crazy ol' fool eat 'em like candy. He don't die, but he shit mo' in a day than you or I does in a month. That be the truth!"

"So his shit is loaded with deadberry juice?" said Julian.

"That's right," said Boudreaux. "Now think about that. That's just the juice, done been mostly digested already. And look what it do to yo' outsides." He gestured at Dave. "Now think about what a fresh berry gonna do to a man's insides."

"Why didn't it have any effect on Cooper?"

"He was protected by a layer of filth."

"How long are we going to be like this?"

"Not long," said Boudreaux. "Shaman gonna fix you up."

The fat lizardman in the alligator tooth skirt, the shaman, removed a membranous pouch, tied off at both ends with a cord, from around his neck. He untied one end of it and reached his hand inside. When he pulled it out again, it was covered in what looked like infected puss. When he spread it on Julian's face, the smell offered further evidence to support his hypothesis.

"Ew!" cried Julian. "That's so fucking gross."

The shaman laughed at him as he lathered on the slimy yel-

low substance. Then he turned around and waddled over toward Dave.

By the time the shaman reached Dave, Julian could feel a noticeable decrease in the severity of the burning and itching.

Once Dave's head and Tim's hand had deflated to their appropriate sizes, the shaman waved his hand, loosening the vines that held them all.

Julian's face didn't itch anymore, but he scratched it anyway, just because he could. His skin was equally smooth on both sides, if not a little slimy and smelly. Suddenly, a thought occurred to him.

"Where's Ravenus?"

"You bird be all right," said Boudreaux. "He visit with the chief right now as we speak." He must have been telling the truth. Julian would know if Ravenus was in trouble. "We can go join them as soon as you friend wake up."

"How long is that going to take?" asked Tim, wringing his recently un-swollen hand. "We're under some time pressure."

"He a big strong guy," said Boudreaux. "But they done shot him up with six times the normal dosage. He could be out a while."

"Ice his balls," said Dave.

"I'm not going anywhere near his balls," said Tim. "You ice his balls."

"Fine," said Dave. He removed his helmet and filled it with swamp water up to where the face of it opened up. "Julian?"

Julian pointed at the contents of the helmet. "Freeze." A thin, blue beam of light crackled through the humid air. The water in the helmet cracked and groaned as the molecules suddenly expanded, as if the one in the middle had just farted.

Dave turned the helmet upside down, and a helmet-shaped chunk of ice plunked down into the water. He put his helmet back on. "Whoa!" he said. "That feels great!"

He picked up the ice chunk and stomped through the muddy water to where Cooper was still restrained in a thick tangle of vines. He averted his eyes as he reached the ice under Cooper's

loincloth.

Cooper began to squirm, then moan, then giggle. "Knock it off, Buford! That tickles."

"Who the hell is Buford?" asked Julian.

"That's his dog's name," said Tim.

"Ew," said Julian. "I don't even want to think about what —"

"Then don't!" said Tim.

"Hey guys," said Cooper. "What's up? Thanks for chilling my balls, Dave."

Dave dropped the ice and rubbed his hands together in the swamp water.

"Cooper," said Tim. "This is the shaman of the lizardman tribe. He's not going to hurt us. Well, not yet at least. So don't lose your shit when he releases you, okay?"

Cooper nodded. The shaman waved his hand, and the vines loosened their grip.

The shaman led the way, having Boudreaux warn them to follow his lead exactly, for the path they traveled was artificially elevated to a point just six inches below the water, rendering it completely invisible. Any deviation from the path would put the deviant in much deeper, and less friendly, water.

They walked single file. Boudreaux followed the shaman. The rest of the line alternated between captive and captor, with three lizardmen taking the rear. They made no effort to hide the fact that their blowguns were stuffed with fresh darts and ready to fire.

They walked until they reached a peculiar section of swamp, where some of the trees had a strange, conical pattern of vines growing on them. At ground level, the vines grew out of the water about five feet away from the trunk. They came together to wrap around the trunk about fifteen feet up.

Julian was just about to ask about the strange vine formations when some of the vines of one of them parted, and a lizardman emerged, stretching his arms out like he'd just awakened from a nap. Seeing the marching party, he immediately bowed and gur-

gled some kind of greeting to the shaman, who raised his hand slightly in acknowledgement.

"Your people live in those?" Julian asked to any lizardman who was listening.

"Welcome to Q'abbatt," said Boudreaux.

They continued along the submerged trail, which would suddenly change direction at haphazard intervals, only to change back to the original direction just as suddenly. Julian imagined the time a terrestrial army would have trying to chase these guys through their native habitat.

The farther they walked, the higher the concentration of vine huts became, until the base of every tree they saw was surrounded by the conical vine formations. Some of them were noticeably larger, and took on more of a dome shape. Others still connected two trees by vine-covered archway. Julian guessed these larger vine formations were the homes of either the more well-to-do lizardfolk, or maybe just the ones with the largest families. He was so preoccupied in his speculation that the main attraction caught him completely by surprise.

"Oh my God," said Dave.

"Fuck me, that's big," said Cooper.

Julian looked ahead. A massive pavilion, also composed entirely of vines, stood within six of the mightiest cypress trees in the swamp. The trees stood in a hexagonal formation, a thick braid of vines reaching down from the top of each one to support the massive, six-pointed, living structure. In truth, it was probably no larger than a four bedroom, two-story house. But here in the swamp it looked to be about as big as the Superdome.

The shaman stopped, halting the entire procession, and belched out some lizard words.

"He say you's free to step where you like now," said Boudreaux. "But y'all make sho' you mind you's manners in the presence of the chief."

"You hear that, Cooper?" said Tim. "You keep your goddamn mouth shut. Even if your balls catch on fire, you just nudge Julian

and point to them."

The shaman waved his arms, and the vines before them untangled from each other and parted like a theater curtain. The entire party stepped inside.

The vine curtain closed behind them, but the pavilion didn't get any darker. Glancing around the interior, Julian noticed sconces along the walls, providing more than ample light. By their lack of flicker, Julian guessed that the sources of light were some permanently Light-enchanted stones, as he'd seen so much of in this world already.

The largest cypress tree of all grew in the center of the pavilion, supporting the high, pointed ceiling. Floating at its base was a massive, rectangular slab of polished wood. It had a hole in the center, just a little larger in diameter than the tree that grew up through it, and smaller holes at regular intervals along its edge. Several dozen smaller slabs of similarly polished wood floated freely in the shallow black water covering the floor. They had holes in each corner.

The air above them was a cacophony of squawks, chirps, whistles, and caws. Looking up, Julian saw all manner of tropical birds. Some flew freely. Some perched on the lower branches of the great cypress tree. Others sat in cages suspended from the vine ceiling. They ranged in size from that of a hummingbird to that of an eagle, with colors more wild and vibrant than Julian had ever encountered in nature.

"They are beautiful, are they not?" said a lizardman stepping into view from behind the great cypress tree. He didn't look particularly old, for a community which chose its elders as their leader. Neither did he look particularly strong, for a community through which the hierarchy is decided through violence. He didn't even look like a fat, bloated slug, laden with gems and jewelry, like Julian imagined a swamp monarch who had gained his title through heredity alone might look. He wore a simple leather cord around his neck, adorned with a few brightly-colored feathers. The confidence and dignity with which he carried himself left no doubt in Julian's mind, however, that he was in the presence of the chief.

Julian plopped a knee down in the stagnant, black water. "Your highness."

The chief waved his hand dismissively at Julian. "Please. There is no call for such formality. I am not royalty. I am but a humble tribal chief." He turned to the shaman. "Our guests are weary from travel. Please provide them a place to rest."

The shaman grumbled some lizard words and waved his hands around. The giant slab of wood floating at the base of the great cypress tree began to rise on a bed of vines. They secured it in place by worming their way through the holes on the edges. Similarly, vines grew out from beneath the water, collecting the smaller slabs of wood and dragging them in pairs to positions around the perimeter of the larger slab. Smaller beds of vines pushed one of every pair of slabs six inches out of the water, while securing the other vertically behind it. Where a few moments ago there had been a haphazard scattering of floating pieces of wood, there was now a full set of dining room furniture.

"Have a seat," said the chief.

At once, the six lizardmen with the blowguns took places behind every other chair on either side of the table, leaving no room for any of the captives to sit next to one another. Julian, Tim, Dave, and Cooper took their places behind chairs between the lizardmen. Boudreaux and the shaman circled around the table, but remained standing. The chief took his place at the head of the table and sat down, followed by the lizardmen, and further followed by Julian and his friends.

"Permission to speak, sir?" said Julian.

"Of course!" said the lizard chieftain. "I grow tired of my own voice. Please voice whatever is on your mind."

"My familiar," said Julian. "He's a big black raven. I was told he was here."

"Ah, Ravenus!" said the chief. "A fine, mighty specimen of a bird."

"He's okay then?"

The lizard chieftain laughed heartily. "I dare say no bird in the history of the world has had a better day than Ravenus has had today. And the stories he has to tell." He wiped a tear from his eye. "Which one of you is Dave? Please let me see your arm."

Dave reluctantly held up his leopard-skinned forearm.

"So it's true," said the chief. "Remarkable."

"You speak Elven?" asked Julian, switching to a British accent.

"I speak many languages," said the chief, matching Julian's accent.

Cooper, who hadn't spent any skill points to learn Elven, opened his mouth to object, but Tim shut him up with a severe glare.

"May I see him?" asked Julian.

"Well that's up to Ravenus, isn't it?" said the chief. "Ravenus, come hither!" he said into the air.

Ravenus flapped, with the grace of a drunk moth, straight into the trunk of the great cypress at the center of the table. He fell over on his side, his black plumage flecked with foreign, vibrantly-colored feathers. He hopped to his feet and hobbled toward Julian like he'd just spent a full day riding bareback on a galloping horse.

"Ravenus," said Julian. "Are you okay?"

"I think so, sir," said Ravenus. "I'm a little sore, but on the bright side, I'd estimate that five hundred years from now, at least seventy percent of the birds in the world will be able to trace their ancestry back to me."

"Why all the long faces?" asked the chief. "I've traveled around a bit, and I've never met a halfling without a story to tell, or a half-orc without a crude joke. It strikes me as ironic that the elf among you is the most chatty."

From somewhere in the bird-filled canopy above, a white blob landed on Cooper's head and dribbled down his cheek.

The chief burst into loud, raucous laughter. The six blowgun lizardmen joined in the laughter, though theirs was far more controlled and subdued. Cooper stared straight ahead, deliberately tight-lipped. When the bird shit made it to the corner of his mouth, he licked it off. The facial expression that followed suggested that the taste was more bitter than he had expected.

After a long, uncomfortable moment, the lizard chieftain's laughter calmed down. "You'll have to forgive me, half-orc. I... This is silly. I can't keep calling you half-orc now, can I? My name is Feather Dancer. May I have yours?"

Cooper continued staring straight ahead, his lips pressed together tightly enough to turn coal into diamonds.

Feather Dancer frowned. His forked tongue flicked in and out a few times. "Is he ignoring me?"

"I'm sorry, your highness," said Tim. "His name is Cooper. He's deaf and dumb."

Feather Dancer stared at Tim. "Is he now?" He turned his attention to Cooper and placed his elbow on the table. He blew gently on his thumb and index fingers, snapping them as he did so. The sound of the snap came from directly behind Cooper's right ear. Cooper's head jerked slightly to the right.

"Shit," Tim whispered under his breath.

"Well he's certainly not deaf," said the chief. "Tell me, Cooper. Are you dumb?"

Cooper shrugged at Tim and turned to the chief. "I have a below-average Intelligence score, yes."

Tim planted his face on the table.

"We apologize," said Dave. "We didn't want to deceive you, but we thought it best if Cooper didn't talk. His Charisma score is also very low. We didn't want him to offend you."

"Your words are strange to me," said the chief. "Even for mammals." He placed both elbows on the table and leaned forward. "Tell me, gentlemen. Do you know what the most potent weapon in war is?" He looked at Julian.

"Trebuchets?" Julian guessed.

"No," said Feather Dancer. He turned to Tim.

Tim sighed. "Um... I don't know. Fire?"

"Wrong." The chief looked at Dave expectantly.

"Smallpox?"

"What?" The chief rolled his eyes and looked impatiently at Cooper, as if he was only doing so because he felt obligated to let him have a guess. "Well?"

"Fuck," said Cooper. "I don't know. I was gonna guess fire."

"Information," said Feather Dancer.

"If you know the enemy, and know yourself," said Cooper, "you need not fear the result of a hundred battles."

The chief stared at Cooper, eyes wide and mouth slightly ajar. "An astute observation! I believe your friends underestimate your... how did you put it? Intelligence score?"

Cooper grinned sheepishly. "Thank you, but the observation wasn't mine. It's from a book, The Art of War, by Shih Tzu."

"It's Sun Tzu," Tim snapped at Cooper. "Shih Tzu is a breed of dog, dumbass."

"The source of the passage matters not," Feather Dancer said to Tim. "The wisdom rings true. This is why I value honesty over all other character traits when separating my friends from my enemies." He turned his head sharply toward one of the blow-gunners. "Drockmar!"

The lizardman at the far end of the table, next to Cooper, stood at attention. "Sir, yes, sir!"

"Have you ever imagined copulating with my wife?"

"Four times this very day, sir!"

"Thank you," said Feather Dancer. "You may be seated." He turned back to Tim. "You see, little halfling, there is much I can forgive. But dishonesty, the very act of hiding, distorting, or perverting the information I rely so heavily upon... well that is a grievous offense indeed."

"I understand, sir," said Tim.

"And yet the very first words you spoke to me, about your friend Cooper, were bald-faced falsehoods."

"I was only trying to —"

The chief slammed his fist on the table. "Your intentions are not important to me!" he shouted. Birds flapped and squawked wildly above, and their droppings splattered on the table. Feather Dancer's eyes calmed, and he spoke in his normal tone. "My only interest in you is the truth of the information you can provide me. Now let me pose another question to you. Would you prefer to have me as a friend, or as an enemy?"

"If I'm being completely honest," said Tim, "I'd prefer to have you as a distant, fading memory."

"Ha!" said Feather Dancer. "You see? It's not so hard now, is it? You will be given an opportunity to redeem yourself, but first, we dine."

"Thank Christ," said Cooper. "I'm starving."

Feather Dancer looked at the shaman. "We are ready."

The shaman and Boudreaux walked to the back wall of the tent. When the shaman waved his hand, the vines spread apart, revealing there was still more to this vast, living structure. A giant ant, as big as a horse, struggled ineffectively against the tight grip of the vines which rooted it to the ground. They had encountered giant ants before, but this one was different. It's abdomen was huge and swollen, larger by itself than the rest of its body.

Tim's eyes lit up when he saw the ant. Dave licked his lips.

"Fuck yes!" said Cooper. "We've eaten giant ant before. I think it's my favorite food."

Feather Dancer stared quizzically at Cooper. "That's preposterous," he said. "We can't eat the ant. She provides us with eggs."

"With what?" said Tim. The brief light in his eyes had gone out.

Boudreaux and the shaman returned, each carrying an armload of what appeared to be slightly deflated white footballs. They placed one before everyone seated at the table. Julian looked down at his. Something was moving beneath the leathery exterior.

With the clawed tips of their fingers, the lizardmen at the table sliced open the eggs, revealing the squirming ant-maggot within. Cooper followed their example. Julian, Tim, and Dave,

lacking clawed hands, simply stared down at their own eggs. Julian hoped they might be spared having to eat dire-maggots, but the lizardman to his right graciously swapped his own open egg for Julian's. The lizardmen next to Dave and Tim did the same. Tim looked pleadingly at Julian, his mouth pouty, and his eyes welling up with tears. Julian just gave him a weak shrug, and nodded for him to man up and eat his maggot.

"It's not as bad as you think," said Cooper through a mouthful of larva. "Once you bite the head off, it stops moving, see?"

Dave picked up his ant-maggot. "I can't bite it while it's looking at me." He turned it around, closed his eyes, and held the back end up to his open mouth. With all of the enthusiasm of someone sawing off their own arm, he bit into it. The thing squirmed violently in his hands as white liquid sprayed out the back of it, all over Dave's face. Dave bent over and threw up.

Cooper had just put the last section of his own maggot into his mouth, and nearly choked on it while he laughed at Dave.

Feather Dancer smiled, but didn't actually laugh out loud. He and the other lizardmen were happily eating their own maggots. He looked at Tim and Julian. "Something wrong with your larva?"

Julian decided to take a bite out of the middle of his. He held his tongue as far back in his mouth as he could and brought the wriggling creature to his mouth. As soon as he placed his teeth on it, the maggot began to writhe violently. It was too much for Julian to handle. He put the maggot on the table, wrapped the leathery eggshell around its head, and punched it until he felt it pop. Once it stopped moving, he threw caution to the wind and ripped a huge gouge in its side with his teeth. He chewed without thinking about it, and swallowed quickly.

Tim held his own larva in front of him. His cheeks were streaked with tears. He closed his eyes and brought the squirmy thing to his mouth. He put it down. "I'm sorry," he said. "I just can't. It's a fucking ant-maggot, and I'd rather you just go ahead and kill me right now than eat it."

"Can I have yours then?" asked Cooper.

Tim threw the larva at Cooper, smacking him in the face. "Fuck you, Cooper."

"Are you trying to tell me," said Feather Dancer, "that you don't like the food we've provided you?"

"That's exactly what I'm trying to tell you," said Tim.

"You might have just mentioned that earlier," said the lizard chieftain. "I find it astonishing what lengths people will go to in order to avoid being honest. You know, it seems like not so long ago I was having a conversation about honesty. I was —"

"Okay," said Tim. "I get it. Sorry. Jesus Christ. You want some more honesty? Here you go. You're kind of a dick. How about that?"

"Snaptooth," said Feather Dancer.

The lizardman to Julian's right stood at attention. "Sir, yes, sir!"

"Fetch a more suitable meal for our guests, would you?" He pointed up. "How about that big pink one. I don't like the way he's been looking at me."

"Right away, sir," said Snaptooth. He pulled out his blowgun and fired a dart straight into the belly of a fat pink bird sitting on a branch. The mohawk-like green feathers of its crown stood up straight, and the bird fell off the branch. Ravenus barely got away in time to not be crushed when the turkey-sized bird crashed onto the table.

"Better?" Feather Dancer asked Tim.

"Are we supposed to eat it raw?"

"My, but you're particular about your food." The chieftain snapped his fingers. "Boudreaux, be a good lad and take this bird outside and dunk it in the flame-well, would you?"

"Right away, sir," said Boudreaux. He grabbed the bird by the neck and ran out of the pavilion.

"We're sorry," said Julian. "It's just —" Feather Dancer cut him off with a raised finer and a slight shake of the head.

Boudreaux returned in less than five minutes with a perfectly roasted bird hanging from a hook at the end of a chain.

Tim tried to rip a piece off, but pulled his hand away as soon as he touched it. He put his hand inside his maggot's leathery eggshell, using it like an oven mitt, and ripped off a steaming white chunk of bird meat. Julian would have liked to do the same, but the inside of his eggshell was sticky with maggot brain. Tim ripped the legs off the bird and passed them over to Dave and Julian.

"You may be wondering," said Feather Dancer after slurping down the last of his third giant ant larva, "why it is that you're here as my dinner guests rather than as my dinner."

"It had crossed my mind," said Julian, "but that wasn't a flame I wanted to fan. I was happy enough in the knowledge that you weren't going to eat us."

"Tomorrow evening's menu has not yet been written," said Feather Dancer, his tongue flicking in and out. "Do you have any recommendations?"

"If you haven't tried it already," said Cooper. "the giant ant itself is really delicious. We weren't fucking with you."

"Shut up, Cooper," said Tim. He turned to the lizard chieftain. "What is it you want from us?"

Feather Dancer stood up. "I want the same thing I always want," he said. "The truth. My men tell me you spoke of Razorback before you took your little nap. I want to know what you're doing in my swamp, and what your relationship is to my exiled cousin. Now, think carefully before you answer, lest the dwarf and half-orc be introduced to the flame well."

"Why just them?" asked Julian.

Feather Dancer looked distastefully at Cooper. "This one's filthy, and likely crawling with parasites, and the dwarf is way too hairy. They'll need to have all of that cooked away. You and the halfling, however, will be a delight to eat raw. I like to start with the feet. Pray you bleed out before I reach your genitals."

"I'm a lot hairier than you'd think," said Tim. He opened the front of his shirt. "See? It's like a Brillo pad."

"They said they'd kill a human child and frame us with the

murder if we didn't cooperate," said Julian.

Feather Dancer raised his scaly eyebrows. "They?"

Julian looked at Tim.

Tim shrugged. "I don't think there's a whole lot of secret left to keep."

"Razorback is in cahoots with a Kingsguard named Esteban," said Julian.

"We know this," said Feather Dancer. "They bring us meat in exchange for furs and gator skins. What does any of this have to do with you?"

"They demanded that we go kill the crazy old guy," said Julian. "His unpleasantness was causing some of their couriers to ask for more money for their services."

Feather Dancer slammed his fist on the table. "Those sniveling, copper-pinching cowards!" He splashed black water as he stomped toward the entrance of the pavilion. "Keep the prisoners here!" he shouted to no one particular guard. "Shaman! With me!" The shaman scurried out after him faster than Julian thought it possible for that fat little lizard bastard to move.

The waiting was tense and silent. Everyone just sat quietly, picking off a bit of roasted bird here and there. Ravenus pecked on Julian's discarded ant maggot.

When Feather Dancer finally returned through the vine curtain about half an hour later, wearing his calm lizard grin, it did little to quell Julian's anxiety.

"You'll have to pardon my outburst earlier," said the chieftain, taking his seat at the head of the table. "Facts, information, calculated decisions. These are the tools of leadership. Emotions must not be allowed to dictate actions. You have spoken the truth to me, and for that you will be rewarded. I shall see you unharmed back to Cardinia."

"Thanks," said Tim. "I guess being hanged for murder is marginally better than watching a giant anthropomorphic lizard bite my balls off."

"You have nothing to fear in Cardinia," said Feather Dancer. "I assure you. Boudreaux, is my human contact currently in Groulet?"

Boudreaux stepped forward. "Why yes sir, he is."

"Good." Feather Dancer motioned for the shaman to approach and held out an open hand. The shaman produced a scroll tube from beneath his robe and handed it to him. Feather Dancer, in turn, handed the tube to Boudreaux. "See that he gets this. Be swift."

Boudreaux raced out of the pavilion so fast that Julian's eyes could barely follow him.

"I have arranged for the local magistrate to be present at Razorback's weapons shop at midday tomorrow. You tell him what you told me, and they will handle Esteban and Razorback's treachery appropriately."

"What makes you think they'll believe us over Esteban?" asked Tim.

"You speak the truth," said Feather Dancer. "And the truth shall set you free."

"Whoa," said Cooper. "He's like a lizard Jesus."

"That's not how it works," said Tim. "People don't believe the person telling the truth. They either believe the person telling them what they want to hear, or they believe the person they like better. The information we have for the magistrate will be a major pain in his ass, so we won't be telling him what he wants to believe. And nobody likes us."

The chieftain frowned and nodded. "What you say is true. You are by far the most unlikeable halfling I've ever met. They're usually a jolly bunch. But you are not stupid. Neither am I. I know you are unlikeable, which is why I have provided you an edge. Shaman?"

The shaman handed Feather Dancer a large waterskin.

"This contains four doses of a potion which will make you more likeable."

"A potion of Eagle's Splendor?" asked Julian.

Feather Dancer looked at the shaman, who shrugged.

"Call it what you like," said Feather Dancer. "If you split it between the four of you just before you enter the shop, it should give you the edge you need to convince the magistrate of your sincerity."

Julian accepted the waterskin. "Thank you, sir."

"You will always have a friend in the Swamp of Shadows," said the chieftain. "Feel free to visit any time."

Tim bowed his head. "Thank you. I look forward to it."

Feather Dancer's nostrils flared. He crossed his arms, glaring down at Tim.

"I'm sorry," said Tim. "I meant to say I'm so glad to be leaving this sweltering shithole, and if I never step foot in this place again, it will be too soon."

The lizard chieftain's glare softened. He smiled. "I appreciate your honesty. Now be swift. My guards will escort you as far as Groulet."

The journey back to Groulet was made made easier by two wooden, pole-driven skiffs. Cooper and Tim rode with three of the lizardmen on one skiff. Dave, Julian, and the other three lizardmen rode on the other.

"Sleep now," said the lizardman called Drockmar. "You need rest." These were the first words he'd spoken since confessing to wanting to boink the chieftain's wife.

Cooper, Tim, and Dave made no arguments, stretching out on the skiffs and falling out of consciousness almost instantly.

"And you," said Drockmar.

Julian looked up at him. "Oh, elves don't sleep." He offered a friendly smile.

Drockmar didn't smile. He conversed with the other two lizardmen on the skiff in what Julian assumed was the lizardman tongue. It seemed to be an argument, but it was quickly settled.

"Elf sleep," said Drockmar. "Elf sleep now."

"No," said Julian. "You don't understand. If I could sleep, I'd gladly comply with —" Fuck. The dart hit him in the side of the head. It might have even pierced his skull a bit. That was going to hurt like a son of a bitch when he...

When Julian woke up, the first thing he noticed was that his head hurt like a son of a bitch. The second thing he noticed was that the sun was up, with just a sliver of sky separating it from the eastern horizon. They were back on the white shell road past Groulet. He was the first one awake. Even Ravenus was still sleeping.

He tried to shake the sleepiness away, but that only intensified the pain. Shit! The dart was still in there. He plucked it out.

"I think you dropped something," he said, holding the dart up to the lizardman on his right, whom he suspected had been the one to blow it into his head. The lizardman grinned and reached down to accept the dart. Julian tossed it into the water. "Dick."

While he waited for everyone else to wake up, Julian meditated for his daily allotment of spells.

"Wake friends," said Drockmar. "Time is short. Must hurry."

"Don't worry," said Julian. "I've got transportation covered."

Drockmar shoved Dave off the skiff, into the murky water, with his foot.

"Huh? Shit! What?" said Dave, sitting up. His day had begun.

One of the lizardmen on the other skiff kicked Cooper in the gut. Cooper farted, but went on sleeping. Tim, who had been right at the receiving end of Cooper's fart cloud, woke up with a violent cough.

Drockmar looked at Julian and pointed at Cooper. "Ice. Balls."

Julian looked at Dave.

"Fine," said Dave, taking off his helmet.

Once Cooper was awake, Julian summoned three horses. He mounted one, Cooper helped Dave onto the second, and Cooper mounted the third, with Tim riding piggy-back on Cooper. They bade their former captors farewell, and rode off down the shell trail.

The ride was refreshing, the sun and breeze drying the swamp out of their clothing and hair. Ravenus flew above them. Julian could feel his familiar's exhilaration in his own heart. Time was lost to the rhythmic beat of hooves on ground. They had been riding maybe an hour and change without incident, passing only a few travelers this early in the morning, when Julian spotted an owlbear stalking around just ahead of the eastern tree line.

"Horse! Stop!" he said, and the horse obeyed. Cooper and Dave stopped their horses with some effort about fifty feet ahead of Julian.

"What are you doing?" asked Dave.

"There's an owlbear," said Julian.

"Who gives a fuck?" said Cooper. "What do you want? To go and get your picture taken with him?"

"Come on, man," said Tim. "Let's go."

Julian pointed at the owlbear. "Magic Missile." The golden bolt of magical energy zipped through the tall grass until it struck the owlbear in the ass. The creature turned around and screamed. As far away as it was, its roar thundered across the grassy plain.

"What the hell did you do that for?" asked Dave.

"Because fuck owlbears," said Julian. He waved his arms in the air. "Hey shithead!" he called out. "We're over here!"

The owlbear charged, flapping its arms as if some evolutionary memory made it believe it could fly.

"Let's go," said Julian. "Yah!" His horse darted forward. Dave and Cooper's horses galloped quickly behind him.

Just as Julian had suspected, the owlbear's speed was no match for their horses. It had scarcely reached the road when they lost sight of it behind them over the horizon.

"That was pretty stupid," said Dave, his horse galloping alongside Julian's. "But you know what? You're right. Fuck owlbears."

Julian smiled. "Look!" he said. The city walls. We're almost —"

There was a sound like a garbage truck rolling sideways down the side of a mountain. When Julian looked to his right, Dave was no longer next to him.

"Horse!" Julian shouted. "St—" For half a second, he was flying. He met the pavement suddenly and gracelessly. Feet. Knees. Elbows. Face. Though insufficient time had passed for shock to give way to agonizing pain, he was pretty sure he had broken all of the above. His mouth was full of blood and road grit. He wanted to stand up and call out for Dave to heal him, but he couldn't even begin to think about moving. Not a single muscle responded to his brain's commands.

Julian lay on the road, paralyzed and in a state of semi-consciousness, for what seemed like an eternity.

"Master! Master!" Ravenus had landed on his arm, and was pecking him, trying to get some sort of response.

Julian wished he could put his familiar's mind to rest, but he couldn't even manage a weak response. He had a sudden thought which provided no comfort. He hoped Ravenus would allow him to properly die before he tried to eat his eyeballs.

Ravenus left him, and his body turned over onto its back. Someone must have kicked him, but he felt no foot, nor could he see anything.

"Jesus Christ," said Dave.

"What happened to his face?" said Cooper.

"I think that's what's smeared all over the road."

"Well fuck, dude," said Cooper. "Get to it already."

"I heal thee," said Dave.

Suddenly, Julian's face started to burn. It was agonizing, but it was feeling. That was good. The burning sensation was muted away by the cracking and fusing together of his shattered elbows and knees. "Yehehehahahahowowyoyou!" He cried.

"He still looks like shit," said Cooper. "Give him another one."

"I heal thee," said Dave. Julian could feel Dave's hand on his forehead.

The second healing was exhilarating. He still had some bumps and bruises, but he thought he could probably stand up. "Thanks," he croaked up to Dave.

"They really ought to put a spell-duration timer on those magical horses," said Dave.

"Seriously," said Cooper. "The horses are more dangerous than the fucking —"

"Owlbear!" cried Julian.

"Well, yes," said Cooper. "That's what I was going to say. You didn't have to interr—"

"Owlbear!" Julian repeated, pointing at the northern horizon.

Cooper followed Julian's finger. "Well fuck."

"Run!" said Tim.

"I can't run in my armor!" said Dave.

Tim started fumbling with the straps and buckles holding Dave's armor together.

"We don't have time for this shit," said Cooper. "I'm really angry!" His back and arms became rippled with muscle. He gripped the breastplate and backpiece where they met at the neck, and ripped them apart from one another, tearing the padding beneath them as well. In a barbarian rage frenzy, he continued ripping the armor off of Dave's arms and legs, leaving behind only shredded remains of padding. Before long, Dave stood as naked as the day he was born.

Julian knew what fear looked like when he saw a sprinting, naked dwarf, eyes wide with terror and dong flapping around like an unmanned firehose.

Cooper picked up Tim and ran. The two of them had nothing to worry about. With Cooper's barbarian rage in effect, and his Fast Movement class ability, they'd make it to the city gate with plenty of time to spare.

Julian was certain of his own safety, not necessarily because he was faster than the owlbear, but because he was faster than Dave. He ran alongside Dave, trying to encourage him to move faster.

"Come on!" said Julian. "Pick up the pace!"

"Fuck you!" Dave huffed. "Look at my legs!"

"I've seen quite enough of you, thanks," said Julian, jogging backwards in order to keep an eye on the owlbear. It was gaining on them, and it looked pissed off. More pissed off than any owl or bear Julian had ever seen, and those are two animals naturally predisposed to looking pissed off.

Then Julian saw something he didn't expect to see. Cooper breezed past him like a freight train made out of 'fuck you, owlbear', and charged the feathered gorilla-beast.

They each roared beastly, incoherent battle cries as they ran at one another.

Cooper met the owlbear with an uppercut to the lower beak, sending its tip cracking through the roof of the upper beak. Whether that cost it some Hit Points or merely pissed it off some more was unclear.

The owlbear wrapped its huge furry arms around Cooper and squeezed. Cooper's arms flailed about. He looked like he was panicking.

Julian stopped jogging backwards and started running toward the fight. "Cooper!" he cried.

Cooper finally looked like he had a handle on what he was doing. He shoved his clawed thumbs into the owlbears armpits and pushed them in deep. When the owlbear backed off, it did so with a large chunk of skin missing from its chest, which Cooper spat out onto as he caught his breath. The creature howled in pain. Julian stopped running.

Cooper and the owlbear circled one another counter-clockwise for a few steps, and then Cooper made his move. He lunged at the owlbear, trying to tackle it to the ground, but only managed to ram its chest wound.

The owlbear gave another hug. Cooper tried the same thumb-to-armpit maneuver he'd done before, but his arms began to grow thinner. His barbarian rage had expired. He beat frantically at the owlbear's sides, but the beast just hugged him even tighter.

Julian ran toward them. He could at least kick it in the nuts or something... give Cooper a chance to recover. He was only twenty feet away when he heard...

"Elf! Stand down!"

Julian turned around. "Holy shit!" A dozen city watchmen on horseback were pointing crossbows right at him. They were led by a Kingsguard holding a longbow with two arrows nocked. It was all too familiar. He put his hands in the air.

"Get down, you fool!" said the Kingsguard.

"Huh?" said Julian. "Oh, right!" He dropped flat on the ground.

"Fire!" shouted the Kingsguard. The simultaneous Thwack of a dozen crossbows and the twang of a bow sent a swarm of steel-tipped missiles over Julian's head and into the back, neck, and skull of the owlbear.

Cooper fell to the ground, sucking in as much air as his lungs could hold. The owlbear tried to turn around, but Cooper was having none of it. He grabbed the beast by its massive chicken-like foot, and pulled. The owlbear fell backwards, landing on the hard road, the bolts and arrows pushing further into its back.

If the owlbear had any life left in it after that, it provided no evidence. Cooper, either in an attempt to be thorough, or (more likely) because he was really pissed off at the creature, jumped up and down on its chest until its bones cracked. When he was satisfied, he hopped down onto the road.

"You okay?" asked Julian.

"Fuck owlbears," said Cooper.

"Are you harmed?" asked the Kingsguard, riding up alongside Cooper and Julian.

"Nothing a gallon of beer won't fix," said Cooper.

"That was quite a show you put on. I don't believe I've ever seen a person single-handedly attempt to fight an owlbear with his bare hands. Nasty creatures, those are."

Cooper grinned. "Just a big hairy chicken. If you fuckers hadn't interfered, I'd have given you a real show."

"I have no doubt," said the Kingsguard. "Now run along and tell your dwarf friend to put some clothes on, lest he have bigger troubles than owlbears."

*

Julian, Tim, Dave, and Cooper stood across the street from Razorback's weapons shop, knowing they were steps away from entering a shop which they would exit either in chains, maimed, dead, or free. Dave wore Julian's serape, which did little to obscure his nudity from the side and much to inhibit from walking properly. It got them stared at, but did not get them stopped.

"This is it, guys," said Julian. He unstoppered the waterskin Feather Dancer had given him and held it up without taking his eyes off the front of the shop. Cooper took it from him, which was just as well. If anyone needed the extra boost to his Charisma score, it was Cooper. "We've only got one chance to make our case, so everyone be on your best behavior, and let me do the —"

"Cooper!" cried Dave.

Cooper belched. "What?"

Julian looked in horror at the empty, sagging waterskin in Cooper's hand. "You fucking moron!"

"What's wrong?"

"That was meant to be for all of us!"

Cooper frowned at the waterskin in his hand. "You can't split one potion for ways. It won't do anything."

"That was four potions! You heard Feather Dancer. We were each supposed to drink a potion!"

"Well I figured there'd be a waterskin for each of us," said Cooper.

"Look at me, you jackass!" Julian spread out his skinny arms, revealing the lean frame of his body. "Do you see four fucking waterskins?"

"Well I'm sorry," said Cooper. "I just thought —" He doubled over in pain, like he was about to throw up. "I —" sweat started pouring out of his whole body, washing away his layer of filth. The sparse hair on top of his head grew thicker, more full-bodied. His pube-like facial hair grew straight and even-lengthed, forming a stylish goatee. His skin changed color, from sickly grey to polished bronze. His gut sucked into itself, leaving behind a smooth, rippling six-pack. His broad chest glimmered in the sunlight. He smelt of lilacs.

When Cooper stood back up, he had been transformed. He was

still a half-orc. Hell, he was still recognizable as Cooper. But his presence didn't make Julian want to constantly gag. He could be on the cover of a men's magazine for half-orcs.

"Cooper," Julian said, barely above a whisper. "You're beautiful."

Cooper flashed a debonair smile, full of pointed, but straightened pearly-white teeth. "Why, thank you."

Dave and Tim stared up, gaping.

Tim snapped out of it first. "Come on, let's go. We don't know how long this is going to last. Cooper, you go in first, and you do the talking."

Cooper sauntered across the street. Tim and Julian walked behind him, on either side of Dave, holding the edges of the serape together. Those in their way took a step back. Those further away stepped forward. Mouths and eyes hung open, in awe of the mysterious half-orc. He winked and pointed a finger at one woman, who proceeded to collapse in an unconscious orgasm.

When they reached the door to the shop, it flung open at Cooper's gentle touch. He sashayed into the shop, his hips swerving, his loincloth rolling in a wavy pattern atop his buttocks, as if the animal it was made from had come back to life.

The inside of the weapons shop was distinctly more crowded than it had been the last time they were there. Razorback stood behind the counter. It was difficult to read any expression on his reptilian face. Esteban stood with his back to the door, his palms up in an expression of someone trying to sell a story that the customer just wasn't buying. Three men stood in front of him, one clad from head to toe in black, and the others wearing polished breastplates and pauldrons identical to Esteban's. Kingsguard.

Esteban whirled around at the sound of the door opening. "Go away, you!" he cried. His eyes were wide and panicky, like he'd just blown his entire life savings at the craps table, and was trying to make it all back with his last fifty bucks at the slot machines. "This is not a good time! I have urgent business with —"

The man in black stepped past Esteban. "My name is Alfred

Farnsworth." Taller by half a head than Esteban, his flowing black robes were curiously unstained, though they piled into heaps at his feet. How he managed to wade through the horse-shit puddles without so much as a smudge of brown was anyone's guess. His head was covered by what looked like a black ski mask, except that it exposed his entire face, rather than just his eyes and mouth. A pointed, white beard jutted out of the bottom of the headpiece, and the man's steely grey eyes felt like they jutted through Julian's soul when he gave him a passing glance. The best word to describe him was severe. And perhaps the best way to describe the word severe to a person unfamiliar with it would likely be a picture of this man.

The severe man extended a hand to Cooper. "I am Chief Magistrate of the Seventh Commercial District of Cardinia. It is a pleasure to make your acquaintance, Mr..."

"Cooper," said Cooper, accepting his hand, and even going so far as to cup his left hand over it. "Please, call me Cooper. Your service allows myself, my friends, and all the citizens of this fair city to sleep well at night. For that, I owe you my gratitude." He took a knee and kissed the magistrate's hand.

The magistrate's face, which had, up until now, had the color and texture of a piece of paper in the desert, began to turn a little pink."

"Ahem," said Julian.

Cooper stood up.

The magistrate quickly turned his attention to the two Kingsguard accompanying him. "These are my escorts, Bartleby and Krabb." The two men stood at attention even more dutifully under Cooper's scrutiny than they had before the magistrate himself.

"Kingsguard," said Cooper. "A fine and noble station. It's an honor to make your acquaintance, gentlemen."

"Cooper," Tim whispered harshly. "We really need to —"

"The honor is all ours, sir," said Bartleby.

"I have a daughter about your age," said Krabb. "She isn't

married yet. If you ever wanted to pop by and —"

"Enough!" shouted Tim and Esteban at the same time. The magistrate furrowed his brow, staring at each of them in turn while they exchanged glares with each other.

"Mr. Magistrate, sir," said Tim. "I believe my friend Cooper has something to tell you about these men."

The magistrate raised his bushy white eyebrows.

"Your honor," pleaded Esteban. "These men are charlatans and scoundrels. Nothing they say can be trusted. Just look what that one did to this hardworking citizen's office. Razorback?"

Razorback hurried to his office door and opened it. The putrid air exploded out of it. Cooper's shit was still visible on the walls.

Dave shut his eyes and wobbled on his feet. "Dude, you really should have cleaned that up by now."

"Evidence!" said Esteban.

"Is it true?" the magistrate asked Cooper. He was calm and stern, seemingly unaffected by the funk. "Are you responsible for that?"

"I won't insult your honor by denying it. I am responsible. I thought it was a toilet."

A snort escaped through the magistrate's nose, and soon grew to a full-blown gale of laughter. He slapped Cooper on the back. "An easy mistake to make, considering the state of this place."

Bartleby and Krabb joined in the laughter.

Esteban and Razorback stood silent and stunned, like they'd just been kicked in the nuts by a ghost.

When his laughter subsided, Magistrate Farnsworth wiped a tear from the corner of his eye. "You had something you wanted to share with me?"

"Indeed I do, your honor," said Cooper. "These men, Esteban and Razorback, have been running corpses to the Swamp of Shadows, to be consumed by the lizardman tribe of Q'abbatt."

Any residual giggles from Bartleby and Krabb instantly evaporated.

"Is this true?" the magistrate demanded of Esteban.

"Of course not, your honor," said Esteban. He had mustered some confidence back into his slithery tongue. "It's preposterous to think that —"

"Furthermore," said Cooper. "They coerced us into attempting to murder the crazy old man who resides along the borderlands. I'm pleased to inform you that we failed in that task."

"The mad old hermit?" asked Krabb. "That guy's hilarious."

Magistrate Farnsworth shut him up with a sideways glance.

"He even went so far as to threaten to murder a human child and frame us for the deed."

"These are serious accusations, Mr. Cooper," said Farnsworth. "Have you any proof of what you claim?"

Cooper stood tall. "Only my honor, and my word that what I say is the truth."

"Pwah!" spat Esteban. "This miscreant's word against mine! I am Kingsguard. I have served His Majesty faithfully for a dozen years. Surely my word is worth something."

"I'm afraid he's right, Mr. Cooper," said Farnsworth. "I'm sorry, but I'll need more to go on than your word alone."

Cooper put his arm around the magistrate's shoulder. "You don't need to trust my word alone. Use your Sense Motive skill, and see for yourself that he tries to deceive you."

The magistrate's face was flushed. He was beginning to sweat. "I... I beg your pardon? Use my what?"

Cooper leaned in close, whispering in the magistrate's ear. "You needn't trust anything but the Wisdom in your own heart." He placed a clawed fingertip gently at the center of Farnsworth's chest.

"I don't... It's... well... I've never been with a man before." Farnsworth's index finger trailed along the muscles of Cooper's back. Julian was relieved to sit this session out as the group spokesman, but he hoped Cooper would hurry things along a bit. There was no telling how long that potion would last.

"Huh?" said Cooper, backing off just a bit. Tim punched him in the ass. "Oh, right. Um... look into your own heart, and look into his. You can make an Untrained Skill Check."

"A what?"

"Ask him again if my accusation is true," said Cooper. "And see his lie unveil itself before you."

"This is preposterous!" cried Esteban.

Farnsworth stepped away from Cooper, piercing Esteban with his steely grey stare. "Tell me, Kingsguard. Is there any truth to Mr. Cooper's accusations?"

"Of course not," said Esteban, his back pressed against the wall. "I would never... you must believe me. I couldn't..."

Farnsworth stared at Esteban for what seemed like an eternity. "Bartleby! Krabb!" he finally said. "Strip this man of his pauldrons. Secure him and the lizardman in manacles, and escort them to the courthouse. They shall stand trial for treason, attempted murder, conspiracy, and whatever else I can think of between now and then."

"Right away, sir!" said Bartleby.

Esteban and Razorback whined and protested, but ultimately surrendered, making no act of physical resistance. When they were gone, Farnsworth turned his attention back to Cooper, his grey eyes having turned from steely to bashful.

"Now, Mr. Cooper," he said, running a finger between Cooper's huge, shiny pectoral muscles. "What is it you were saying about the wisdom of the heart?"

A small fart broke the awkward silence which followed, like someone stepping on the edge of a whoopee cushion.

"Egads, man!" said Farnsworth. "What was that?"

"It was Dave," said Cooper.

"It most certainly was not!" said Dave.

A mole appeared on Cooper's back, with two thick hairs sprouting out of it.

"Shit," said Julian. "Cooper, it's time to go."

"It's rude to leave so abruptly, without a proper goodbye," said Cooper. "Sir, It's been a pleasure getting to know you, but my friends and I really must be leaving now. I would be most honored if—"

"Cinderella," said Julian. "The fucking ball is about to end!"

"Huh?" said Cooper. A tiny belch escaped is lips. "Oh!"

"Let's go!" said Tim. He and Julian grabbed him by the arms and rushed him out the door, leaving behind a befuddled and profoundly unsatisfied magistrate.

"Visit me at the courthouse!" Farnsworth called out after them. "My chamber doors are always open!"

Ravenus was perched on the shop sign outside. He stirred awake as the group burst through the front door, out into the street. "What's the hurry, sir?"

"Cooper's potions are about to run out," said Julian. "We've got to get him away from here."

They made it two blocks before Cooper doubled over, clutching his stomach, and fell to the ground. A few passers-by looked their way curiously.

"Help me drag him into the alley," said Tim. "Nobody needs to see whatever's about to happen.

Strangely enough, no one seemed to care that three dudes were dragging a fourth dude, crippled with pain, into an alley.

"Fuck," Cooper moaned.

It happened all at once. Cooper shat, farted, sneezed, belched, vomited, and pissed himself.

"The fuck was that?" said Dave.

"I think Cooper just exploded," said Tim.

"Cooper?" said Julian. "Are you okay?"

He was back to his old self, as disgusting and wretched as ever. He opened his eyes. "That was... cathartic."

"So what now?" said Dave. "Back to the Whore's Head?"

"I was thinking we could stop at a bath house," said Tim. "Get cleaned up, have a tall, cold glass of temporary memory loss."

"And how do you propose we pay for that?" said Julian. "We're flat broke. Hell, Dave's almost naked."

"It's Razorback's treat," said Tim. "While Obi-Wan was dry-humping Cooper, I snuck round the back of the counter and snagged a few ornate daggers." He opened his vest, revealing the hilts.

Cooper got to his feet. "Well if there's anything that takes the edge off of being fondled by an old man, it's booze paid for with stolen money. Come on guys. Tonight we're gonna party like it's 1399."

The End

ABOUT THE AUTHOR

Robert Bevan took his first steps in comedy with The Hitchhiker's Guide to the Galaxy, and his first steps in fantasy with Dungeons & Dragons. Over the years, these two loves mingled, festered, and congealed into the ever expanding Caverns & Creatures series of comedy/fantasy novels and short stories.

Robert is a writer, blogger, and a player on the Authors & Dragons podcast. He lives in Atlanta, Georgia, with his wife, two kids, and his dog, Speck.

Don't stop now! The adventure continues!

Discover the entire Caverns & Creatures collection at
www.caverns-and-creatures.com/books/

And please visit me on Facebook at
www.facebook.com/robertbevanbooks

Made in the USA
Columbia, SC
15 December 2017